A BOLDLY DARING SCHEME

A Regency Cozy

LYNN MESSINA

potatoworks press · greenwich village

For everyone who asked for a Flora story

Beatrice Hyde-Clare Mysteries

Chapter One

Finally, I have wrested the narrative away from Bea! Grasped firmly now in my own two hands is an exceedingly suspicious death desperately in need of investigating.

That is a metaphor, of course, as one cannot actually hold a murder mystery in one's grip. You would be excused for thinking otherwise, however, from the way my cousin has hoarded the assortment of corpses that have populated her life recently. Jealously, she clutches them to her chest, refusing to acknowledge to anyone that they even exist.

No, Flora, I am not conducting interviews with suspects. I am attending a political salon because I am merely interested in the process of governance.

No, Flora, Mrs. Norton is not trying to undermine my social standing by embroiling me in a nefarious plot that could end my engagement. She is just being friendly.

No, Flora, I did not have a tussle with Lord Taunton. He was only showing me how to extinguish a torch using my dress.

Again and again, Bea issues weak-sounding excuses to

discourage my interest in the strange events in her life. I would not say she lies to me exactly.

Evades, yes.

Equivocates, without question.

Endlessly defers follow-up questions by drawing Mama into the conversation so that she can ramble on a wholly unrelated topic, absolutely.

Why is she so determined to withhold her adventures from me?

The answer is obvious: She does not trust me to act with wisdom or caution.

Like Papa, she believes I am the veriest peagoose and that if I attempted to pursue a killer, I would promptly end up with a gun pointed at my own head.

Oh, yes, that is *exactly* as insulting as you think it is.

She would argue that she has every right to be concerned.

As the elder by six years, she *has* pulled me out of quite a few scrapes, some of which *were* the result of my inability to properly judge my own proficiency. When I jumped into the lake at Welldale House to capture a turtle, for example, I did not yet fully know how to swim. (It was such a perfect specimen, with bright yellow markings, and I had been splashing near the shore for ages.) It was a poorly considered decision, yes, but I was six at the time. Surely, I can be relied upon to have learned something about responsible behavior in the intervening fourteen years.

Furthermore—and this is not an insignificant point—*she* is the one who got herself and the Duke of Kesgrave bound to a desk in a pitch-black room in the desolate basement of a theater on the Strand.

Boldly and without any concern for her safety, Bea marched into the dressing room of a murderer and brazenly searched through his belongings for proof of his guilt.

Was anyone surprised when the villain came upon her in

the act, aimed a pistol at her heart and insisted she and Kesgrave accompany him to the dingy cellar?

I don't think so, no.

Even my chuckleheaded brother, Russell, would have seen that development in the offing.

Oh, but there was a twist!

Me. I was the twist.

Unable to accept that Mrs. Norton's offer of friendship was sincere and did not in some way bode disaster for Bea, I kept an eye on my cousin to ensure her safety, and as soon as I observed the fix she had got herself into in the basement, I rushed to the rescue.

Had I not stolen into the building and snuck down the stairs to free them from their prison, they would be in that room still.

Did Bea give me my due?

No, she did not.

Rather, she was so ungracious as to insist that Kesgrave would have freed them from the room as soon as he turned his attention to unlocking the door. (Turned his attention— ha! When I arrived, he was otherwise occupied in an activity that would appear to muddle one's thinking, not clarify it, and the fact that Bea was wholeheartedly engaged in the pursuit signified, I believe, a worrying lack of seriousness on her part.)

To be sure, I believe unequivocally that a young woman should have consuming faith in her husband, but the fact remains that the door was locked and they were trapped inside.

(An impertinent actress also tried to undermine my achievement, but as she was a member of the theater company, I cannot see what act of heroism she performed other than climbing down the stairs and walking along a darkened corridor, something I do almost every night to fetch a snack from the kitchens.)

With my daring and perfectly executed rescue, I had proved myself capable to Bea, and she unbent enough to relate the details of several curious incidents that I had long suspected were connected to murder investigations. At last, I possessed all the pertinent details of her strange confrontation with Taunton on the terrace at Larkwell's ball. I *knew* the story about her accidentally lighting his lordship's hair on fire with one of the torches was a complete plumper, for despite her social awkwardness, Bea has never been clumsy, and the idea that she had tricked Kesgrave into offering for her was patently ridiculous. That he was inexplicably fond of her was obvious from the beginning.

Well, not the *very* beginning because when we first met him at a country house party in the Lake District, he was severe and terrifying and positively relished quelling his fellow guests with haughty glares, of which he seemed to have an unlimited supply.

Good gracious—Lakeview Hall!

Even now I cannot think of that horrid visit without shuddering.

But that is where it all began.

Bea, I mean.

The Bea who hoards mysteries and marries dukes.

I can still remember the exact moment in the Skeffingtons' elegant drawing room when everything changed. The air was heavy with grief at the untimely death of that wretched spice trader and yet there was Bea, her cheeks flushed prettily and her eyes glimmering brightly, asking the Duke of Kesgrave a *direct question* and *pressing* him for an answer.

Oh, the mortification!

We were all beside ourselves—me, Russell, Mama.

Poor Mama tried so valiantly to intercede to spare the

family further humiliation, chattering on about one thing or another in the way only she can do. It was a remarkable effort, but Bea, demonstrating what turned out to be backbone (although one could be forgiven at the time for assuming it was obliviousness), stayed the course and compelled the duke to respond. Kesgrave appeared annoyed at her impudence but in fact was actually charmed by it.

Yes, yes, *I know*. It all seems so utterly unfathomable. How could he not prefer any one of the literally dozens of Incomparables offered to him daily like options for his waistcoat? And yet there is no other way to account for the fact that the perpetually drab Beatrice Hyde-Clare is now a duchess.

Oh, dear. *Drab* seems so harsh, maybe even a little cruel.

I don't mean it that way.

Really.

I am simply stating a fact.

Bea *is* drab.

Her hair is an indiscriminate shade of brown and lies limply on her head as if it cannot be bothered to retain a style. Her skin is pale, her eyes are beady, and her lips are narrow.

Even so, it was never really her appearance that was the problem but her disposition. The poor darling was always as timid as a dormouse trembling under a chair, her button nose jumping ever so slightly at the fear of discovery. Whenever someone addressed a comment to her, she would recoil anxiously as if being called upon to recite some long, tedious document like the Magna Carta rather than simply give her name.

If only she had shown just a *little* vivacity during any one of her six seasons.

Alas, she did not, and I was forced to make my debut in the shadow of my dreary spinster cousin. It was intolerable, having her looming over me as a reminder of the horrible future that awaited if I failed to sparkle enough.

Does it sound as though I resented Bea?

It must *sound* as though I resented her terribly, but the truth is actually much worse: I did not think about her enough to resent her.

And why would I have?

She was always so quiet, and when she wasn't fetching things for Mama in her dressing room, her head was tilted down in a book.

I thought she *wanted* us to ignore her.

Truly, I was doing the kind thing by leaving her to herself (and making her feel useful because I too had things that needed to be fetched from various corners of the house).

It is only now that I look back and wonder if perhaps she was lonely.

She was almost certainly bored. With her vibrant mind, the way it jumps from one thing to another, drawing conclusions from seemingly unrelated events, she must have been bored to flinders attending to our needs year after year.

No wonder she seized so zealously on Mr. Otley's murder. His corpse must have felt like a breath of fresh air.

Exceedingly morbid, I know, but having my own suspicious death to investigate I won't pretend not to understand the appeal of deciphering clues, outwitting a killer and attaining justice for the victim.

And who is *my* victim?

His name is Theodore Davies.

You may have heard of him because he figured prominently in Bea's past. He was a lowly law clerk and her former beau. Their love was torn asunder by the young man's cruel father, who wanted something better for his son, which seems despotic but was actually an act of good fortune because it left Bea free to marry a duke. (Assuming one's affections are equally engaged by both suitors, then it is *always* better to marry the duke.)

He was killed a few months ago in a tragic carriage accident.

Or was he?

The evasive look that entered Bea's eyes when I recently asked about his death indicates otherwise. She had been completely candid about everything else. She gave me all the details of her interactions with Taunton and Wem. But as soon as the topic switched to Mr. Davies, she became uneasy, shifting her gaze downward and changing the subject to something inconsequential.

I defy you not to find that behavior highly suspicious.

Ah, and now you are wondering why, if Bea thought his death was more sinister than mere misfortune, she did not look into the matter herself.

The answer to that is simple, I believe: Kesgrave.

From the very beginning he has assisted Bea in her inquiries, and despite her audacity, I think even she is disinclined to ask her current beau to help her investigate the death of her previous one. The situation is simply too rife with the potential for misunderstanding, and furthermore it is impossible to ignore the great disparity in their positions. Having nabbed a duke, she must be slightly mortified by her willingness to settle for a clerk.

It is the ideal time for me to launch my own investigation because the demands of newly married life have thoroughly consumed her attention. (A full week wed and we have had only one communication—a brief missive thanking us for attending her nuptials. Mama huffed, as if gravely insulted that we did not merit more than a few lines, but I do not know what she was expecting. A book-length dissertation on the challenges of overseeing a large household staff that resents her for possessing neither noble blood nor beauty? Actually, yes, that is exactly what she is waiting for.)

Bea's preoccupation is only temporary, I am sure, and as soon as she feels confident in her new position, she will raise her head and look around again. By the time that happens, I will have brought Mr. Davies's murderer to justice.

Why am I so determined to do this courageous if slightly dangerous thing?

A reasonable question, to be sure, and in response I will supply three answers.

First of all, because my debut season was only a modest success.

I had many admirers, of course. Mr. Holcroft, for example, remarked on the uncommon pertness of my nose, and Mr. Cuthbert described my laugh as enchanting. I received, however, no proposals of marriage.

That I was not eager to marry any of the men among this assortment is wholly beside the point. (Mr. Holcroft's breath smells of kippers, and Mr. Cuthbert has a dreary fascination with horseflesh.) A young lady simply wants to be asked regardless of her intention to decline.

Bea's experience unequivocally demonstrates that an investigative female is curiously attractive. Naturally, I am not embarking on a mystery in hopes of securing a duke like my cousin, but I would not be offended if an earl glanced my way.

Second, because what young lady does not yearn for an adventure?

The heady sensation of creeping down the staircase at the Particular to rescue Bea and Kesgrave was almost as exhilarating as slipping on a gorgeous new ballgown made out of yards and yards of the finest silk. (Or so I imagine, as Mama has never stood the expense of fine silk.)

Lastly, because it is our fault.

Yes, *our* fault, all of us: Mama and Papa and even me for not discouraging their effort to locate Mr. Davies.

What happened is this: After discovering Bea had had a secret love affair with a law clerk, Mama resolved to seek out the young man and learn more about him to help us find a match for my cousin. Prior to the revelation about Mr. Davies, the case had seemed utterly hopeless because Bea appeared incapable of attracting a man. But if she had managed to charm one law clerk, perhaps she could charm another.

The reasoning, I concede, is a *little* foolish. But you must understand it had been *years*. Mama was desperate and so was my father.

Consequently, Papa devoted himself to finding Mr. Davies. It was a difficult endeavor because Bea refused to supply any useful details. As she was too embarrassed to tell us the address of his home or place of business, we had only his physical description with which to work. Luckily, that was distinct, for the poor man sported a disfiguring scar that ran from his right temple to his left nostril.

A genuinely distinguishing feature and yet everyone my father spoke with claimed not to know him.

The scar.

Dozens of people.

Not one spark of recognition.

And then he is dead.

Less than a week after my father started his search, the target of inquiry's body was mangled under the wheels of a carriage.

A coincidence?

I hardly think so.

Only one thing could have transpired: An associate of Mr. Davies, misunderstanding the nature of Papa's interest, elimi-

nated the law clerk to ensure that the terrible secrets he had
unwittingly uncovered would never come to light.

Well, actually, there is another possibility: His wife
learned of our interest and, driven mad by jealousy, killed him
before he could succumb to the irresistible lure of true love.

Furthermore, I cannot eliminate the father. He has
already shown himself to be deeply immoral and cruel.

In fact, there are several options.

Even so, I will start with his employer.

Papa made no progress in his investigation because he did
not know where to look. In the wake of her former beloved's
death, however, Bea was far more forthcoming. I know both
the name of his employer (Mr. Brooks) and the location of his
office (Lyon's Inn).

My first step, then, will be to pay a visit to the lawyer to
discover more about his business. Possibly, he is a decent man
who discharges his duties honorably, and Mr. Davies was a
corrupt dealer who sought to engage in unethical activities
under his employer's nose.

It is possible, yes.

But also highly unlikely.

Knowing Bea as I do now and having observed her regard
for Kesgrave, I cannot believe she would develop a fondness
for any man lacking a keen intellect and a firm moral
backbone.

Bea would never love a villain.

(And, yes, I *have* observed her regard for Kesgrave and
cannot comprehend how we failed to notice her affection for
Davies. Her heartbreak after the relationship ended would
have been easy to overlook because her complexion is so
pallid she always appears to be wearing the willow. But her
joy! Bea in love is a giddy creature with a hint of mischief
glinting in her eyes as she thinks of an outrageous thing to
say. How on earth did we miss *that*?)

If Davies cannot be the villain of the story, then the blame must rest elsewhere.

What terrible misdeeds did he uncover? What horrible truth did he stumble upon? Is Brooks the architect of his demise or another victim trapped in an elaborate web of deceit?

A thorough investigation is the only way to answer these questions.

But first I have to make myself sick.

Chapter Two

✥

Although one's instinct is to make a great show of suffering when affecting a stomach ailment, it is actually more persuasive to display restraint. Instead of doubling over in agony, it is better to tighten one's lips as if struggling to stifle a moan and press one's arm tightly against one's belly. The effort to bear one's pain with dignity is far more convincing than a procession of groans and whimpers.

This is true, at least with my mother, whose own fondness for dramatics runs so deep only the prospect of actual death would overcome it.

But figuring out the best way to exhibit one's symptoms is only half the battle. The larger challenge is finding the appropriate source of one's complaint.

The last time I needed to slip out of the house undetected, which was a week ago, when I rescued Bea and Kesgrave from certain death, I used a plate of oysters. I let them sit at room temperature for an entire day, which made them so pungent that when my mother came to my bedchamber to attend to me, she flinched at the smell. Fervently, she ordered me to take to my bed (I was already there) and remain supine for at least four and twenty hours (barring episodes of gastric distress, in which case I was to get to the commode as quickly as possible to spare the linens).

Obviously, spoiled shellfish is the ideal culprit and should always be one's first choice if they can be found in the larder. Variety, however, is also essential to a successful scheme, and since I have already used oysters, this time I pretended to eat rotten eggs.

As the patterns of the household are familiar and unchanging, I know that a half hour after my mother wakes up in the morning is ideal for sneaking into the kitchen. That is when the servants are at their busiest, running in every direction to make sure Mama's tea is served promptly and the rooms are up to her standard of cleanliness. At that time, I can boldly stroll into the pantry and rifle through the shelves without Mrs. Emerson noticing I am there.

But on this occasion I did not boldly stroll. I unobtrusively crept.

Although deceiving the entire household was easier than I had expected, it was still a fraught enterprise and I worried about being caught with a trio of eggs in my hands. I fabricated a story about being hungry and impatient, but I knew it would fall flat and invite suspicion.

Better to pass unnoticed.

Likewise, when my mother ordered me to retire to my bed for the rest of the day, I remained tucked firmly under the covers for a full hour. Ordinarily, I would not consider the precaution necessary because illness makes her very uncomfortable and she usually stays far away from the sickroom. But this was my second stomach ailment in seven days, and she was worried that I was suffering a pernicious relapse of oyster poisoning.

"I said this would happen," she grumbled with a hint of triumph when I complained that my stomach was hurting.

We had been sitting in the drawing room quietly embroidering when I decided it was time to have the first wave of pain, which was promptly followed by a rush of nausea. "When you were called from your sickbed to attend Bea's wedding before you were well, I said it would set back your recovery. I knew it would cause you undue harm, but nobody would listen to me. You and your father dismissed my concerns and look at you now, deathly pale and your skin clammy to the touch."

In fact, Mama had not touched my skin at all—that is how discomfited sick people make her.

"What if your health is permanently damaged?" she asked as she led me up the stairs, her legs moving with unprecedented speed in order to ensure she remained two or three steps above me at all times. "How very vexing of Bea! After causing such egregious damage to your health, the least she could do is send a note inquiring after your well-being. I am of half a mind to send her a letter apprising her of your condition."

Goodness gracious, I certainly hope she does not do that.

If Mama has the presence of mind to mention the eggs, then perhaps Bea would not grow suspicious. But her rambling on about oysters would be fatal.

As a precaution, I reminded her that my sickness was caused by rotten eggs.

"Eggs," I repeated with emphasis, "not oysters."

Mama, however, refused to believe it, forcing me to pull two malodorous orbs out of my pocket to prove that I had made another wretched choice. Although the smell made me feel genuinely queasy, she paid them no heed. They might as well have been roses for all the reaction they elicited.

By the time we arrived at my bedchamber, she was convinced that I would never regain my pre-oyster robustness *and* that she had caught my ailment from me.

"I am quite warm, Flora," she said, breathing heavily. "Quite, quite unduly warm."

Of course she was—she had practically run up the stairs, which was a significant exertion for a woman who rarely takes exercise.

Distressed, she wondered if she should summon the physician.

As this was the very last thing I wanted, I agreed ardently with the proposal and lauded her for being willing to stand the cost of a doctor's visit. "I know how frightfully expensive they can be."

At once, her expression turned thoughtful and she pressed her palm against her forehead again, pleased to note that her skin had cooled a little. Since I was the one who was reportedly suffering a stomach complaint, it was a little difficult not to take offense at her action. If anyone's temperature should be gauged, it was mine.

Clearly, if I ever truly got sick, I would have to rely on Mrs. Emerson for proper treatment.

"Let's hold off on the doctor for now, as oyster poisoning relapse usually runs its course within a day or two," she said firmly. "What you need is a good, long nap. I will have Mrs. Emerson send up some broth in a few hours."

I nodded weakly, as if almost too exhausted to speak, and suggested that the housekeeper leave the tray by my door so that my sleep would not be disturbed.

Mama readily agreed and left.

That was little more than thirty minutes ago.

It is almost noon now, and I wait until the clock strikes the hour before climbing out of bed. I retrieve my green dress from my wardrobe and put it on without the help of my maid, which is a little more challenging than I expected. I also select a dull-colored poke bonnet with a wide brim and an assortment of clashing feathers to hide my face. Then I pull a slim black leather case from under my bed, which contains the drawing of Mr. Davies that I made from Bea's description. I check my reticule and count the number of coins to make sure I have enough money to get me to and from Wych Street. The last time I ventured out by myself, I underestimated how much it would cost to take a hack all the way to the Strand and found myself without sufficient funds to pay for the return trip.

Although this might have been a deeply problematic discovery, it caused me no trouble at all because I was able to apply to Bea for a loan. Freshly freed from their underground tomb by my humble self, she and Kesgrave were more than happy to return me safely to Portman Square.

By any measure, my first solo outing had been an unqualified success. Not only did it give me the opportunity to heroically save Bea and Kesgrave from certain death, but it also provided me with a valuable lesson on the economics of public transportation.

Confident that my second expedition will prove just as fruitful, I slip out of my room and proceed silently down the corridor. When I reach the bottom of the staircase, the first floor is also deserted and I dart quickly down the empty hallway to the front door.

Then I am outside and the cool air feels lovely on my heated skin. I realize my right hand is clutching the black case so tightly my nails have pressed half-moons into the fine leather.

Apparently, I was a *little* anxious about escaping the house undetected.

I hurry to the pavement and turn right, holding to my rushed pace out of fear that one of the neighbors might catch a glimpse of me in the square without my maid.

For the first time, it strikes me how vulnerable I am to gossip as a young lady by myself. Although I am not as popular as an Incomparable such as Miss Petworth (oh, yes, the angelic Miss Petworth, who floats around the assembly rooms at Almack's and the gardens at Vauxhall with ethereal grace), I am not entirely unknown among the beau monde and any number of persons would recognize me if they looked out their window. I am cousin to a duke now, yes, which increases my stock on the Marriage Mart, but not even Kesgrave's consequence would be enough to overcome the scandal if I am discovered walking the streets of Mayfair alone.

Curiously, I did not feel this anxiety the last time I went out by myself. On that occasion I was wearing my brother's clothing and knew myself to be sufficiently disguised. Even if a passerby noticed I was female, he or she would not have known *which* female I was.

Unsettled by the exposure, I increase my speed until I am almost running down the block, then halt abruptly when I realize how much worse it would be if I were observed unaccompanied *and* trotting. To be caught—*gasp!*—breathing hard was really beyond the pale of acceptable behavior. Mama might as well pack up my things and send me back to Sussex in disgrace.

Determinedly, I assume a sedate pace.

The walk to the corner feels intolerably long, but finally I reach Orchard Street and raise my hand to hail a hackney cab. One stops almost immediately, and I climb inside, grateful for the privacy the conveyance affords.

Wych Street is in the same direction as the Particular, the theater from whose basement I rescued Bea and the duke, but farther along the Strand. (Oh, dear, quite a good distance farther. I do hope I have enough money for the return journey. Yes, of course, I do. Only a ninny would make the same mistake twice.)

The conveyance circles a large white church with a high

bell tower and turns onto a lane lined with three-story buildings with lofty gables, deep bay windows and dark timber beams. Wych is narrow and close, with thin pavements providing little room for passersby and an air of impenetrable gloom that is unmitigated by a few shards of sunlight glinting against the windows.

I know this is my destination and yet my stomach lurches with unpleasant surprise when the hack stops in front of a buff-colored building bearing a coat of arms barely distinguishable from the grime surrounding it. The shield depicts a lion with its front paws raised, as if it's about to pounce, and I cannot decide if it's the creature's pose that appears so menacing or the muck partially concealing it.

Slowly, I climb out of the vehicle and stare at the entrance to Lyon's Inn. A wrought-iron gate, tall and severe with sharp spikes, stands before a dim passageway leading to the courtyard. Uneven cobblestones, many cracked or broken, line the long path, which is lit by a single lamp. At the far end, a patch of murky light reveals the trunk of a large tree and the thin edge of a building.

It is an inauspicious sight.

Indeed, it is quite intimidating, with its determinedly gothic feel, as if seeking to repel any guests who would dare to visit its dark and distant shore.

But this is London, I remind myself, not the wilds of Italy, and the banks of the Thames are near if not bright.

All very true, and yet I cannot bring myself to move.

The heavy ominousness of Lyon's Inn is daunting, and a frisson of apprehension passes through my limbs, impossible to ignore.

This would never happen to Bea.

Oh, no, not her.

She would not only have accounted for the unlikely prospect of a second-rate Udolpho but also scoffed dismissively at the looming peril of the spiky gate and grimy lion. She had, after all, confronted Lord Taunton with his crime on a deserted terrace and Lord Wem with his sins in the middle of a crowded ballroom.

She is fearless.

Bolstering my courage, I take a step back (yes, yes, I know, *the wrong way*) and examine the buildings surrounding the inn's entrance. They are neat and tidy, with freshly scrubbed windows advertising their wares. To the right is a bookseller, and several well-known titles are displayed. *Guy Mannering* is front and center, and its familiarity is oddly reassuring—oddly because it is the most dreadfully dull book and when I returned it to the lending library, I vowed to never look upon it again. On the other side is a shop selling men's footwear, with a pair of fashionable two-tone top boots prominently exhibited. Papa and Russell regularly sport the popular style.

The resolute ordinariness of both stores is comforting and tempers the menace of Lyon's Inn. If Udolpho were flanked by Carlton House and Kensington Palace, then Signor Montoni would not have been able to get away with quite so many crimes.

I am in the middle of a city.

Furthermore, it is an astoundingly lovely day, bright and sunny and a little bit warm like spring.

Nothing bad will happen.

Staunchly, I pull my shoulders back, as if bravery actually resides in the stiffness of one's spine, and take a step forward, then another and another. Drawing closer to the entrance, I see that it is not *so* unwelcoming. A coat of paint has been recently applied to the gate, which is open to admit visitors. Clearly, the administrators of the residence are devoted to the upkeep of the building's frontage and simply have not had the opportunity yet to clean the rest of the structure. No doubt the mucky lion is scheduled for a thorough bathing later this week or next.

It is my timing that is problematic. Had I come in the middle of April rather than the beginning, I would have been greeted with a pristine facade.

Truly, there is no cause for anxiety. The passageway looks like a gloomy abyss only because the new lamps have not been installed yet.

Encouraged, I take another step forward.

"Miss Hyde-Clare!"

I am focusing so intently on the darkened corridor, with the sliver of courtyard at the other end, that I do not immediately turn around. For a fleeting moment, it seems as though the void itself has called my name.

Silly goose!

As if a void would speak with such cultured assurance.

It would growl, wouldn't it? Or murmur with an oozing sinisterness that sends a tingle of fear up your spine.

"Miss Hyde-Clare," the voice says again.

A very silly goose indeed, I think silently, woolgathering when a gentleman has requested your attention!

Smiling brightly, I turn around to reply with warmth even though I am more than a little peeved to be addressed in the middle of Wych Street. I realize my ugly bonnet and unflattering dress are not a masterful disguise, but surely both suggest a desire to pass anonymously?

Who among my acquaintance is such a bore that he would ignore these clear indications and initiate conversation?

Oh, yes, fish breath.

A man who does not have the sense to chew on a leaf of parsley after eating kippers *would* address a young lady who is clearly on a secret mission.

It is much better, however, than someone important

discovering me. A dandy like Lord Nuneaton, for example, would stare in horror at the minty shade of my dress, and a gossip of Mrs. Ralston's stamp would ensure that word of my strange unaccompanied appearance spread quickly among the beau monde.

Mr. Holcroft, by contrast, holds little sway over the *ton*. He is respectable in every way, possessing a generous fortune and a mild demeanor, but has none of the fascinating originality of other gentlemen I have encountered. When we danced at Lady Leland's affair, he asked me if I was enjoying the clement weather.

The clement weather whilst we were twirling in a glittering ballroom under an array of exquisite flowers!

Truly, if I had to think of one word to describe him, it would be staid.

Well, staid *and* fishy.

It is actually rather vexing because his appearance is quite appealing. His eyes are an unusual green, deep and soft, and his features are gently molded. He has chestnut hair that is thick and wavy but wears it closely cropped in an insipid style that seems to sum up his wasted potential perfectly.

Although I am looking directly at him, Mr. Holcroft seems to think he possesses some special ability that makes him invisible because he raises his hand as if to wave at me and repeats my name yet again.

That is three times in total.

What does he hope to accomplish with his lack of discretion? To summon Mrs. Ralston like a witch in a fairy story?

"I say, Miss Hyde-Clare, are you all right?" he asks as he leans forward to examine me as if I am a specimen under a plate of glass. "You do not look well. Has your maid gone off to fetch help? Do you need to sit down? The spot is not ideal, but I am sure we can manage something."

His concern is genuine if overdone, for I have only taken

a moment to consider the situation before responding to his greeting. Is that not permitted? Am I not allowed to indulge in thoughtful contemplation? Must I answer him immediately without deliberation?

Because his impatience has increased my churlishness, I make him wait another few seconds as I inhale deeply before replying. "Good afternoon, Mr. Holcroft. How lovely to see you again. I trust your family are well?"

For a man whose conversational topic of choice during the waltz is the weather, he seems unduly taken aback by my prosaic remark.

Now *he* requires a moment to think before speaking, and although this meeting has already caused me a delay, I do not wave my hand at him as if calling for a hack. I merely smile and wait.

When he finally does respond, it is to ask again about my maid, puckering his lips and twisting his head this way and that to look for her. Now he does not only smell like a fish but looks like one as well.

"I cannot conceive what she is about, leaving you by yourself on a street like this," he says with disapproval tempered by confusion. "It is reprehensible."

As we are standing only a few feet from a window displaying an assortment of highly fashionable boots, I think this comment is also a *little* excessive. Mr. Holcroft, for all his seeming dullness, has a penchant for hyperbole.

"My parents are well, thank you," I say pointedly, "and as you may know, my cousin recently wed, which was a happy event for all of us. We are delighted with the match."

I stop just short of mentioning the duke because it is impolite to be profligate with one's illustrious relations, but I do want to remind him that I am well connected now. Although the information is interesting on its own, for anyone who had observed the Hyde-Clares anytime in the past two decades would not have imagined our elevation, it also signifies my determination to proceed civilly despite an eagerness to be gone. I am sure Bea is not half so decorous in her pursuit of murderers.

Mr. Holcroft's lips compress into a straight line as he stops looking around for Annie. "I can only assume something rather dire has delayed her. Obviously, it is untenable for you to remain here by yourself. If you will give me a description of your maid, I will leave my tiger here to explain the situation while I accompany you to your home," he says.

His tone is decisive and satisfied, as if he has arrived at the only solution to a troubling problem, and although I find his attitude offensive, I do not let my smile waver. There is nothing to be gained from allowing a gentleman to know you are cross with him. Cheerfully, I thank him for his kind offer but assure him his help is not required. "I have everything I need," I say.

Mr. Holcroft, however, is determined to impose his assistance on me and gestures to a compact man in blue livery who is standing beside a curricle. "Herman will look out for her."

My vivaciousness dips as I realize I cannot smile my way out of the muddle. I must address the matter directly, a task I do not relish. Few men possess the ability to blithely accept correction, preferring to believe that the fault lies elsewhere, most likely with the woman standing nearest to them. "You are so very lovely to be concerned about me, Mr. Holcroft, but you must believe me when I tell you it is not at all necessary," I insist before turning to the tiger. "Your willingness to serve is greatly appreciated, Herman, but you may return to your post."

Naturally, the groom remains firmly at his employer's side.

Although I have stated it clearly, Mr. Holcroft persists in misunderstanding the situation. I cannot perceive what he thinks has happened. How could I have arrived in Wych Street by accident? What strange events occur in his world that people inadvertently wind up at unexpected destinations?

Fortunately, he has enough sense to realize that I won't meekly climb into the curricle at his bidding (oh, but it is a very dashing daisy, is it not, with its wooden gadroons and mustard yellow color) and returns his tiger to the horses so that he may browbeat me in private. "Do you mean to tell me, Miss Hyde-Clare, that you are here without your maid?"

"To be entirely candid, Mr. Holcroft, I don't *mean* to tell you anything," I explain somewhat severely. "If you will recall, you were the one who hailed me. I was quite content to go about my business and you were quite free to go about yours."

It is a sensible response, and if either one of my parents were present, they would gape at my demonstrating such straightforward pragmaticism. Rarely have I spoken so sensibly.

Mr. Holcroft shakes his head in denial and argues that he had not been at liberty to ignore me. "No gentleman worthy of the description would abandon a lady in this part of town."

As he has already revealed a penchant for histrionics, his extravagant framing of the situation does not surprise me. Verily, I thank him for his display of chivalry, however misplaced it is, and seek to release him from the obligation of seeing to my welfare. "You had no hand in my arriving here and therefore *cannot* abandon me."

Although my intent is to put his mind at ease, all I succeed in doing is agitating him, for Mr. Holcroft immediately stiffens. "You cannot relieve me of responsibility, for I answer only to my conscience."

Now I have insulted him.

Men can be so prickly in matters involving their integrity, for they are always so concerned about how others perceive them. They worry about *appearing* caddish more than *acting* caddish. Russell treats me with utter contempt when we are alone together, but the moment we step out of the house, he is all civil and accommodating.

It is such a bother.

Nevertheless, I am not above soothing the male ego if it will help me move matters along and Mr. Holcroft's curricle *is* so elegant. I could easily see myself enjoying a ride about Hyde Park with various members of the *ton*, which may or may not include Miss Petworth, looking on in awe as I drive by in the company of a gentleman whose appearance is not objectionable.

Coquettishly, I flutter my eyelashes and smile sweetly in precisely the way my mother taught me. (Mama believes ardently in the power of a well-executed simper. There is no awkward moment or social faux pas that cannot be overcome with an artful look and a shy giggle.) Then I arrange my features into my most sparkly, endearing expression. "Why, Mr. Holcroft, I am simply overwhelmed by your desire to spend time in my company. Yes, thank you, I would love to take a ride in your curricle. Shall we say something later in the week? Five-thirty in the afternoon perhaps? You may send a note around to my house to settle the details."

But the pose that quelled Mr. Mercer and charmed Mr. Taylor has no effect on Mr. Holcroft, whose lips thin as he regards me with impatience.

Fine thing for *him* to be impatient!

He is not the one whose investigation has been impeded by an officious busybody.

"I am not courting you, Miss Hyde-Clare," he says stiffly. "I am trying to remove you from a dangerous situation, of which you appear to be completely unaware. Wych Street is filled with ruffians and thieves and men who brutalize women. I do not know what brought you here or how you came to be alone, but I cannot allow you to remain. You will permit me to escort you to your home at once."

As Mr. Holcroft seems determined to quarrel, I fear there is no way to avoid an argument. Even so, I make one last attempt. Coyly, I say, "Ah, but you *did* ask me to dance at the Leland ball, so you have *some* interest in advancing our acquaintance. It is flattering, to be sure, and I look forward to our drive in Hyde Park. Now if you will excuse me."

"I must insist that you cease with this nonsense and accompany me to my curricle," he says firmly. "And there will be no drive in Hyde Park. The dance request at the Leland ball was merely a courtesy."

"Is *that* why you spoke of the weather?" I ask, feeling as though a puzzle piece has finally fallen into place. Ah! That also explains the fish on his breath during our dance. Only a man who has no interest in securing a lady's affection would be so indifferent to his presentation.

"Since my intentions are known and clear, I trust you will —" He breaks off suddenly and looks at me suspiciously as if I am trying to trick him. "What do you mean? The weather is a perfectly acceptable topic of conversation."

"It is boring, Mr. Holcroft," I state forthrightly, "as is this conversation. Now excuse me, I have business inside."

For a moment he does.

Stunned by my condemnation of his social address, he lets me take several steps toward the gate before putting himself in my path to impede my movement.

"Inside?" he repeats, aghast at the notion. "But Lyon's Inn is the most vile lair of blacklegs, adventurers and attorneys who have been removed from the rolls. You can have no business there."

I will not pretend that my stomach does not lurch slightly at his description of the establishment, which aligns with the premonition I felt upon observing its facade. Having devoted considerable energy to overcoming my anxiety, I do not relish its return.

Then I recall his habit of overstatement and realize he is exaggerating again. Lyon's Inn cannot be thoroughly disreputable, I remind myself, because Bea's former beau worked there and Bea would never fall in love with a reprobate.

"I must beg to differ, Mr. Holcroft. I do have business here," I say calmly, "and as I have tried to subtlety imply without stating outright because I was raised never to disagree with a gentleman, it is none of yours. I do not know how I can make it any clearer. Please allow me to pass."

But Mr. Holcroft remains resolutely in my way.

"What you are asking is impossible," he explains. "I would not be able to look at myself in the mirror if I let a young lady proceed unaccompanied into that den of iniquity."

I do not doubt the words sound very noble in his own ears. To mine, however, they sound domineering and conceited. "How very fortunate, then, that you have a valet to see to your appearance. I am sure he will be the first to alert you when your swelled head returns to normal size. In the meantime, I must be off. It has been delightful talking with you, Mr. Holcroft, and I hope you will reconsider that drive through the park. My new bonnet would be shown to perfection in your charming curricle."

Although I have little expectation that this maneuver will bear fruit, I am surprised by how darkly Mr. Holcroft considers me. He appears angry at my refusal to yield to his concern, which is rather odd, for he is nothing to me, not even a suitor, so why would he have sway over my decisions?

His expression remains thunderous for another few seconds, then the wrinkles in his forehead smooth and his eyes lighten. "Forgive me, Miss Hyde-Clare, for handling this exchange poorly. My high-handedness has offended you, and it is little wonder you are resorting to insulting me."

"Insulting you?" I wonder aloud, confused. "But I have just lavishly praised your curricle."

He continues as if I had not spoken. "It was overbearing of me to tell you what to do. Rather, I should have ascertained the nature of your predicament before issuing orders. For some reason you are determined to visit a solicitor at Lyon's Inn, and although I find that troubling, it is not my place to question it. Please tell me the reason for the call, and I will take care of the matter on your behalf."

"Commanding me to share my private business is an example of your *not* being high-handed?" I ask with a laugh.

Displaying no corresponding amusement, he says, "Yes. An example of my behaving high-handedly is leaving here, paying a call on your parents and relaying the substance of this conversation."

I stop laughing.

Mr. Holcroft notes the change and nods with approval. "Now tell me the purpose of this visit and I will execute it for you."

There are two reasons I cannot comply with his request, the first and foremost being that this is *my* mystery to investigate and if I hand it over to Mr. Holcroft, then it will become *his* mystery to investigate. Second, it is a deeply painful matter pertaining to my dear cousin Bea and not a trifle for public delectation.

My hesitation annoys him, but his tone is understanding when he promises to tell no one about what happens at Lyon's Inn today. "You have no cause not to trust me. And you must not worry about my judgment. I already know your errand is unsavory if your parents are unaware of it."

"You misrepresented yourself as a suitor," I say.

For the first time since he hailed me, he looks utterly bewildered. "Excuse me?"

"You said I have no cause not to trust you," I explain, "but

I do. You misrepresented yourself as a suitor rather than a gentleman fulfilling an obligation to a female who lacked a dancing partner."

His confusion deepens. "You sought my interest?"

As Mr. Holcroft is thirty years old, reasonably handsome and plump in the pocket, any young lady desiring a suitor with a slight fish smell would be over the moon to nab him. "Of course not. You spoke of the weather and offered a tepid compliment on the pertness of my nose while calling no attention to my grace as a dancer or the becoming blush in my cheeks or my lovely gown."

He apologizes for the oversight at once, and although I am disinclined to accept it, he forestalls the necessity by adding that his comment on my nose was not meant as a compliment, tepid or otherwise. "I was merely stating a fact, for it is unusually petite and sharp. That said, yes, the blush in your cheeks was becoming—as it is now."

But the color in my cheeks at the moment is not a flattering blush. No, it's a mortified flush, and I am sure he knows it.

Determined not to succumb to my own embarrassment, I calmly report that it was in fact *very* becoming. "Which you would know if you had been the suitor you purported to be. Regardless, I have no wish to debate the issue. I was merely explaining why I am reluctant to trust you with the details of my mission."

"I have no wish to debate the issue either," he says amiably, "for I have allowed you to waste enough of my time. You have two options: Trust me to address the matter either for you now or with your parents later. The choice is yours."

His tone is an infuriating mix of languor and confidence, and I can hardly believe the temerity of his statement. *I* wasted *his* time? If not for this conversation, I would not only already have entered Lyon's Inn and discovered the office where Mr. Davies worked but also interviewed the solicitor for whom he served as clerk.

"Ah, see, *now* the blush in your cheeks is very becoming," Mr. Holcroft says mockingly. "I do not have to be a suitor to be observant, Miss Hyde-Clare."

The angry red in my face deepens at his teasing, and I imagine bashing him over the head with my garish bonnet, its bright feathers adding a hint of interest to his otherwise boringly cropped hair.

But obviously I do no such thing. Attacking a gentleman with one's ugly hat on a public thoroughfare is decidedly not good *ton,* even if the lane is narrow and in a bad part of town. It is also not conducive to anonymity, and although I never had the pleasure of meeting Mr. Davies, I am positive he would not want my reputation to suffer in the pursuit of justice for him.

Even if the clerk was indifferent to my fate, there is nothing to be gained from venting my spleen in such a satisfying manner. If Mr. Holcroft were to follow through on his threat to speak to my parents, then my investigation will be at an end. I would cross the threshold of Lyon's Inn but go no further.

I have no choice but to accept his offer.

Still, one never likes to feel as though one has been outmaneuvered by a staid gentleman with a history of fish-scented breath, so I smile radiantly at the tyrant, my eyes sparkling prettily, and apologize for conscripting him in the service of my errand. "I know you are impatient to continue with your day, Mr. Holcroft, but I must insist that you linger a little while longer to accompany me into Lyon's Inn, for it is a terrible place for a female to go all on her own."

For a moment, he looks as though he is going to object, which I find fascinating. Does my treatment of the situation make a difference to him? Is there an imaginary record in his head that must contain an accurate accounting of the transaction? Does it really matter either way?

But he does not argue. Instead, he compliments me on having a conscious knowledge of my own limitations and applauds my wisdom in recruiting him. "You could not have found a man more suited to the task."

Clutching my case tightly in my hands, the better to resist the urge to clomp him on the head with my bonnet, I explain my business at Lyon's Inn.

Chapter Three

I trust it goes without saying that I do not explain my *entire* business to the interfering gentleman whose assistance I neither sought nor desired. Certainly, I would never reveal a secret that would expose my family to scorn or threaten Bea's social standing. But even if public exposure were not a concern, I would withhold information anyway because I do not believe meddlesome behavior should be rewarded.

Instead, I tell him that I am seeking the son of Papa's steward, launching into an exciting tale of filial rebellion filled with raised fists, sworn oaths and heartbreaking betrayals. The younger Mr. Davies, incapable of meekly submitting to the life his father had laid out for him, sneaks away under the cover of darkness to seek his fortune in London. There, he disappears amid the clamoring masses and is never heard from again.

But wait!

He is discovered through a remarkable (and too complicated to explain here but trust me it is *really* extraordinary and your mouth would drop open upon hearing it) coincidence to be working as a clerk at Lyon's Inn, and I have taken it upon myself to arrange a reunion.

As I am making up the story as I go along, adding more and more details to heighten its sense of reality, it's impossible to account for every narrative contingency. The longer I speak, the more issues arise.

Why, for example, am I the one who is conducting the search? Is there no one who is better qualified?

Um...yes...but, you see, the elder Mr. Davies is like a second father to me and knowing how dearly he longs for this reunion, I could not bear to impose the responsibility onto someone else.

Not even my own dear papa?

Because...hmmm...because the younger Mr. Davies is like a second son to *him* and I do not want to get his hopes up. For that would be cruel, wouldn't it, to make him believe a happy event is imminent and then fail to produce the fatted calf. No, it is far better to find out the truth first and then share it with everyone. Yes, because the younger Mr. Davies was like a second son to Mama as well.

How dearly everyone in the family loves Mr. Davies!

Despite being a haphazard patchwork of lies, the explanation makes sense because Mr. Holcroft does not interrupt a single time to ask questions. When I finish, he merely nods and says, "An unfortunate situation indeed. I hope the gentleman's mother recovers from her convulsive fit to resume gardening. It would be a shame if her radishes died."

I lower my head, as if to observe a heartfelt moment of silence for Mrs. Davies's struggling vegetable plants, and thank him for his concern.

"Given the purpose of your visit," he adds, "it is very fortunate you requested my assistance because I happen to know a solicitor with rooms in Lyon's Inn to whom we can apply for information."

As that development is a little too convenient, I eye him warily. "I thought you said only blacklegs, adventurers and attorneys who have been removed from the rolls work there."

"Oh, they do. It's a veritable breeding ground of ne'er-do-wells and scoundrels," he affirms mildly. "But we happen to have one of those in our family."

Since no one among my acquaintance would readily own to having a black sheep among their relations, I find this claim even more dubious.

Sensing my distrust, he laughs. "Miss Hyde-Clare, we are having an honest exchange, are we not? You have given your unvarnished opinion of my conversation, which I will take under advisement, although I am unlikely to alter my behavior, as I still think the weather is an appropriate topic of conversation between strangers, even on the dance floor. And I have admitted with unprecedented candor that I have no romantic interest in you. Why would I lie to you now? I have no cause, especially when it can be quickly disproved."

His argument makes sense—not the part about our honest exchange, for I have told many lies during our conversation and cannot believe he has not done the same. But laying claim to a family member who doesn't exist is a needlessly brazen falsehood. And what purpose could it serve? To lure me into a building I was already determined to enter? If he had wicked designs upon my person, he could have allowed me to proceed unimpeded. Instead, he tried to dissuade me from my course.

Given his penchant for exaggeration, it is possible that Mr. Holcroft has devised some elaborate scheme to entrap me. Only a fool would dismiss the concern entirely. Nevertheless, I think it is highly unlikely. Squalid little deceptions are simply not in his character, which is too sedate.

I believe not in his goodness but his staidness.

"Very well, then," I say. "Tell me about the Holcroft black

sheep."

He shakes his head vigorously. "Not a Holcroft. Never a Holcroft. Cousin Charles hails from a branch on my mother's side of the tree. He's a Caruthers through and through. Even has the hairline. He's the son of my mother's first cousin, so a little bit removed, which gives us breathing room when it's necessary to deny the connection. He is quite a disgrace, old Charlie. Disbarred for accepting payments from his client's opponent, which is utterly shameful. It would not be quite so wretched had it happened just the one time, but he made a regular habit of it. So very distasteful. The family are quite embarrassed and do not talk about him at all, except to lament the moral laxity of the other side of the family. Needless to say, my mother has cut all ties to her cousin and his family."

Suddenly, I am suspicious again. If the connection has been severed, why would he be willing to reestablish contact for me, a woman he admits to having no romantic interest in at all?

Once again, he finds my lack of trust amusing and smiles at my doubtful expression. "Miss Hyde-Clare, how do you think I came to arrive here, at the entrance of Lyon's Inn, at the same time as you? It was not, I assure you, to buy boots at the mediocre establishment next door. Despite my mother's abhorrence, I visit once a week. I am determined to reform him."

Of course he is. What else is a staid gentleman to do when saddled with a disreputable family member?

I nod, satisfied with his answer. (Although I am actually not satisfied because how does one go about performing a rehabilitation: Bible study? Brisk exercise? A strict diet of turnips and pork jelly?)

Mr. Holcroft gestures toward the entryway and asks if I am ready to proceed to his cousin's rooms. I agree and we walk through the gate into the passageway, which is as dark and dank as it appeared. There is a coldness about the air, and I am surprised to find myself grateful for his presence.

The sliver of courtyard seen from the pavement expands as I draw closer, revealing worn stone paths and anemic patches of grass and dirt. Sunlight filters through the trees as we pass the hall, elegant despite its ramshackle surroundings and smudged windows. A pouncing lion perches in the middle of a gracious pediment, its paws as dirty as its twin over the gate.

"Through here," Mr. Holcroft murmurs as he opens the door to a brick building with narrow corridors.

We pass several men in disheveled waistcoats, and although I examine them each keenly, none pays any attention to me. It is a relief to be ignored, and I try to imagine what it would be like to walk the dark hallway by myself. Scary, I think, possibly terrifying. I might have taken two steps into the building and promptly turned around.

Having never been inside an Inn of Chancery, I could not conceive what one was, and now that I am here, I realize it is like a large hostelry. It is hallways and doors, hallways and doors.

After we climb a second set of stairs, Mr. Holcroft stops at the first door on the left and raps twice. I hear a manic shuffling sound inside as a voice calls, "One minute."

"It will be two," Mr. Holcroft says. "He always underestimates how long it takes him to put on his shoes."

While we wait, he reveals an important aspect of reforming one's ignominious relations: employing the element of surprise. Visiting at the same time every week or sending a note apprising him of one's plan will give one an inaccurate picture of his progress.

"I thought he was making great strides," Mr. Holcroft explains, "because every time I called, Charles was neatly

presented and his rooms were clean. There was never a hint
of brandy on his breath, even when I came in the evening.
Then one afternoon I arrived an hour early because my business concluded sooner than I anticipated and found him in
his shirtsleeves drinking out of a bottle while sitting on a pile
of dirty linens. It was unpleasant but illuminating. Since then,
I have stopped announcing my visits and listen at the door
while he straightens up. He is getting faster and faster. The
first time I had to wait a full ten minutes. It is a positive sign,
but I am not sure of what. Either he is wallowing in less filth
or growing more efficient at hiding it."

Both possibilities seem like a step in the right direction to
me, for getting better at anything is always an achievement.
After five years of lessons, I still cannot play the pianoforte
with any degree of skill and my French is adequate at best and
totalement inutile at worst. And I have never learned the knack
for keeping my bedchamber neat. Russell's room has always
been pristine, with every glove in its place, while mine looks
like a garden after a windstorm.

Before I can voice my opinion, the door opens and Mr.
Caruthers greets his cousin with a scowl. There is a family
resemblance, slight but marked, in the color of his eyes,
which are the same dark green as Mr. Holcroft's. But that is
where the similarity ends because the face of the former
solicitor bears all the hallmarks of dissipation. His cheeks are
drawn, his eyes are inflamed, and his nose is sprinkled with
broken blood vessels.

He might have become proficient at hiding the brandy
but is somewhat less skilled at concealing its ill effects.

"Good God, Seb, it can't be that time again," Mr.
Caruthers says in a rough grumble before coughing several
times as if to clear his throat. When he speaks again his voice
is smoother. "You were just here three days ago."

"It has been a full week," Mr. Holcroft says as he exam-

ines his cousin, "although you may be forgiven for the confusion, as you look as though you've barely slept three nights in
the interim."

The solicitor's frown deepens as he glowers at his visitor
with ardent dislike, but he steps aside to allow us entry.

As it would be indecorous for me to enter the rooms of a
gentleman I have never met, I wait for Mr. Holcroft to make
the introduction, which he does promptly.

"Allow me the pleasure of introducing you to Miss Hyde-
Clare," he says smoothly. "Miss Hyde-Clare, this is my cousin
Mr. Charles Caruthers."

Mr. Caruthers turns his angry gaze toward me and laughs
without humor. "Oh, I see, phase three of my rehabilitation:
make banal conversation for twenty minutes with an insipid
miss."

"Don't be absurd, Charlie," Mr. Holcroft says with languid
calm. "You have yet to complete the first phase, which is to
remain sober for seventy-two hours."

While Mr. Holcroft corrects his cousin, I stiffen with the
intolerable insult of being called insipid. I am many things to
many people and I am sure my father's perception of me as a
silly peagoose is not entirely without merit, but I have never,
ever been insipid. Miss Adams is insipid. Miss Williams is
insipid. Bea before her transformation was excessively
insipid.

Why?

Because they all have hair of an indiscriminate brown
shade?

No!

(Well, yes, because it is a well-known fact that indiscrimi-
nately colored hair leads to a lack of confidence, which leads
to insipidness. My hair, in contrast, is a rich auburn.)

It is because none of them have anything to say. Lacking
conversation, they stand mutely in drawing rooms and ball-

rooms and dip their heads in agreement. If they can manage any statement at all, it is something prosaic like the quality of the lemonade or the weather.

Yes, the weather!

Mr. Holcroft is the insipid one with banal conversation.

"As we have just met, Mr. Caruthers, I will take no offense at your comment," I say, flashing him my brightest smile. Insipid misses do not sparkle. "I am not here to provide you with banal conversation, as I lack the capacity for it. I would be happy to indulge you in a spirited exchange if you so desire. If you *are* yearning for banality, I suggest you ask your cousin about the weather."

The gentleman, seeming to desire neither, stares at me with blank-eyed confusion, which I assume to be an effect of the brandy. I turn to Mr. Holcroft to see if he is offended by my criticism, but he is watching his cousin with a faint smile on his lips.

I pause to allow one of them to speak because it is not proper for a lady to dominate the conversation, especially in the presence of men. Mr. Caruthers's silence I understand, for his ability to think clearly has been muddled by the liberal consumption of alcohol, but it is not like Mr. Holcroft to be so quiet.

Finally, after an awkwardly long interval, Mr. Holcroft speaks. Striding into the room and sweeping aside worn blue curtains to reveal filthy panes and weak sunlight, he says, "It is a bright spring day with a hint of warmth in the air, but you would never know it buried in this crypt of yours."

Mr. Caruthers flinches at the sudden shock of light and growls that if his rooms really were a crypt, then he would at least be allowed to rest in peace. "But I am denied even that small luxury. Go away, Sebastian. Go away and leave me to decompose without your interference."

In response, Mr. Holcroft opens one of the windows and

fresh air enters the room in a pleasing rush. Papers on the desk flutter. For a tomb, the space is decidedly unmusty, although there is a thin layer of dust on many of the surfaces. Law books in a small bookcase near the window look as though they have not been touched in years, and the soot-covered mantel is much in need of a wet cloth. The furniture is in good condition, for there are no nicks or dents in the weighty desk or chest of drawers, but the maroon rug is frayed and the plaster walls are chipped. There is a hole in the ceiling, about eight inches in diameter, which reveals part of a wooden beam.

Displeased with his cousin's presumption, the disgraced lawyer closes the window with a forceful thud. Mr. Holcroft, mere steps away, easily reopens it. Mr. Caruthers, his face thunderous, slams it shut again. Undaunted, his cousin calmly lifts the sash.

Clearly, they could do this all day.

Having no desire to get in the middle of a family squabble (although, yes, I do, for *this* family squabble is fascinating), I step farther into the room and address its tenant. "Although you have taken an adversarial stance against me, Mr. Caruthers, I think you will find that we are in fact allies. You see, I also did not seek your cousin's assistance but rather had it foisted upon me. I was actually going about my day minding my own business when he insisted upon taking control of matters. Perhaps we may join forces to overcome his tyranny once and for all."

Mr. Caruthers, whose arms are poised to lower the window yet again, halts his movements and gapes at me with a stunned expression.

"I have come to Lyon's Inn on a benevolent mission to reunite an estranged family, and I think you can help me with that," I continue. "If you assist me in my effort, then I will endeavor to assist you in yours. I do not know the particulars of your situation, but with a glancing acquaintance, I think the best way to get your cousin Mr. Holcroft to leave you alone is to provide him with another distraction. I understand you have been disbarred from the legal profession. Is there anyone else in your family who is in greater disgrace? A defrocked priest, perhaps, or a traitor who spied on the English for Napoleon? If not, maybe we can find an orphanage in need of a patron. These are just the ideas that occur to me in the moment, and I am sure if we put our heads together and think about it, we can come up with something viable."

As I outline my proposal, the astonishment on his face gives way to amusement, and by the time I am done he is grinning broadly. The change is remarkable, for suddenly he looks ten years younger and I realize with surprise that he is the same age as his cousin. They must have grown up together.

In humor, the lines of dissipation on his face soften, making them appear almost natural, and there is life in the green depths of his eyes.

I can see now why Mr. Holcroft is so determined to redeem him. He wants his childhood friend back.

Mr. Caruthers removes his hand from the window and steps away. "Redirecting his energies to another victim is an ingenious plan, Miss Hyde-Clare, and I cannot think why that did not occur to me."

"Really?" I ask, raising an eyebrow because the answer is so readily apparent. "Perhaps if you drank less brandy you would realize drinking less brandy would help you think better."

I expect another scowl because gentlemen are notoriously prickly when it comes to their drink. They cannot abide any criticism about the amount they consume, especially from women, whom they consider to be abstemious and bothersome. (I am sure this is unfair, but again I refer you to the debilitating effects of insobriety and the general tendency of men to blame women for things they either do not like or that give them discomfort.)

Mr. Caruthers's expression, however, remains amiable and he agrees with my assessment, saying perhaps he should have had the good sense to abstain from all alcohol until after his problem had been resolved.

I nod approvingly. "Exactly, *then* you may be free to kill yourself by inches without officious interference. It is very convenient that you already have a crypt."

His smile does not falter, but a hint of confusion enters his eyes, or maybe it is regret, and he looks around the shabby room. His gaze settles on an armchair with carved cabriole legs. It is covered with loose sheets of paper and a wrinkled cravat, and bundling the assortment in his arms, he begs me to take a seat. "I am unaccustomed to callers," he explains apologetically as he delivers the items to the next room, "except for Holcroft the Holy here, and I make him stand during the visit so as to discourage his return."

"No," says Mr. Holcroft, who is placing a kettle on the fire, "he makes me clear a space for myself, which is more inhospitable."

"And yet he keeps returning," Mr. Caruthers murmurs, "so you can see my predicament."

His cousin ignores this remark and scavenges a third teacup from a cabinet along the far wall. He places it on a tarnished tray next to the other two before retrieving a canister of tea. His proficiency is a little startling and at odds with his elegant appearance.

Mr. Caruthers notices nothing amiss, and taking the other seat in the room, a simple chair with a torn back, asks how he may be of service.

I open the black case and pull out my drawing of Mr.

Davies. "I am trying to locate this man or his employer. His name is Theodore Davies and he has a connection to my family," I explain vaguely. Although I will repeat the story I told his cousin if necessary, I would rather not. I am certain I included particulars that are impossible for me to remember now because I do not have Bea's skill for recalling every minor detail of a situation (which, to be honest, can be a little vexing because sometimes there are things you are deliberately forgetting, such as whose turn it is to help Mama count the silver). "My information is unreliable, but I've been told that he is a clerk for a solicitor at Lyon's Inn, a Mr. Brooks."

He takes the proffered drawing and examines it thoughtfully, as does Mr. Holcroft, who has stepped away from the fire to peer over his cousin's shoulder.

"That scar is quite distinctive," the latter says.

I nod because I am grateful to have its distinctiveness acknowledged. From Papa's failed search, one would think every second clerk in London sported such an eye-catching disfigurement.

"Although I won't claim to know every occupant of Lyon's Inn, I am familiar with the majority of them and there is no Brooks," Mr. Caruthers says, destroying my hopes.

"How did he get the scar?" Mr. Holcroft asks thoughtfully. "It seems as though only a blade could have made a mark that is so long and thin. Does he fence? How much function does he have in that eye? I cannot believe he has full function because of the way it cuts across. It must be very difficult for him to read. I wonder why he chose law as a profession. Something manual would be more suitable to his disability."

I have no answers to these questions because I myself never asked them. I thought them, for it is impossible to see such an extravagant mark across someone's visage and *not* wonder how it got there. But Bea was always so uncomfortable whenever we raised the topic of her lost love and it felt cruel to make her talk about him more than necessary. Furthermore, disfiguring marks, no matter how dashing and appealingly piratical, are always the result of a painful incident and it is discourteous to explore another person's anguish simply to satisfy one's own curiosity.

Of course, I am not bound by the truth. Having created an alternative history for the law clerk, I am free to add whatever details I would like. *My* Mr. Davies, for example, might have suffered a terrible injury on the night of his departure from Welldale House after being set upon by a pack of thieves determined to rob him of his last few possessions.

A harrowing duel!

A grievous wound!

A daring escape!

But I do not want to add anything because it seems foolhardy to tell new lies when I am barely capable of remembering the old ones.

Fortunately, I am spared the necessity of a reply by Mr. Caruthers, who says pensively, "There *is* a Brooke, Walter Brooke, but he cannot be the person for whom you are looking, as he is known to be a scoundrel."

My ears perk up at this information.

A scoundrel is *exactly* the sort of person I am looking for.

Grateful, I smile brightly at Mr. Holcroft just as the water begins to boil, then return my attention to the former attorney. "A scoundrel?"

He nods slowly. "I realize it is a case of the pot calling the kettle black but he is—"

"Gray," Mr. Holcroft interrupts.

His cousin's brow furrows at the interjection.

"It is a case of a *gray* pot addressing a black kettle," Mr. Holcroft explains mildly as he pours the water into the teapot. "You are once again inflating the depravity of your misdeed. Your reputation has been tarnished, not blackened.

I beg you to recall the difference, for it is getting tedious reminding you."

"Not as tedious as being reminded," Mr. Caruthers mutters under his breath.

Mr. Holcroft, remaining silent, either did not hear the remark or chose to ignore it.

"Mr. Brooke?" I prompt.

"I do not know him personally so I cannot attest to his character or the extent of his immorality, but I have been advised by several people whose situations are similar to mine to contact him," Mr. Caruthers says. "I have been told that he can give me work, and the general tenor of these conversations leads me to believe the assignments are not entirely honorable. More broadly, they say he uses his position to gather information about his clients' valuables and then arranges for the items to be stolen. If that is true, then he is a man without conscience, and I cannot believe that anyone with a connection to you, Miss Hyde-Clare, would be associated with such a blackguard."

Ordinarily, I would be the first person to agree with that sentiment. My family is unremarkable, and we occupy a narrow slice of the social sphere. Papa does belong to a club, of course, where he has no doubt interacted with dozens of men of questionable ethics, but he has befriended few, and Mama also keeps to a small circle. She has several intimates with whom she visits regularly, and if they are not entirely circumspect in their chatter they are all perfectly respectable (although one of her dearest friends from childhood *did* turn out to be a murderess).

But accidents happen, and no matter how hard one tries to account for the moral worthiness of one's acquaintance, a rogue or a rascal slips into the mix. Given Bea's regard for Mr. Davies, I can only assume he was completely ignorant of his employer's wicked reputation when he accepted the position.

As the father of two young children and a mostly devoted husband (he could not give to his wife the piece of his heart that he long ago surrendered to Bea), he did not have the luxury of being overly selective in his situation. Presented with a seemingly golden opportunity, he would have had no choice but to pursue it.

From Mr. Caruthers's description, it seems apparent that Brooke is a man who works in the shadows, making his villainous deeds harder to detect. Mr. Davies probably discovered them inadvertently, perhaps by overhearing a furtive conversation or reading a document that was not meant for his eyes.

Once cognizant of the solicitor's villainy, Mr. Davies could not have helped but alter his behavior slightly. Maybe he could no longer look his employer in the eyes or let slip to a colleague that he was thinking of taking a new position. Something in his conduct made Brooke suspicious, which is why, when Papa began asking questions, Brooke decided his clerk had to be eliminated.

The theory is pure speculation, but one has to begin somewhere and Brooke seems like a very good starting point.

Am I concerned that the attorney's name is slightly different?

No, I am not.

My inability to correctly recall the particulars of Mr. Davies's fictitious history only a half hour after relating them makes me aware of the alarming limitations of my own memory. That I would misremember the name after several weeks does not shock me. It certainly makes more sense than attributing the similarity to coincidence.

Since I cannot affirm Mr. Caruthers's statement, I evade it by asking how a man who works out of an establishment as unsavory as Lyon's Inn manages to find clients with objects worthy of being stolen.

It is the wrong thing to say, and I hear the cruelty of my words the second they leave my mouth. In an instant, the smile vanishes from Mr. Caruthers's face. But it is not replaced by a frown or a ferocious scowl. No, he keeps his expression blank, which is somehow worse.

Horrified, I look to Mr. Holcroft, hoping, I suppose, that he can smooth over my faux pas. He does not say anything but carries over the tray and places it on the nearby table. Then he hands us each a teacup, and I clutch mine tightly despite the heat emanating from the hot brew.

I want to apologize.

Of course I do.

It is a terrible thing to insult a gentleman by mistake and not at all as satisfying as offering an intentional slight.

But trying to remedy the problem would only exacerbate it by drawing further attention to it. There are few things more humiliating than having one's humiliation openly acknowledged by other people. I have seen it happen to Bea, and you can read the horror in her eyes and her ardent desire to disappear into the floorboards.

Unable to mitigate the situation, I simply ignore it, raising my eyes to meet Mr. Caruthers's empty gaze in expectation.

He darts a look at the cup of tea near the edge of the table, contemplates it silently for several seconds and then responds. "As notorious as the inn is for the poor quality of its occupants, it is still an Inn of Chancery. My general understanding is that Brooke has cultivated clerks who work for the courts and can refer business to him."

"Cultivate?" I ask, uncertain what the term means in this context. Obviously, Brooke does not bat his eyelashes and giggle with appreciation at their sallies.

"Bribes," he replies. "The clerks refer clients to him and he compensates them generously for the business. Any concern a prospective client might feel at entering the insufficiently hallowed halls of Lyon's Inn is usually calmed by the clerk's enthusiastic recommendation. Brooke's chambers, as well, are quite luxuriously appointed, which tends to quell concerns. He does not *appear* to be a scoundrel."

The best ones never do, I think, raising the teacup to my lips.

But it explains, does it not, how Bea's morally upstanding former beau failed to comprehend the illicit nature of his position until it was too late.

Although the tea is still a little too hot, I take a sip as I try to figure out how to word my next question. If I am going to present myself to Mr. Brooke as a potential client—and obviously I am going to present myself to Mr. Brooke as a potential client because it is the surest way to gain access to the inner sanctum—then I require the name of one of the referring clerks. But how to get it without alerting either man to my plans?

Indicating in any way that my interest is personal would be fatal. Mr. Holcroft, who has already proved himself to be an inordinately meddlesome bystander, would redouble his efforts to interfere. He would threaten again to tell my parents about my shocking behavior and I would immediately fall in line, promising to abandon my pursuit, although really I would just be delaying it. Then I would have to wait another day and arrange yet another stomach ailment before continuing my investigation.

Such a lot of bother!

For the sake of justice and all that is good, Mr. Holcroft must be made to believe that I believe that Mr. Brooke is not the solicitor for whom I am looking.

It should not be difficult to convince him. Sons of old family retainers never get mixed up in ignominious business. They are far too honorable. It is exactly as Mr. Caruthers said: I cannot possibly have a connection.

And yet I must justify my curiosity somehow.

My interest cannot pertain specifically to my situation, but it *can* relate generally. I am, after all, an English citizen and take great pride in the moral rectitude of its legal institutions. The Chancery Court is vital to the functioning of the country because it provides fair distribution of...of...

Well, to be completely candid, I am not entirely sure what the Court of Chancery does. I know it has something to do with noncriminal matters and cases can sometimes take a long time to work themselves out. Every so often, Papa will mumble incoherently about a claim's endless journey through the system while reading the *London Morning Gazette* over breakfast. It peeves Mama to no end, for she claims his grumbling upsets her digestion.

Regardless of its actual purpose, I am certain the court serves a vital function in our society and its clerks should not be accepting bribes from a scoundrel (or anyone else). Having learned of this corrupt practice, I cannot allow it to stand.

It is a matter of civic responsibility!

As this line of reasoning sounds persuasive to me, I own myself to be quite distressed by Mr. Caruthers's report and ask if he knows the names of any of these dishonest clerks. "I will have their employment terminated immediately."

It is a lavish boast, to be sure, and I am not at all insulted by the look of amused condescension that overtakes Mr. Holcroft's expression. His cousin, however, is startled by the assertion and seems to wonder what aspect of my person he has failed to notice.

Confidently, I tell him. "I am related to the Duke of Kesgrave, who wed my cousin Beatrice Hyde-Clare last week. You may have heard of him, most recently in connection to the murder of an actor at a theater on the Strand? He subscribes wholly to the cause of justice and believes ardently in holding villains accountable. I am certain that as soon as he is made aware of this issue, he will exert his authority to ensure that the clerks in question are removed from their positions at once. If you will give me the names, Mr. Caruthers...."

As there are several things in my statement that are difficult to comprehend, not the least of which is that my cousin Bea managed to marry so well, I am not at all insulted when he turns to Mr. Holcroft for confirmation. "The Duke of Kesgrave embroiled himself in the murder of an actor?"

His cousin nods.

"The Duke of *Kesgrave?*" he asks again, as if to clarify a case of mistaken identity.

"Yes," Mr. Holcroft says, his lips curving into a smile. "The Duke of Kesgrave."

Even with this reassurance, he remains in doubt. "The same man who refused to cross the road to lend "Golden" Rod Felton his umbrella or allow the widows of the Peninsular War to have a picnic on his lawn?"

"A lot has changed since you last frequented your club," Mr. Holcroft says. "Brummell's debts continue to mount, and there is talk of his fleeing to the Continent."

That the staid gentleman with a history of slightly fish-scented breath (no sign of it today—thank goodness!) is unable to come up with a more thrilling tidbit is hardly surprising. Even his disgraced cousin realizes it is stale news and rolls his eyes. Nevertheless, he is convinced. "If the influential Duke of Kesgrave takes an interest, then I do believe it is possible that unethical clerks will be removed from their posts," he says, rising to his feet. He strides across the room to the desk, extracts a slip of paper and begins to write.

"I am composing a list of five names," he explains with more than a hint of eagerness. "I am almost certain that the first two are in Brooke's pay. I had heard whispers about them before discovering the connection. The other three names I am less confident about but have good reason to suspect they are too. I trust the Duke of Kesgrave to tread carefully and not take action against anyone without a thorough investigation," he says.

Any satisfaction I feel at the success of my ruse is undermined by the optimism in the broad strokes of his pen. He is hopeful.

I had not anticipated this reaction. Given his own history of depravity and exploitation, I naturally assumed he would be indifferent to their plight or perhaps even sympathetic. If anyone would be able to understand how easy it is to succumb to venality, it would be a man who had succumbed to venality.

But Mr. Caruthers genuinely desires that the corrupt clerks be held to account.

Devil it.

I suppose this means I will have to raise the matter with Kesgrave.

Although the duke does not know me well enough to wonder at my sudden interest in the cause of legal justice, Bea will find it highly odd. Will she find it so bizarre that she will ask me uncomfortable questions and take it upon herself to scrutinize my recent behavior? It is possible, of course, for Bea comprehends far more than we ever gave her credit for.

Even if my conduct alarms her, what could she possibly do?

She is a wife now and cannot don my brother's clothes to ask intrusive questions of strangers. She has the dignity of her position to consider—and Kesgrave! He cannot possibly want his duchess wandering around London alone.

It would be extremely unsafe.

Having settled one qualm, I am confronted by another when I realize Mr. Holcroft is regarding me with a look of deep mistrust. Unlike his cousin, he is not entirely swayed by my display of civic-mindedness, and rather than chance his intercession, I walk over to the desk to collect the list.

Then, to both distract him and bring the interview to a close, I advise Mr. Caruthers to consider looking in on his club in the near future. "As it is apparent to me that you cannot rely on your cousin to provide you with gossip that is au courant. I would never quibble with a man's desire to take to his crypt in disgrace but to do so without the latest *on-dit* seems unduly punitive. And while you are at your club, you can befriend a hapless gambler up to his elbows in vowels whom you can present to Mr. Holcroft as a new project. That would, I believe, be the ideal arrangement for the three of you."

Mr. Caruthers laughs, just as I had intended, and more importantly, the expression on his cousin's face lightens as he hears the sound and affirms my assertion. "If you emerge from your rooms to visit your clubs, Charlie, then I will reduce my visits to fortnightly."

I laud the spirit of the offer but caution Mr. Caruthers against accepting what is clearly the opening salvo in a protracted negotiation. "Counter with one visit per month and settle for three every eight weeks with *specific dates* to be decided later."

As he would rather his cousin did not drop by his rooms without prior notice, forcing him to quickly straighten his appearance and dump his glass of brandy into the bedpan, Mr. Caruthers nods enthusiastically at this concession and calls me a savvy horse trader. "Yes, I think perhaps Seb and I could come to an agreement if he is willing to stop clucking around me like a hen with her chicks."

"Yes, well, if the chick would stop drinking himself into an early grave...." Mr. Holcroft mutters.

His cousin pays him no heed, which seems wise because by all appearances he *is* trying to drink himself into an early grave, and directs an apology to me for not being more help-ful. "I wish I could have provided you with the information you need to find Mr. Davies. Unfortunately, I do not think he is here at Lyon's Inn. Or fortunately, depending on your opinion about reprobates and moral degeneration."

Oh, but he has been *very* helpful, and because I don't want to reveal that fact, I tilt my head down to briefly avoid eye contact as I arrange my features into a moue of disap-pointment. "I am sorry too. Luckily, I had the presence of mind not to mention the possibility that he was here to anyone in his family or mine. So they will not be disappointed."

He agrees with the wisdom of this precaution as he escorts us to the door.

The window has been open for a full thirty minutes, and the sun's position has shifted so that it is now casting light directly onto the worn maroon rug, filtering through tiny particles of dust and glinting off the porcelain teacups. The room is far more cheerful than when we had arrived. Indeed, it is almost warm and welcoming, not at all like a crypt.

Mr. Holcroft thinks so too because the broad grin he directs at his disgraced relative is relaxed and sincere, bearing no resemblance to the tight grimace he had worn upon entering the residence.

Despite his affability, he bids Mr. Caruthers a stern good-bye and promises to see him next week. "Or the one after that if you put in an appearance at Boodle's. I do not have Miss Hyde-Clare's shrewd talent for bargaining, but I will always stand by a reasonable offer."

Mr. Caruthers demurs with a shake of his head.

No, he has no intention of trading the comfort of his crypt for the judgmental interest of his peers.

Truly, I cannot blame him.

Chapter Four

As final as Mr. Caruthers's silent refusal appears to me, something about it strikes his cousin as hopeful. The moment the door clicks shut, Mr. Holcroft sighs with satisfaction. His mood almost buoyant, he leads me down the hallway of the residence to the staircase, which he trips down with a vigor bordering on spritely.

It is utterly bizarre.

To be fair, I do not know Mr. Holcroft well and cannot say with any certainty which aspects of his conduct are *not* utterly bizarre. He might tramp around gloomy corridors with a lighthearted step *all the time*.

But it *seems* wholly out of character for him.

That is to say, why, if he had any capacity for joy, would he talk about the weather while waltzing?

Doesn't the ability to feel the former preclude the compulsion to do the latter?

Nevertheless, he is happy about his cousin's progress, which is good news for me because it means he is preoccupied and not wondering about what I plan to do next. If he *had* suspected that I intend to continue my search in Mr.

Brooke's office, the notion has slipped his mind. His thoughts are elsewhere, possibly in the billiards room at Boodle's, where he will meet his cousin for a glass of claret.

Wine outside of the crypt.

Progress indeed!

We emerge from the gate onto Wych Street, and although the sun is not as bright in the narrow lane as it was in the courtyard, I have to squint to see clearly. I turn to Mr. Holcroft and thank him for his help. "Truly, sir, I do not know what I would have done if you had not insisted on providing your assistance. You have performed a great service for me and I do not know how to express my deep and abiding gratitude for your kindness other than to say a heartfelt thank you."

Is my speech a little grandiose?

Yes, definitely.

But we are at the end of an association that proved quite useful for me and I can afford to be gracious. Additionally, he is a gentleman of some favor, with well-sculpted features and a sizable fortune, which makes him a catch on the Marriage Mart. *I* am not interested in him for the various reasons already stated, but it would only increase my stock to be seen in his company.

Despite his shortcomings, I could bear to dance with him again, especially as a turn around the room would most likely enhance my popularity. His conversation might be ploddish, but his steps are light and airy. Furthermore, a young lady can never have too many suitors.

(Except Miss Petworth. Miss Petworth has too many suitors.)

Consequently, I smile brightly at him, my eyes squinty but sparkly, as I thank him once more for his help.

Mr. Holcroft, however, shakes his head and insists that he has done nothing. Then he devalues his contribution even further by saying he has actually done *less* than nothing. "I have taken away your only promising avenue. What will you do now?"

Spin swiftly on my heels.

Reenter Lyon's Inn.

But obviously I cannot say that.

Instead, I sigh deeply with the *utmost* dejection and admit that I cannot proceed. "As you have just pointed out, I have no promising avenues to explore. Mr. Brooks was my only lead, and now that it has come to naught, I will have to abandon the project."

"Nonsense," he says firmly.

Fleetingly, I think he is challenging me on my lugubrious performance, but then I realize he objects to my attitude.

"You cannot give up so easily," he says with bracing cheerfulness. "Mr. Davies is out there, and you will find him. Never doubt it."

Although I think woeful is the better note to strike in this situation, I yield to his demand for optimism and raise my chin to what I believe is a sanguine angle. "No, I will not doubt it. I will keep hope alive and know in my heart that one day soon I shall reunite Mr. Davies with his dear parents. Thank you, Mr. Holcroft, for your heartening faith. I will take much comfort from it as I wait for more information about him to reach me."

I pause because it is his turn to speak. I have thanked him, he has encouraged me, I have thanked him for his encouragement. We have been as courteous and polite as both our mamas could wish. Now all that remains is for him to say good-bye and leave.

He nods approvingly, which is a step in the right direction, for it indicates that my remarks conform with his expectations.

Excellent. There is nothing out of step here.

Bid me good-bye now and leave.

"To make sure of it," he says, "I pledge to pursue the matter unwaveringly until he is found."

He speaks fervently, his words full of conviction, but they are not the ones I want to hear because they are neither *good* nor *bye*. How much longer will I be forced to linger on the pavement? True, the day is not yet half over, so there is still plenty of time for me to infiltrate Mr. Brooke's office, but I am brimming with confidence now and do not want to waste it. That is not to say I will *lose* my nerve but—

Wait a moment.

Did he just say that *he* would pursue the matter unwaveringly?

He, Mr. Holcroft?

But...but...*I* am the one who is supposed to be steadfast in my pursuit. Mr. Davies is the imaginary long-lost son of *my* father's steward, not his! Mr. Holcroft has nothing to do with my family's deeply personal fictitious trauma.

How dare he insert himself!

Observing my stunned silence, Mr. Holcroft praises my reaction but insists that I must not be in awe of his generosity. "I know it seems overwhelming, but I assure you it is the very least I can do to repay you for your own great benevolence."

My own great benevolence?

Is he mocking me?

Have I done something horribly selfish and horrible, and now he is shaming me by saying the opposite of what he thinks?

But what did I do?

I teased him about his conversation, yes, but there was nothing malicious in my tone and he appeared to take it as a varying preference in style, not as a harsh judgment. And of course I said *nothing* about his unpleasant fish smell because I know the difference between gentle ribbing and mortifying criticism. Even if Mama had not drilled me on the vital necessity of never giving offense from my very first step, I would have known instinctively that a lady does not notice the quality of a gentleman's breath.

Was it something previous to this meeting?

Had I offended him dreadfully before we danced at the Leland ball and *that* is why he discussed the weather with me?

For some reason, I find the idea of earning Mr. Holcroft's disgust highly upsetting.

Suspecting nothing of my turmoil, he regards me with an air of expectation and I am more flummoxed than ever.

Am I supposed to *thank* him for insulting me?

Is the onus now on me to maintain the pretense and affect gratitude for the affront?

If that is the case, I am not sure I can do it because there are no words in my head. I know what Mama would have me say and can even picture the endearing blush that should tinge my cheeks, but I cannot produce either.

My mind is blank.

Is this what it was like for Bea all those years?

Knowing but unable?

When I do not respond, Mr. Holcroft perceives at last my confusion and says, "Your kindness to Charles. You struck the perfect note of matter-of-fact yet sympathetic, and he responded to it. I have not been able to achieve that. During your visit, his demeanor changed, becoming less self-pitying, and it is the first sign of hope I have seen in a year. For that, I am grateful, Miss Hyde-Clare, and I will always be grateful. You must allow me to do you a service in return. I can see how much finding Mr. Davies means to you. I would like to help you locate him. Please let me do that for you."

His heartfelt belief in my benevolence is somehow more bewildering than his incomprehensible contempt for my meanness because it has no grounding in reality. My treatment of his cousin was motivated by a desire to elicit information from him. If the tone I took to do that somehow resonated with him, it was merely an accident. I did not intend to alleviate his self-pity.

His self-pity was of absolutely no concern of mine.

Because it is so discomfiting to be credited with a kindness one did not intend, I explain this to him candidly. Freely I admit that I had acted solely in my own interest. "I was being selfish," I say earnestly, "and you must not be grateful for that."

But Mr. Holcroft cannot be swayed from his path. He is *determined* to admire me. "If that is true, then you must have an innate sense about people. But that hardly signifies. I am offering you my assistance, Miss Hyde-Clare, and I would advise you to accept it. Look how helpful I have been to you already. If we put our heads together, I am certain we will find Mr. Davies before the month is out."

Before the month is out?

I do not have a *full month* to devote to this mystery.

Just think of the horrifying amount of rotten foods I would have to pretend to consume to spend that much time away from home.

Mama would be beside herself with anxiety.

And my diet!

It would be limited to thin porridge and toast.

I would waste away to nothing long before I found the killer.

Fluttering my eyelashes apprehensively, I profess myself overwrought by his offer. "I could not *breathe* if I allowed you to make such a significant sacrifice of your time on my behalf. If you genuinely wish to repay me for my treatment of your cousin, Mr. Holcroft, you will not encumber me with that burden."

He nods as he contemplates the unpleasant prospect of being a millstone around my neck, and I am relieved because the argument *should* dissuade him. Whatever being a gentleman entails, it should not include crushing a lady with your generosity.

But when he replies to my plea, it is not to take a step back from my investigation but to embroil himself further. "And I will not encumber myself with the burden of your ill treatment, abuse and possible assault at the hands of Brooke or one of his henchmen. Do not ask me to assume that responsibility, Miss Hyde-Clare, because I will not."

Gasp!

Mr. Holcroft smiles with grim humor at my shock. "Yes, my dear, I know exactly what you are thinking because it is the obvious conclusion. If Charlie's wits weren't so addled by drink, he would have also realized the names are too similar to be anything but a mistake on your part and refused to provide you with a list of Chancery clerks. I assume you intend to introduce yourself as a client and claim you were referred by one of the clerks? Very well," he says mildly, his manner oddly placid for a man outlining a devious scheme that was meant to be undertaken without his knowledge. He does not appear offended or put out. "Let us proceed now to Brooke's office and see what we can discover about your Mr. Davies."

Ah, so that's why he is so phlegmatic, I think, narrowing my eyes as a ray of sun creeps over a gable and shines directly in my face. He means to trick me by...by...

If I cannot conceive exactly how he plans to deceive me, it is because I am not a swindler at heart. Lying to my family about my various stomach ailments is very difficult for me, and I devoutly wish it were not necessary.

Alas, there are few opportunities for a well-bred young

lady to find evidence and examine clues outside the confines of her bedchamber.

Mr. Holcroft eyes me expectantly because he thinks I am so goose-witted as to accept his suspicious offer. He would never blithely volunteer to escort me into the company of a known scoundrel.

Obviously, it is a trap, and the moment I confirm the accuracy of his assumption, it will snap closed. Mr. Holcroft will return me to my parents posthaste and will reveal to them every little detail of my day's activities, starting with the fact that I ventured to disreputable Wych Street without my maid.

He has had enough of me and Mr. Davies, for he had come to Lyon's Inn only to needle his disgraced cousin for a little while before sauntering over to Bond Street to buy a new tailcoat. Having devoted so much time to my misadventure (although, reminder: Nobody asked him to!), he is determined to bring it to a conclusion by ensuring I am not allowed to leave my home for several months to come.

That is how he plans to evade the burden of my ill treatment at the hands of Mr. Brooke or his henchmen.

I remain silent as these thoughts occur to me, and Mr. Holcroft shrugs and walks away.

But he does not go toward the street, where his tiger is waiting with his horses. No, he goes in the complete opposite direction, striding briskly toward the austere black gate that marks the entrance to Lyon's Inn.

Stunned, I stare at his back, appalled that he thinks he can treat me like a recalcitrant toddler who refuses to obey her mother. Pretend to walk away and the small child will follow.

It is excessively insulting.

Unlike a parent, however, Mr. Holcroft does not peer over

his shoulder to see if his ruse is working. He passes through the gate and disappears into the passageway.

Devil it!

Humiliated beyond words, I run after him.

Yes, you read that correctly—*run*.

I, Flora Hyde-Clare, am running on the pavement in Wych Street.

That is what he has reduced me to with his childish ploy.

And I thought fish breath was bad.

He is at the far end of the passage by the time I catch up to him. I am a little out of breath, and he slows his stride as a concession. But he does not stop despite my request that he do so.

"I do not know what you think you are doing, Mr. Holcroft," I begin heatedly, although I know exactly what he is doing and it won't work, "but you are interfering in a matter that is very important to me and I could not resent it more. You may think informing on a young lady to her parents is an honorable action to save her from abuse, but it is in fact disgraceful behavior and I would have thought better of you."

He stops.

We are in the middle of the courtyard, and a gentleman with heavy black brows grunts at me as I halt suddenly in his path. I step carefully to the side to allow him to pass.

Because he was walking with great speed, as if to get away from me, I expect him to be angry when he addresses me. But his expression is placid and he calmly assures me that he is well aware of how important the matter is to me.

"On that head, Miss Hyde-Clare, you have no cause to worry," he says. "Now, to be clear, I *am* acting honorably to save your person from abuse by accompanying you on your visit to Brooke's offices. I made that exact offer not three minutes ago, and you are the one who dawdled by refusing to respond. Personally, I am not a devotee of slapped-together plans and would prefer to proceed with delicacy and caution. That is why I said we would have the matter resolved within the month. But you are so determined to talk to Brooke now, today, that you refused to even discuss it. As I have some inkling as to the cause of your impatience, I decided to fall in line with your schedule. Today. Now. Is there something else you wish to discuss before we call on Brooke?"

Do I still think it is a trick?

Yes, some small part of me cannot comprehend the generosity of his offer. There is no rational reason why he would insist on entangling himself in my escapade, and telling on me to my parents is a reliable way to ensure my safety and end his involvement.

But I cannot deny the sincerity with which he proposed his overture, and if he is such an accomplished thespian that he can lie so convincingly, then I am powerless against his deception.

Solemnly, I nod.

When I imagine myself swooping down from on high and bringing a murderer to justice, I am alone in the picture. (Well, actually, there's a disgruntled killer in the picture as well as a small audience who are so impressed with my savvy they are incapable of speech, but I am *alone* in my heroism.) The prospect of sharing my accomplishment with another person had never occurred to me, and I am slightly disheartened to consider it now.

Some of that sensation, however, can be attributed to shame because I am relieved not to have to pursue Brooke alone. Lyon's Inn is bleak and gloomy and not at all delightful to look at like Brighton Pavilion, and I am not certain that I would have got the nerve to pass through the gate had Mr. Holcroft not insisted on introducing me to his cousin. Very possibly, I would still be standing on the pavement trying to convince myself to enter.

Bea would have entered.

Brashly and bravely, she would have strode through the spiked gate and entered Lyon's Inn.

It is strange to contemplate your own weaknesses in light of the strengths of someone who you thought feeble for so long.

And yet for all her brashness and bravery, Bea has the duke, I remind myself, and he is no minor addition. When I saved them from certain death in that theater cellar on the Strand, she insisted it was Kesgrave who had been on the verge of ensuring their freedom.

Kesgrave, not herself.

If the situation called for the duke's intervention, that means Bea herself was unequal to the task. My clever and dauntingly competent cousin was helpless and required assistance.

In view of that development, the most un-Bea-like thing I could do would be to turn *down* Mr. Holcroft's offer.

Obviously, I cannot be that foolish.

Tilting my head thoughtfully, I own myself to be quite fond of delicacy and caution as well and suggest we discuss our approach before charging into Brooke's chambers to demand answers. "We must first establish our story."

"Our story?" he asks quizzically.

"Yes," I say firmly. "The reason we are looking for Mr. Davies."

His eyebrows knit as he contemplates me in the shadowy light of the courtyard. "Our story is he is the obstinate son of an old family retainer whom we wish to reunite with his parents."

Well, yes, that is *his* story, I think churlishly, told specifically to allay any suspicions *he* might have about my presence at the Inn of Chancery.

But what am I going to tell Brooke to allay *his* suspicions?

Forced to devote all my energy to extricating myself from Mr. Holcroft's company, I have not yet had the chance to properly consider my ruse. A venal uncle would be convenient, for they are always trying to steal one's inheritance and—

"I know you think an elaborate tale of intrigue will better serve your cause," Mr. Holcroft continues, "for that is why you asked Charlie for the list of clerks, but you must trust me on this: The truth is always better than a lie. Especially when the truth is so utterly benign, as in this case."

Naturally, I am gratified by his description, for one does want to come up with credible fabrications, and it appears I have achieved that end swimmingly. But the convincing falsehood has hampered to a large extent his ability to make useful recommendations about the current circumstance, and I have to take a moment to decide if repeating the story to the men in Brooke's office will help or hinder my investigation.

The main drawback is that I know what happened to Mr. Davies so to visit Brooke and ask him what happened to Mr. Davies will merely elicit information I already possess. It will provide nothing of value and force me to return another day with another ruse, one that will necessarily have to be more elaborate to overcome the fact that we have previously met.

It is, I think, a rather significant disadvantage.

But it is not entirely without its positive aspects, for it would also extricate me from Mr. Holcroft's officious presence once and for all. Kindly, he will offer his condolences on my loss, escort me home and, responding to my subtle hints, offer to take me for a drive in Hyde Park in his splendid curricle.

Fresh air is wonderfully consoling.

LYNN MESSINA

Furthermore, it would provide me with a useful introduction to Brooke, to whom I could then apply for help regarding the unpleasant matter of my wicked uncle. Where else would I turn in my moment of need other than the trusted former employer of my dear childhood friend?

On the whole, repeating the story I told Mr. Holcroft is beneficial to my investigation, particularly as there is no way I can avoid a second visit, so I thank Mr. Holcroft for his wise counsel, assure him that I also believe honesty is the best policy and suggest we locate Brooke's office at once.

"As Mr. Davies's parents have been waiting four years for word of their son," I explain, "I am sure you can understand my impatience."

"Indeed, yes, Miss Hyde-Clare, I understand it perfectly," he says with smooth conviction.

We proceed to the solicitor's office, which we locate after a brief consultation with a passerby. It is on the first floor of the building, in the middle of a long corridor that is as poorly lit as the one leading to Mr. Caruthers's rooms, and when we step inside, I expect to find the same careworn desolation that pervades all of Lyon's Inn. Instead, I am greeted with a cheerful interior, tasteful in its comfort, prudent in its luxuries and possessing an air of modest success. The walls are a serene blue, pale in its cast and slightly greenish, with curtains of a deeper aquamarine and a floor cloth that is a little lighter than navy. White bookshelves flank the cheerful fireplace, whose mantel displays a trio of small green vases with yellow arrangements.

There is a desk near the far wall and a square table with four chairs with silk cushions and latticework backs. Open books are scattered on various surfaces, including the small settee next to the fireplace, creating a sense of genteel productivity. The feeling is enhanced by the pair of clerks who are engrossed in their work and belatedly realize our presence.

Both men rise to their feet, greeting us warmly, and the one with sandy hair crosses the floor with a slight smile on his face. He is younger than I would expect a clerk to be, only a year or two older than my brother, but appears knowledge-able and competent as he invites us to tell him how he may be of service.

Having failed to anticipate such a reassuring atmosphere, I am thoroughly taken aback by it. As Brooke is a villain, I assumed some aspect of his villainy would reveal itself in his surroundings. I am not such a ninnyhammer as to expect cloven hooves or horns, but a faint whiff of brimstone would not have given me pause.

Examining the lovely office, all I can think is how easily I would have succumbed to its charms had I not known better. If I had in fact possessed a sinister uncle with dastardly designs on my fortune, upon entering the space I would have felt confident I had come to precisely the right man to save me from a life of penury and deprivation.

I am aghast to realize how effortlessly I can be gulled by well-coordinated drapery and brightly colored flowers.

Mr. Holcroft, however, is neither appalled nor dismayed, and he quickly explains the purpose of our call. Forthrightly, he introduces us, using our actual names, not false identities, and offers no lies or misdirection. Just as he had said he would in the courtyard, he tells the story of Mr. Davies exactly as he knows it, describing in straightforward terms the anxiety of his family and my hopes in reuniting them.

The sandy-haired clerk listens intently and nods kindly and when Mr. Holcroft finishes his explanation, he turns to me and says, "How very distressing for you and your family, Miss Hyde-Clare. I myself am from Wiltshire, and when I announced my intention to begin my training as a solicitor, my father and I exchanged harsh words. We patched it up quickly enough, but I learned then the ease with which one can say terrible things that he will long regret. For that reason, I do wish I could be helpful to you, but we do not have a Mr. Davies in this office."

If Mr. Davies had been killed to conceal the truth about Brooke's nefarious deeds, I am not surprised that an underling in his office would deny his existence. One expects criminals to lie about all sorts of things, even seemingly minor details.

And a man's murder was *not* a minor detail.

Mr. Holcroft, appearing to conclude the clerk's lack of familiarity is due to the brevity of his tenure in the office, turns to the other man, who is at least a decade older, and asks him if he recalls Mr. Davies.

The clerk takes a few steps forward upon being addressed and then shakes his head, unable to remember such a person. "But I have been here for only a few months. Mr. Altick has been here for several years."

Turning back to the clerk with the sandy hair, Mr. Holcroft confirms that he does not recall anyone with the name of Davies. "What about a man with a scar? He has a scar running across his face. Miss Hyde-Clare has a drawing. Mayhap you would recognize him."

Goodness gracious, my drawing!

How could I forget?

"Here," I say, removing it from my case and passing it to Mr. Holcroft, who holds it out for Altick to inspect.

The clerk examines it carefully but to no avail. He has never seen anyone even vaguely resembling the man in the picture. "As I said, I am very sorry that I cannot be of more help. Although finding lost people is not one of the functions of this office, my employer, Mr. Brooke, is astute and resourceful. He might be able to provide you with ideas for how to proceed with your search if you would like to schedule an appointment. He is appearing in court today, which is why he cannot meet with you now."

As Brooke is my most likely suspect, I open my mouth to accept the offer. Altick and his associate can insist all they want that they have never heard of Mr. Davies, but I will not believe it until I have spoken to the solicitor himself.

And most likely not even then.

Before I can agree to the meeting, however, Mr. Holcroft assures them it is not necessary. "We have other avenues to explore," he says.

We do?

That is certainly new information to me.

To be sure, there are still Mr. Davies's wife and father to interrogate, but I have no intention of shifting my focus until I am satisfied with Brooke's innocence.

"I am relieved to hear it," Mr. Altick says.

"May I see the drawing?" the other clerk asks as he slips a pair of spectacles on. "It is unlikely that I will recognize him, but it's important to leave no stone unturned, is it not?"

Slightly startled by the oversight, for he is clearly a man who prides himself on the inspection of stones, rocks *and* pebbles, Mr. Holcroft agrees at once. He unfolds the sheet of paper as he takes several steps toward the table as the other man crosses the rug, meeting him halfway.

"Mr. Roberts has an eye for detail," his colleague explains, "which makes him a credit to this office."

It is a futile effort, I am sure. Mr. Roberts is no more likely to admit to recognizing the image than his associate, for the subordinates of corrupt solicitors are inevitably immoral themselves (with the exception of Mr. Davies, of course, who was almost certainly too decent to suspect the worst and possibly lost his life attempting to intercede on the behalf of all that is good and righteous). Consequently, I am not surprised when he follows the thoughtful squint of his eyes with a shake of his head.

Oh, but I *am* astonished by what happens next.

Mr. Roberts sneezes with great ostentation and then pats the sides of his coat as if to locate an item. Unable to find what he requires, he apologizes to his colleague with a self-conscious smile, explains that he has lost his handkerchief yet again and asks Mr. Altick if he may borrow a clean one.

With an impatient nod, Mr. Altick sighs and turns to open the top drawer of his desk.

As soon as the other man lowers his head, Mr. Roberts slips a note into Mr. Holcroft's pocket.

He thinks he has been very deft, very subtle and sly, for he looks in the opposite direction and his arm barely moves. Only his wrist twists and his fingers shift.

Mr. Holcroft, as well, gives nothing away. His expression remains placid, a slightly curious furrow between his brows as he waits for the clerk to respond to the drawing.

Indeed, his features are so resolutely unchanging that I cannot be sure he even knows what has happened.

I noticed only because the sneeze was so emphatic, like something you see in a comedic opera at the Haymarket, that I thought an unpleasant emission might sully my drawing.

"No, no," Mr. Roberts says now, raising his head just as his colleague hands him a fresh white square. "I have not met him, nor ever seen anyone with a scar that long. I am confident I would recall if I had, for it is certainly memorable." He blows his nose noisily, causing Mr. Altick to flinch and return to the other side of the office. "I am sorry that I cannot be of more help."

Mr. Holcroft assures him that he has been quite helpful. "Knowing where Mr. Davies is not is almost as informative as knowing where he is," he explains before thanking both clerks for their time.

Smiling broadly, Altick says, "It was our pleasure. And if you would be so good as to leave a card with us, we can contact you at once should a man bearing Mr. Davies's name and description ever apply for employment at the firm."

Of course he is smiling broadly.

He is relieved we are leaving before discovering anything about Mr. Davies.

Little does he realize we have just had every wild supposition confirmed.

Chapter Five

I topple Mr. Holcroft.

Really, there is no other way to describe the maneuver by which I pitch myself forward and knock him to the floor. Carefully, aware that I have only one chance to make it appear natural, I wait until we are at the end of the long corridor, only a few feet from the door to the courtyard, and trip. It is difficult because I am actually quite graceful, but I bend my knees a little bit so that my feet may become entangled in the hem of my dress and I flop onto Mr. Holcroft. He teeters encouragingly, then regains his balance with annoying speed, forcing me to slacken my muscles and drop all my weight onto him.

Finally, he falls.

Huzzah!

Does my gambit lack the finesse and subtlety of Mr. Roberts's tactic?

Well, yes, naturally. As a gently bred young lady I was not instructed in the art of discreetly lifting a letter from the pocket of a gentleman. Instead, I have learned how to leave the presence of royalty (curtsy three times, then back out of the room) and perform a variety of dances with grace and precision (cotillion, scotch reel, quadrille, waltz).

I should like to see Mr. Roberts execute a skip-change step with a little hop, ending with his feet together without launching *immediately* into the next step.

Nevertheless, in this endeavor he plainly possesses the advantage, a reality of which I become even more aware when Mr. Holcroft makes a deeply felt *oof* sound as he lands on the hard floor.

Fortunately, he falls on his left shoulder, providing me with access to the right side of his coat. Swiftly, before he gathers his wits, I dip my fingers into the pocket, extract the note and read it: *Western Exchange, flower stall, 3 p.m.*

A meeting?

A meeting!

Roberts has arranged a secret meeting.

Well, that is highly suspicious. What important information does he have to—

Mr. Holcroft groans.

Oh, yes, Mr. Holcroft!

Following his lead, I groan as well, more loudly than he and with greater intensity, as if to make it clear that my suffering is more acute than his.

If he believes I am in pain, then he will be less likely to examine my clumsiness for an ulterior motive.

Muttering incoherently, I slip the note back into his pocket and then make a great show of patting his torso as if searching for damage. It is excessively shocking for me to take such liberties with his person, but I can see no other way to ensure he does not guess the truth.

Justice must take precedence over propriety.

Mr. Holcroft shifts his position, tilting his shoulders

backward, and now he is looking up at me with an expression of surprise mixed with apprehension. His eyes are so close I can see each individual lash, sooty and long, and I am startled to discover his irises are a deep verdant shade of green, lush and luxuriant, like a rolling field. In the ballroom, when he was discussing the weather, they appeared to be a muddier color, more like olive than emerald.

But now—

"Miss Hyde-Clare," he says sharply, shaking me slightly as I continue to stare blankly at him. "Are you hurt? Can you stand?"

Suddenly aware that *my body is pressing against his,* I leap to my feet and take several steps backward until I bump my head against the wall of the corridor.

"Careful," he murmurs with concern as he stands, "you might be dizzy for a moment. What made you fall?"

It is not difficult for me to affect confusion because I am genuinely baffled by the attraction I feel toward him.

Mr. Holcroft!

With the fish breath!

"I don't know," I say.

He nods understandingly and seeks to mitigate my embarrassment by saying the stone floor is uneven. His kindness, however, only increases my discomfort because now I feel mortified *and* guilty.

It is possible that I was a little precipitate in my abuse. Just because he did not tell me about the note as soon as we left the office or when we were several feet away in the corridor does not mean he has no intention of telling me about it. He could be waiting until we are in the courtyard or the passageway or even his curricle.

Perhaps he simply desired an opportunity to read it first before sharing its contents.

As reasonable as that course of action might be, I did

not have the luxury of biding my time until he was ready. The hallway was my only viable option. The courtyard, which is overlooked by half the rooms in Lyon's Inn, is too exposed to prying eyes, the passageway to Wych Street is too dark to effectively read anything, and Mr. Holcroft's lovely curricle is too intimate to execute any sneaky gambits.

By necessity, it had to be the hallway.

Even so, I am not immune to shame, and unable to bear his bright gaze, I look down at my feet. Seeing the dirt on my gown, I lift my skirt slightly and explain that I tripped over the hem.

Another understanding nod!

If Mr. Holcroft suspects the truth of my maneuver, he gives no indication as he brushes dirt from his overcoat.

Belatedly, I inquire about his own condition. "I fear your left side hit the floor with a rather hard thud."

He shrugs both his shoulders as if to confirm the pair are in good working order and assures me he will suffer no lasting effects. "My greatcoat, on the other hand..."

Although he trails off, implying something quite dire, I observe no tear in the material and optimistically announce that his valet will have the superfine in pristine condition quickly enough.

He allows it is likely and, convinced that the wave of dizziness has passed, escorts me into the courtyard.

"I am sorry about your friend," he says as we pass under a cluster of trees that block out the sunlight.

Briefly, I am confused and almost repeat his statement as a question. Then I realize he means Mr. Davies and sigh heavily, emphasizing my disappointment, which is *very great*. Nevertheless, I remain optimistic and repeat his own comment about all information being useful. "At least now I know he isn't at Lyon's Inn, which is a blessing, I suppose, for it is such a disreputable place. His father would have been so disappointed, I think."

Mr. Holcroft praises my cheerful outlook and pledges to continue with the search through other avenues. We are in the passageway now, and I watch him out of the corner of my eye, waiting for him to indicate his awareness of the note. If it were in my pocket, I would be compelled to run my fingers over it just to confirm that I had not imagined the moment when it was passed to me.

He does nothing.

"Avenues?" I say. "Pray tell, Mr. Holcroft, to what avenues you refer. I am most intrigued."

It is presented as a straightforward question, but in fact it is a disingenuous query designed to prove that he does not intend to deal honestly with me. What he *should* do at this juncture is assure me we have a very promising avenue indeed as he withdraws the secret missive from his pocket and owns himself eager to discover its contents. But what he *does* do is offer to return me to my house and advise me to allow the matter to rest in his hands.

Then his steward enters the conversation, which is a little bit of a surprise. "Mr. Rees is a wonder of proficiency and ingenuity with many acquaintances among the lawyering class. I am confident he will find your missing clerk with ease and quickly supply us with an address for both his home and business. You must not give it another thought, Miss Hyde-Clare," he says, as we step out of the dark passage into the dingy bustle of Wych Street. "I will have you reunited with Mr. Davies in no time at all."

"His parents," I amend.

"Excuse me?" he says, his eyes sweeping the lane in search of his curricle and tiger. It has been more than an hour since he climbed down from the elegant conveyance, and the horses would have grown impatient during the interval.

"We are reuniting Mr. Davies with his parents," I remind him. It would never do for him to believe I have an excessive interest in a law clerk. It is all right for Bea to bear the indignity because she is a duchess now and her consequence could withstand a minor imbroglio.

Not that her devotion to a lowly law clerk would become public knowledge.

Darting his eyes to me, he nods in agreement as his curricle comes into view. "Right, yes, his parents. You are very thoughtful to be doing this service for *them*."

He is correct to hail my consideration, for it is quite noble of me to bring a murderer to justice, but he puts just enough emphasis on the last word to make it clear he doubts my motive. Despite my assertion, Mr. Holcroft remains convinced I have formed some sort of inappropriate romantic attachment to the missing law clerk.

Stubborn creature!

As protesting again will only further entrench his belief, I dismiss the matter entirely and thank him for his assistance. "Your help has been immeasurable, and I do not know what I would have done had you not been so ruthless in your determination to foist it upon me," I say with a good-natured smile before adding that I look forward to receiving word from his steward. "You are very kind to do me this service."

Mr. Holcroft nods at his tiger, then directs his attention toward me. "Why does it sound as though you are taking your leave of me?"

"Because I *am* taking my leave of you," I reply. "I arrived by hack and will return by hack."

But he shakes his head and insists he cannot allow a young lady to ride through the streets of London alone. He will deliver me safely to my home in his curricle.

With a delighted expression on my face, I firmly explain why his proposal is impossible. "Even as we converse on the pavement here, I am ensconced in my bedchamber with a devilish case of food poisoning. If I allow you to drive me to Portman Square in your charming curricle, half of London would observe me out and about and word would surely get back to my mother. I trust you can see the problem. *But* I do find your curricle very charming indeed and have no objection to riding in it on general grounds. I hope you ask me again at a more propitious time."

The simplicity of my logic, however, is no match for the manifold obligations of gallantry, and he remains determined to see me home. After a moment of consideration, he announces he will join me in the hack.

"Very good," I say because it is actually the ideal solution for me. If he assumes responsibility for the fare, I will have just enough coins to cover the cost of getting to and from the Western Exchange.

Despite the lessons learned during my first outing, I am embarrassed to admit that the full expense of embarking on a murder investigation still escaped me.

As Mr. Holcroft has a brief conversation with his tiger, I look down the lane for a hack to hire. Finding none, I realize we will have to proceed to the Strand, which is a busier thoroughfare, a conclusion with which my escort agrees.

We are silent as we walk. I do not know what concerns dominate Mr. Holcroft's thoughts, but I am preoccupied by the meeting that is soon to occur. Mr. Roberts is a mystery to me, and I cannot fathom what his game is. Is he a villain who suspects we are aware of his misdeed or is he a noble bystander determined to do the right thing?

Either way, it is clear that he knew Mr. Davies.

If his tenure did not start until after the law clerk had been murdered, perhaps he has heard Brooke talk about him or read his name in a report.

I will find out the truth as soon as we meet.

Ordinarily, I would never consider attending a secret assignation with any man, let alone one who might be a criminal. I am eager to catch the man who murdered Mr. Davies, yes, but I certainly would not do so at the expense of my own life.

There is a line between courage and stupidity, and I am determined not to cross it.

But the location of the encounter is not a terrifying alleyway in St. Giles or a rough tavern near the river. It is a popular shopping emporium that I have visited dozens of times with Mama to purchase ribbons and gloves and bonnets. It's lofty and bright, with wide skylights and tall columns topped with elaborate capitals. Merchants sell their wares from tidy booths on the main floor while purveyors of art arrange private exhibitions in the galleries above.

It is crowded and cheerful and full of lovely things, and I am certain that nothing horrible can happen there.

For goodness' sake, it is on Bond Street!

Readily, Mr. Holcroft hails a conveyance and he kindly assists me in climbing up before boarding himself.

As he has yet to read the note smuggled into his pocket and is unaware of what lies ahead, I ask how he intends to spend the rest of his day.

Naturally, he cannot resist drawing my attention to the weather and replies that he will go for a ride in Hyde Park. Then he will call on Mr. Caruthers's father to report on his cousin's progress, which he does once a month despite the man's insistence that he does not care to know anything about his son. "And what do you plan?"

"Feigning a slow recovery from a wretchedly debilitating stomach ailment," I remind him.

He nods and asks what disastrous food I consumed to cause such a terrible illness.

"That depends on whom you ask," I reply.

"I am asking you," he says.

"Eggs that had turned."

"And if I ask…"

He trails off but the implication is clear and I supply the answer. "Mama. She is convinced it is oysters I ate a week ago."

His brow furrows. "Were you sick from oysters you ate a week ago?"

I answer truthfully. "No."

Slowly, he nods, and it occurs to me that I should show a little more consideration for my mother. Her belief is not wholly rooted in the puff of smoke it appears to be from my conversation.

"It is fortunate, then, that we have decided to leave the matter in Mr. Rees's capable hands," he says with a satisfied air. "It spares you from causing that kind woman more distress."

Although I find his complacency infuriating, I smile serenely and say that my true good fortune was meeting him in front of Lyon's Inn. As this observation aligns perfectly with his own understanding of events, he agrees at once and further congratulates himself for visiting his cousin at regular intervals.

Mr. Holcroft continues to speak, and I wonder about the hour. It must be approaching two o'clock by now. That is awkward, for it leaves me with just enough time to return to my bedchamber before having to leave it again. The advantage to that is making my presence felt to the household would allay any suspicions that might have arisen during my absence. But I do run the risk of getting caught either entering the house or leaving again. Also, Mama could decide to stay for an extended visit at my bedside, trapping me at Portman Square when I should be dashing to the Western Exchange.

Vexingly, there is no alternative. I cannot linger outside my house or in the square or on the corner.

Oh, but there *is* another option, isn't there? I can go directly to the Western Exchange and arrive early. It would be only a short interval, and I can even do a little discreet shopping while I am there. If I keep my head down and do not ask to see anything in particular, I will hardly be noticed.

If that turns out to be inaccurate and I find myself unduly exposed, I can always hide in a corner or behind one of the columns.

Having settled the matter, I return my attention to Mr. Holcroft, who is silently considering me.

When did he cease speaking?

I have no idea.

Although I can readily fill the extended lull with insightful observations and queries, for I number among my accomplishments ease of conversation, I remain quiet. Rather than asking him about his interest in botany or French politics or the theater, I wait to see what he will do now that he has regained my attention.

It is the perfect moment for him to confess that Mr. Roberts slipped him a note that he is excessively eager to read.

But he says nothing about it at all, which I find simultaneously very annoying and remarkably reassuring.

Clearly, I was right to topple him in the corridor of Lyon's Inn. Any injury his greatcoat suffered was well earned and necessary.

And yet how dare he not share information that pertains directly to me? Mr. Davies is *my* missing clerk, not his.

For all his talk of chivalry, his behavior is deplorable, seizing from my grip the mystery I had wrested with considerable effort from Bea!

The hack dips into a hole in the street, and I grasp the

edge of the seat with both hands, not because I feel myself falling over but because the urge to speak is almost overwhelming. Having been taught to fill silences that tilt toward awkwardness with engaging chatter, it feels like an abdication of my duty to remain mum.

Mr. Holcroft apparently does not suffer from the same affliction, and unable to hold myself back anymore, I remark on the bumpiness of the carriage. "I am sure your curricle provides a much smoother ride."

He acknowledges my statement at once, agreeing that the conveyance is indeed well-sprung and explaining that he had taken a particular interest in devising the design. "I have always been fascinated by how things work."

Although I do not share his interest in the mechanical workings of vehicles, I was just this week brought to a demonstration of Mr. Tarwick's steam carriage by my father, who thought the experience would be enlightening. It was not as I expected—it was grimy, to be sure, and loud—but I did find myself intrigued by the prospect of a future with horseless equipages.

Mr. Holcroft also attended the exhibition and converses energetically about the event. He shows himself to be quite capable of holding a proper discussion, asking me questions that lead me to reveal my thoughts and opinions.

It is a thoroughly engaging exchange, but I do not for one moment forget Mr. Roberts and the secret missive and Mr. Davies's tragic end. I am smiling pleasantly whilst seething privately.

When we arrive in Portman Square, the carriage stops a few doors short of my home, per my request. Mr. Holcroft alights and helps me down.

Deeply resentful of his refusal to tell me about the note, I bid him a stiff good-bye. I do not flirt or slyly let drop how much I would enjoy a turn about the park in his curricle.

Because I have been raised correctly, I do thank him yet again for his assistance, but my tone is cool and a little distant.

Mr. Holcroft promises to be in touch in the very near future with information about Mr. Davies's whereabouts. He says it anticipatorily, as if he truly expects to have the answer for me within the next day or two. He is unfamiliar with the substance of Mr. Roberts's note and yet confident it will lead to a resolution.

I nod abruptly and walk toward my house; my steps slow and close as I wait for the clatter of hooves as the hack drives away. Alas, I hear nothing but birdsong from the trees that line the street and I realize he is going to wait until I am inside my house before leaving.

Bother!

Ah, but Mr. Holcroft cannot know which residence is actually my home. Our acquaintance is slim, and my family is generally beneath his notice. If we resided in an august mansion of architectural significance, such as Kesgrave House, then our address would be widely known.

As a consequence, I walk all the way to the end of the square and disappear into the foliage that swathes the townhouse on the corner. Anyone watching from a goodly distance away would think I had crossed the threshold.

Happily, this ploy works according to plan and a few seconds later I hear the fall of hooves as the hack drives past the shrubbery.

Even so, I wait another minute just to be sure that the danger has passed, then return to the road to secure a hack to Old Bond Street.

As Mr. Holcroft noted, the weather is well suited for outdoor activities and quite a few people are enjoying the pleasant spring day. Drawing my bonnet forward to further disguise my appearance, I alight from the hack and almost immediately bump into a familiar figure.

Miss Petworth!

I gasp in horror and fight the overwhelming desire to lift my skirts and run as fast as I can in the other direction.

Oh, but that would be fatal.

A lone woman in a plain gown and an ugly bonnet is easy to overlook. One haring at top speed through a crowded shopping district is impossible to ignore.

Resolutely, I remain planted in my spot and tilt my eyes downward.

Miss Petworth, as regal as ever, brushes past me with an annoyed huff. She does not deign to look at me, although her lip furls slightly in disgust.

I know it is to the good, for my reputation would be in tatters if she were a little less of a stiff neck, and yet I am insulted by the easy dismissal.

How highly she holds herself!

But taking a pet is a luxury I cannot afford at the moment, and keeping my eyes down, I cross the pavement to the Western Exchange. Ordinarily, stepping inside the shopping emporium causes me to gape in wonder at the endless possibilities. Ribbons, gloves, shoes, umbrellas, bonnets, linens, shawls, *jewelry*—so many wonderful things laid out for my adoration. (I would love to say *consumption,* but the truth is Mama rarely lets me purchase anything, and when she does relent it is always the least impressive version of the item. That is how I wound up with a bonnet so horrendous it does not even rise to the level of Miss Petworth's contempt. Although, yes, I know it is actually impressive to sport a hat that makes one invisible.)

Entering today, however, I feel an entirely different sort of anticipation, for at this moment it is thrilling to know that my suspicions are correct. Far from dying in a routine carriage accident, Mr. Davies was ruthlessly run down by a violent criminal who possesses no respect for the sanctity of life.

Determinedly, without lingering to admire the wares at any stalls, I walk across the floor toward the flower kiosk.

Do I happen to notice out of the corner of my eye a gold necklace with flat-cut garnets and seed pearls that would perfectly complement my blue ballgown?

Well, yes, of course.

I am en route to a clandestine meeting to discover secret information, not dead.

The arcade is crowded, with scores of people milling about, and the pleasing hum of conversation fills the air. I brush by another acquaintance, Miss Caroline Flexmore, whose moderately pretty features and blonde curls are offset by a pair of comically large ears that seem almost specifically designed to endear her to me. She is arguing with her older sister about a fichu in jonquil. Obviously, I cannot stop and lend my support, but I think Mrs. Clement is being unduly harsh in calling the shade horrendous. Nevertheless, her point is well taken: It *would* clash horribly with Caroline's hair.

Reaching the other side of the room, I dismiss these thoughts from my head and consider how to proceed. The flower stall is slightly larger than the others, occupying a corner of the spacious bazaar and consisting of three rows of blossoms and bouquets. As I approach, I glance at the large clock that overlooks the main floor and confirm that I am indeed early. It is only a quarter to three.

Very good.

Now, where should I position myself?

Naturally, I adore flowers, especially ones delivered by a suitor the morning after a ball, and could easily peruse the selection of tulips and roses for hours. There is nothing like a vibrant bouquet for making a room cheerful and warm, especially on a rainy day when one is stuck in the drawing room embroidering an emblem onto a slip of muslin.

Yes, the flower stall will do quite well, for there are already several people inside it browsing and it is unlikely anybody will notice me among them. If I keep my head down and—

Caroline is coming this way!

Having lost the argument with her sister, she is striding toward the kiosk.

Anxiously, I look around for a place to hide. There *must* be something behind which I can conceal myself.

Not the counters.

No, obviously not them.

But there are so many columns.

Yes, but not a single one is accessible. They are all—*all!*—incorporated into stalls, providing, for example, a divider between the glove merchant and the cravat vendor.

Dash it!

Caroline draws nearer, and I back away.

My eyes travel upward, toward the skylights (wretched invention, making everything so easy to see), and settle on the upper-level galleries.

Of course, the galleries.

There is a staircase in the rear of the emporium that leads up to the second level. It is tucked away discreetly in a corner. To the right, I believe.

Swiftly, I spin on my heels and find myself face to face with Mr. Holcroft.

"Miss Hyde-Clare!" he cries in a shocked tone.

Yes, *cries,* as if we are in the drawing room in his mother's home.

Does he want to ruin me utterly?

Frantically, I shush him.

He stiffens his back as if offended but perceives my

concern and lowers his voice when he asks me what I am doing here. I glance behind me to make sure Caroline has not noticed me, and seeing her greet Mr. Arbuthnot (goodness gracious, is the entire *beau monde* shopping for accoutrements today?), I feel some of my anxiety lessen.

Nevertheless, it would never do to become overly confident, and I tilt my head to the left to indicate we should conduct our conversation somewhere else.

Mr. Holcroft glowers at me as he repeats his question, then smooths his features as he nods to a passerby. He consents to my suggestion and leads me to the right, away from where I think the staircase is and closer to the flower stall.

"I cannot believe you are here," he says, the outrage thick in his voice.

Oh, but his indignation is no match for mine and I scathingly respond that his shock is not surprising as he withheld the time and place of our meeting.

"It is not *our* meeting," he growls.

"No, it is mine," I say seethingly, "and you stole it."

Mr. Holcroft snarls but does not otherwise reply, and I realize he is waiting for the opportunity to chastise me properly.

I have no objection to that, for I am eager for the same thing.

He leads me past the flower stall, and I discover he has a particular place in mind, an alcove behind an especially wide column. As we approach, veering slightly to the right, I catch sight of a pair of shoes first, and I think his private meeting spot is occupied by a gentleman already conducting private business. But the shoes are facing the wrong direction, with the tips of the toes pointed downward, toward the floor, and then I see his legs and waist and torso and head—

Gasp!

On a sharp inhale, I open my mouth to scream, but Mr. Holcroft, vile villain that he is, *slams* the palm of his hand against my mouth, ruthlessly silencing me.

He killed Roberts and is going to do the same thing to me.

Chapter Six

Imminent death makes everything still.

The low hum of conversation stops, my limbs freeze, and my brain seems to empty like a bucket that has been tipped over. Even my heart pauses for one ineffably long moment.

At the center of the stillness is a clarity so crystalline it feels as though I can see every particle of dust in the air. Easily now, I perceive the whole plot, and there's almost an inevitability about the law clerk's death.

How did Mr. Holcroft know?

Ah, yes, that is the question, isn't it?

I have no idea. Did he have an inkling of what was to come when he danced with me at the Leland ball? Had his conversation been deliberately banal to lull my suspicions?

Impossible.

I myself was without a clue.

And yet there was nothing coincidental about our meeting in front of Lyon's Inn. It was far too convenient, the way he just happened to discover me as I was contemplating the entrance's gothic shabbiness. Gaining my trust required little more than a firm hand and an authoritative tone.

And now a man is dead.

Mr. Roberts's murder is on my conscience. I led Mr. Holcroft to his door. He trusted him because I trusted him.

Now I must find justice for two victims.

It seems like a futile task, given the heaviness of Mr. Holcroft's hand on my mouth, the pressure he applies to keep me silent and compliant as he plans my own gruesome end.

Oh, but this is not the end.

Just as abruptly as my heart ceased, it starts up again, beating wildly, and with furious determination, I raise my foot and drop it forcefully on top of Mr. Holcroft's.

Stamp!

All my weight!

It does little.

How can it not?

My slippers are silk, flimsy and slight, and he is wearing boots of the stoutest leather. They do not yield an inch to my heel.

Worse, the soft bottom of my shoe actually slides off the hard tip of his.

But he is surprised.

This useless gesture startles him, and his hand slackens just enough for me to drive my teeth into it.

He gasps in pain, tugging his hand toward his chest, freeing me entirely, and he stares down at the bite mark on the side of his little finger and then at me and then down again, astonished.

Why is he astonished?

Did he truly think I would go unresistingly to my death just because I am a gently bred lady who was taught to defer to men in all things? Does he honestly believe that the rules governing proper decorum do not contain a proviso on the preservation of one's life?

While he is still staggered by surprise, I run past him toward the crowded floor of the exchange, but his hand darts out and grabs my arm. Firmly, he tightens his fingers and says with impatient disgust, "For God's sake, I knew you were silly but this—" He breaks off with a shake of his head, unable to come up with a word properly descriptive of my silliness. "I did not kill Roberts. I had nothing to do with his death. Use whatever small amount of intelligence you have, Miss Hyde-Clare, and think! Why would I have brought you here? What purpose would I have in harming him, a man who is a complete stranger to me, and then bringing you to the same spot to...what? Harm you as well, here in this public place where anyone may discover me at any moment? Is that what you think my dastardly scheme is?"

He is offended.

Every muscle in his body is taut with insult, but not because I believe he is a villain in league with Brooke. No, he is affronted because the dastardly scheme I have ascribed to him is so facile. If he were a villain, he would be masterful and clever.

It's an idiotic response to the charge of murder but also persuasive. If he were actually the dull-witted ruffian I think him to be, he would not have been shrewd enough to find the slight in my behavior.

I stop struggling as the worst of the panic subsides. I am not about to be brutally slain, and that is a positive development. Mama will not have to spend the rest of her life wringing her hands over my inexplicable murder in a large shopping emporium that many of her friends frequent. That would have mortified her utterly, and the purity of the despair she felt at my passing would have forever been tainted by a hint of churlishness at my exposing the family to speculation and disapproval.

Moreover, I would be dead, which is a terrible thing to be at the beginning of one's second season (or at any point during one's subsequent ones).

But even without the threat of Mr. Holcroft killing me, the situation is fraught with peril. Mr. Roberts has been ruthlessly dispatched by an enemy, and we are in a small alcove in the Western Exchange. Danger lurks in every direction. The killer himself could be nearby, observing the scene with interest and adding names to his grotesque list of people he must eliminate. And of course there is Miss Caroline Flexmore perusing the flower stall only a few feet away. At any moment, she or her sister or any of the dozens of members of the *ton* shopping for ribbons and fans could turn the corner and discover me standing over a bloody corpse.

Truly, I cannot decide which prospect is more horrifying: being targeted for murder or being branded a murderess.

Both possibilities make my knees weak.

But the fact that I am able to contemplate the horrors of my situation is a sign of my good fortune. The law clerk does not possess that privilege. Splayed on the floorboards, blood pooling around him, he thinks nothing, feels nothing, sees nothing.

His poor mother.

What will she think of the horrible way he died?

Does it even matter?

Heartbreak is heartbreak.

Mr. Holcroft shakes me slightly, his impatience tempered now with concern as he tells me not to look. "No good will come of it," he insists.

Yes, yes, he's right. Of course he is. It is a grisly sight, and I have spent much of my life turning away from grisly sights.

But I do not know *how* to turn away.

This ghastly scene is all my fault. Mr. Roberts was only at the Western Exchange to impart secret information about Mr. Davies because *I* insisted on discovering what really happened to him. Had I not walked into Brooke's office two hours ago asking questions about Bea's former beau, the law clerk would still be alive.

His mother would have no reason to mourn.

Mr. Holcroft, his hand gentle as he takes my arm again, says we must go. "We cannot risk being discovered."

And still I stare.

At what exactly, I'm not really sure because it is impossible to fully comprehend what I am seeing. I can separate the elements—the body, the blood, the boards—but putting it all together requires closer scrutiny.

My stomach clenches at the thought of drawing nearer to Mr. Roberts.

It is an abomination, pressing one's nose against a corpse, and yet what choice do I have? I created this situation and must see it through. I cannot scurry away like a frightened mouse.

Bea would not run.

She would not allow herself to succumb to a fit of nerves or be repelled by the sickening seepage of blood.

Resolutely, she would examine the body. It is the only way to discover how he was killed.

Mr. Holcroft, perceiving my intention by the sharp stiffening of my spine, says, "For God's sake, Miss Hyde-Clare, you cannot just..."

No, I cannot *just*.

But Mr. Roberts is dead because he bravely answered the call to decency—*my* call—and I must do the same.

I shrug off Mr. Holcroft's concern and cross the five or so feet separating me from the victim. Avoiding the blood is futile, so I do not even try. Without thought for my gown or shoes, I lower myself beside the body and look for the wound. The greatest concentration of blood is next to his left shoulder, and when I lean over to get a better look, I see the slash in his side. It is a gash about four inches long that begins under his arm and slices toward his heart.

Far too easily, I imagine the thrust of the knife as it ravaged Roberts's body, tearing first though his clothes, then through his flesh. I picture the look of surprise on his face as the first wave of pain overtakes him, then the horror as he realizes he is about to die.

How many seconds did he stand there, a man on the precipice of death, before he fell like a brick to the floor? Did he feel the ground as it rose up to meet his body or was it already too late?

Oddly dizzy, I close my eyes and press a hand to the floor-board to steady myself. The lightheadedness passes quickly, but when I open my eyes again, Mr. Holcroft is there in front of me, crouched as well, his head tilted with concern.

"Are you all right?" he asks softly.

I nod.

"You've gone white."

I imagine I have. "There is so much blood, and the cut is terrible."

Now he nods and says again we must go. "You cannot be found next to a dead body."

The observation is a striking understatement. "Neither can you."

"So let us go," he says, rising to his feet and offering his hand.

I shake my head. "We have to gather information."

The idea shocks him. He cannot conceive of remaining one moment more, let alone rifling through the pockets of the corpse. I do not blame him, for I cannot imagine it either. And yet I must.

Despite his dismay, his tone is mild as he tries to persuade me to leave. "Come, please. I cannot allow you to ruin yourself. It would be the height of irresponsibility."

Ah, yes, the noble Mr. Holcroft, always so worried about how my terrible decisions will negatively impact his high opinion of himself.

"Yes, let us talk about *responsibility*," I say, laughing bitterly, "for this man's death is mine and I will not let it be in vain. You may scuttle off to protect yourself, Mr. Holcroft, but I cannot worry about my reputation when a life has been lost. I may be silly, but I am not frivolous."

Ardent and sincere, I mean every scathing word I say. I am appalled by the prospect of his cowardice and do not know if he can be shamed into remaining by my side. The dangers of the situation are manifold, and I have to hold myself in check lest I begin to shake from fear. Blood is seeping into the hem of my gown, I am inches from a slain law clerk, and despite my claim to the contrary, I am in fact a *little* frivolous. The thought of ruination actually turns my bones to jelly.

I adore donning beautiful gowns and dancing to lovely music and fluttering my eyelashes at handsome gentlemen. I do not want to lose any of that, certainly not to an act of violence over which I had no control.

But having resolved to stand by Mr. Roberts, I must now stand by Mr. Roberts.

With all my determination, it is still a daunting task, and I stare at my hands and picture them soaked with blood—red, warm, thick. I can almost feel the odd tackiness of it sticking my fingers together. And that is the least of it, I realize, because in order to search him properly, I have to roll him over. I cannot do that without putting my whole body into the effort and drenching the front of my dress.

The shaking grows worse as I wonder how I will manage

to get home if I am stained with blood. No respectable hack driver would stop to pick up a woman covered in gore.

Obviously, I cannot walk home. The distance is far too great, and to be seen by every passerby—

"The man who did this is assured," Mr. Holcroft says matter-of-factly.

Startled, I look up. Far from leaving me to my examination, he has applied himself to the cause, lowering to his haunches to gather the information I had insisted we needed.

"There is only one puncture wound, indicating that his hand was steady and his aim true," he adds. "You know what that means?"

Baffled, I stare at him and shake my head.

"He is experienced," Mr. Holcroft says. "He has done this before. A man who lacked proficiency would have stabbed him several times, either missing the vital spot on the first attempt or not believing that a single stab was enough to accomplish the goal. This assailant, however, struck once and fled. That is the mark of an expert."

As grim as the explanation is, I take comfort in the cool appraisal because it means that Mr. Holcroft is not panicked. Whatever fear he has about my ruination or his own reputation, it is not so intense that it has corrupted his ability to think clearly. He is able to draw useful and informed conclusions.

Determined to ape his manner, I press my shaking arms tightly to my side to hold them still and say, "An assassin?"

The effort is only partially successful. I am able to restrain my body from shuddering, but I cannot control the tremble in my voice.

If Mr. Holcroft has noticed my anxiety, his response makes no reference to it. "Brooke, perhaps, or an associate of his if the organization is large. Either way, Roberts had information someone did not want us to discover. Now let us see if there is anything to be learned on his person. If you will move away, Miss Hyde-Clare, I will flip his body over and check his pockets."

Responding to the calm authority in his tone, I scoot back more than a foot as he positions his hands under the law clerk. With seemingly very little effort he lifts the poor slain man at his shoulder and waist and pushes. Mr. Roberts lands with a dull thud, his blind eyes now staring up at the ceiling, and blood splatters. A few droplets stain Mr. Holcroft's sleeves, but he pays them no heed as he looks through the victim's pockets. His fingers are spry, his movements efficient, and I watch as he withdraws a white slip of paper from the fob. In an instant, it is gone, inserted into his own coat pocket.

I do not say a word because now is not the time.

Mr. Holcroft finishes his search by making sure nothing is hidden in his socks or shoes, then rises to his feet. Firmly, he says, "Now we must go."

Yes, now we must.

Although I stand eagerly, I don't move because suddenly leaving feels as fraught as staying. Around the bend of this alcove is Miss Caroline Flexmore and possibly Miss Petworth and half of the beau monde, and the hem of my dress is trimmed with blood. I cannot walk past Miss Caroline Flexmore and possibly Miss Petworth and half of the beau monde with the hem of my dress trimmed in blood.

One glance and I would be ruined.

Even if the source of the stain is not traced back to Mr. Roberts's corpse (an utterly useless hope given the circumstance!), its presence alone is enough to turn me into a nine days' wonder.

A more popular young lady might be able to brazen it out, but not me. I do not possess nearly enough credit to withstand the virulent speculation that is sure to follow such a sighting. Even if I wanted to make an attempt to ride out the scandal, my family would not have the spine. At the first harsh word, Mama would have our bags packed and all four of us on the road to Bexhill Downs to bear out the rest of the season in disgrace. It would make no difference to her that Bea is a duchess now and could lend us her support.

Mr. Holcroft, not perceiving the cause of my hesitation, waves his hand impatiently as he tells me to come. "I have done as you asked against my better judgment. Now you must do as I ask. Let us go."

In fact, he is not asking. He is ordering. I do not quibble, however, because I remember how highly he values the propriety of his own conduct. He will see me safely removed from the premises because it is what he owes to himself, not me.

Although self-importance is not an attractive character trait in a suitor, it is an appealing one in a protector and I bow to his command.

My trust is almost immediately rewarded when we bend to the right upon exiting the alcove. Instead of returning to the large hall of the busy shopping arcade, we enter a wide passageway that leads in the opposite direction. It is partially lit by lamps, and I can see daylight at the other end.

Determinedly, I keep my eyes down, presenting my ugly bonnet to anyone who passes. Although the corridor is not especially long, it feels endless, which is unsurprising. Having blood on the hem of one's dress changes everything, even distance and the passage of time.

Finally, we emerge and I raise my eyes. We are still on Old Bond Street, but several buildings away from the Western Exchange, and the pavement is bustling with people.

We are not out of the woods yet.

"Stay here," Mr. Holcroft says and then dashes off, crossing the road before I have a chance to protest.

I don't wish to remain here, in the bright daylight, surrounded by interested onlookers. I want to be back in the darkened corridor or, better yet, safely home in my bedchamber, where nobody can gasp in shock at my bloody dress. Even without the stained hem, I am a curiosity—a lone young lady standing on Old Bond Street.

That is enough of a scandal.

Fleetingly, I wonder how Bea could bring herself to do this, expose herself to public censure, over and over again. The answer of course is obvious: She was a spinster. Nobody notices a spinster, and even if they did, they would not bother to comment on her behavior because it would serve no purpose. The only reason to gossip is to demonstrate how fully one occupies the center of the social whirl, and chattering about a nonentity accomplishes the opposite.

Conclusively, a woman of no status cannot be brought low.

Why waste all that effort on someone whom you cannot cause harm?

All that was true of Bea in the past, but her situation is wildly different now. Not only is she the Duchess of Kesgrave; she is also the scheming nobody who nabbed the Marriage Mart's most glittering prize from the clutches of more deserving Incomparables.

Make no mistake: It was an act of intolerable audacity, and many members of society will not rest until she is returned to the obscurity from which she had no right to emerge.

Oddly, contemplating Bea's destruction at the hands of thwarted society matrons and their beautiful daughters soothes my apprehension. It reminds me that the place I occupy in society is not so exalted as to merit more than a few days of wagging tongues. It would be horrible and I would spend endless hours crying into my pillow about the vile treatment, especially as I imagine Miss Petworth's titters of amusement. But the *ton* would lose interest in me soon enough. More fascinating quarry would step out of line and attention would move on.

Ultimately, I am simply not important enough to sustain a scandal. The wonder would last three days, maybe four.

Contemplating my own insignificance (and I *had* a successful first season), it is easy to imagine how utterly inconsequential Bea probably felt for all those years.

Plain, silent, spinsterish, she barely existed.

Perhaps that is why she has been so brazen in her investigations—because she does not know what it feels like to be seen.

She is very visible now.

I can see her.

Mrs. Ralston can see her.

The whole beau monde can see her.

Verily, she will have to alter her behavior to comply with her new prominence.

Lady Abercrombie, a friend of Bea's mother who has taken an interest in her welfare, believes all she has to do to see the new duchess established is throw a lavish ball in her honor.

Ply the spiteful society matrons with caviar and compote of peaches and their bitterness will melt like ice in the sun.

I do not think it will be so easy.

Their indignation runs deep, and Bea has done little to assuage it. Only days after becoming engaged to Kesgrave, she created an astounding scene in the middle of Lord Stirling's ball.

To be sure, *I* thought it was a remarkable display of wit and courage, not only staring down the man who killed your parents but also getting him to own his atrocities in front of the entire *ton,* but many of the guests thought it was horribly gauche.

Confessions of one's multiple homicides should be done in the privacy of one's own drawing room.

Obviously, Bea will not be doing anything like that anymore.

Gaining acceptance will be challenging, but I am determined to lend her my support no matter how many extravagant parties for the new duchess I am obliged to attend in the process (nor lovely red silk dresses with ivory lace netting and delicate rosettes edging the hem I am obligated to wear).

The vision of Madame Bélanger's creation is so engrossing, I am momentarily taken aback to see Mr. Holcroft standing before me.

"That was quick," I say with relief as I accept his arm and allow him to lead me across the street to where a hack is waiting.

"I am glad you think so, for it took a full ten minutes to find and hail," he says. "This is the second time today I have forgone the pleasure of my own curricle for a public conveyance, and my tiger is quite cross about it. Since getting into a skirmish over the matter would cause an unnecessary delay, I submitted to his disapproval without comment, which I fear will cause his vanity long-term harm. He already considers himself superior to me."

The image of Mr. Holcroft being berated by his servant is humorous, and I laugh, which is, I believe, what he intended. He knows as well as I do the argument that is about to take place. In a moment, he will sit down across from me and regard me with avuncular concern. Pursing his lips, he will claim that the situation is now far too dangerous for me to be involved. He will assure me that he will handle the matter going forward. He will insist that I must trust him not only to locate Mr. Davies but also to find the man who assassinated Roberts.

Mr. Holcroft is a wealthy man. He has resources and subordinates and will almost certainly assign the unpleasant task of resolving this awful situation to Mr. Rees. The steward, in turn, will most likely hire a group of men trained in the art of investigation to discover who killed Mr. Roberts, and now the mystery I wrested from Bea with considerable exertion will be in the hands of complete strangers.

Do I find that thought a little bit of a relief?

Well, obviously, I do, yes.

When I decided to embark on this quest it was not with the expectation of being confronted with a bloody corpse.

Just the opposite, in fact.

Mr. Davies's highly suspicious carriage accident occurred in February, and he was buried two months ago.

Bea herself attended the funeral. (*And* found herself the target of horrible abuse by her former beau's father for her efforts. Apparently, he took violent exception to the interest she was showing in his newly widowed daughter-in-law. Are you bewildered by the tale? Trust me, you are not alone. Several things about the story do not quite make sense, and realizing she was wearing my brother's clothes at the time improves one's understanding of it only a little. Bea makes a charming man but not an entirely convincing one. I can only assume she could not stop herself from staring openly at the woman who had won her lover's heart and that the elder Mr. Davies had been driven mad with grief.)

But now that hideous confrontation has occurred, and I cannot make myself comfortable by allowing someone else to handle the consequences. It was my actions that led directly to Mr. Roberts's death, and it must be my actions that secure justice for him. Anything less would be cowardly and immoral.

To be sure, I do not live my life by the same rigid code of honor with which Mr. Holcroft abides, but I know the difference between right and wrong.

And *that* is why Mr. Holcroft and I are about to have a heated argument.

He sweeps the door to the carriage closed, and as I wait for him to settle himself, I run through the conversation that is about to take place.

It will start with a request, firm but polite, to see the slip of paper he found on Mr. Roberts's person. Mr. Holcroft, his brow furrowed as if confused by this puzzling non sequitur, will claim to have no idea what I am talking about, forcing me to remind him with more than a modicum of contempt that I was *right there* when it happened. Arrogantly, he will insist it is none of my concern, and seething at the supercilious display, I will explain in mind-numbing detail why his assertion is patently absurd. Then he will respond with more high-minded nonsense about his duties and responsibilities as a gentleman.

On and on it will go as the carriage bumps along, drawing us closer to my home in Portman Square.

We have yet to say a word, and already I am annoyed by his tiresome lecture on the obligations of chivalry.

If only I could just topple him to gain access to the information and bypass the exchange altogether.

Alas, the maneuver is unlikely to work a second time. Mr. Holcroft is a man of reasonable intelligence and has no doubt figured out by now *how* I knew to appear at the Western Exchange at the appointed hour. Any attempt to tumble him to the ground would arouse deep suspicion, and my ability to feign clumsiness is not well honed. I did not know it was a skill I needed to master like waltzing.

Determined to get through the tedious scene as quickly as

possible, I open my mouth to demand the scrap of paper. But Mr. Holcroft forestalls the entire exchange by *offering it to me*.

Extending his hand, he says with mild interest, "I assume you want to see this."

It is a trick.

Of course it is.

After withholding the first note and trying to shield me from Roberts's bloody corpse, he cannot be willing simply to *hand over* the slip.

It must be a fake.

Yes, that is exactly what it is.

While claiming to be in conference with his tiger, he hastily substituted a fake scrap for the real one. The sham note probably has nothing at all written on it or it says something innocuous like "teacakes."

The swap would have been easy enough for him to arrange. His curricle was too far away from me to see his movements, and it was not as though I was paying careful attention. In fact, I was woolgathering almost the entire time.

Ah, but what is the likelihood that he or his tiger just happened to have a slip on hand to substitute? It is not exactly high, is it? So perhaps his scheme is even simpler. Maybe he just wants to draw me out and prove my interest so that he will not be caught off guard again. As soon as I admit that I do want to see the note, he will snatch his fingers away.

If that is the case, then I should feign indifference.

Or should I?

It hardly seems to matter because we will have an argument either way.

The coach jostles slightly as it begins to move, and I wonder where the driver has been told to go. The fact that Mr. Holcroft gave him directions without first consulting me seems to underscore the fact that he is determined to mislead me.

Noting the suspicion on my face, Mr. Holcroft laughs softly and assures me it is not a trick. "This is the actual piece of paper I retrieved from Roberts's fob pocket. Please take it. You were going to steal it through some heavy-handed deception, and this way my greatcoat is spared further abuse."

I narrow my eyes in disbelief (and, yes, in insult, because my so-called heavy-handed deception was in fact smooth and undetectable) and accept the folded sheet. Holding it between my thumb and forefinger, I realize there is another option I have yet to consider: He has already read the contents and knows they are meaningless. "What does it say?"

"I do not know," he replies.

I find that very hard to believe. "You haven't opened it?"

Mr. Holcroft says no.

And *that* I find utterly impossible.

Thoughtfully, I tell him I do not trust him.

He is undaunted by the information. "I know."

"You do not want me involved," I say, compelled to state the obvious even though it is not at all necessary. There is something strangely coercive about his abrupt answers. They are like little nuggets of gold pulling me deeper into a dark cave. He could just strike a flint and illuminate it all at once.

"I do not," he says.

Pressing my lips together, I unfold the note and read an address: 5 Turnbury Street. It is neither a main thoroughfare nor a road located in the immediate vicinity of my home, and I do not recognize it. Even so, I do not believe for a moment that it is genuine. "Is this where your former governess lives or did you make it up entirely at random?"

Mr. Holcroft smiles, then shakes his head with an air of exaggerated disappointment. "Really, Miss Hyde-Clare, your cynicism is wildly out of control. I have no idea what that slip of paper says, but I assume from your query that it is an address. Rest assured, I had nothing to do with it. To prove it, I suggest you compare the handwriting on this slip with the original. Or do you suspect I rewrote that note and forged this one in the same short interval?"

Although he asked the question to make me feel ridiculous, I am impervious to his mockery and agree at once to his proposal. "I would like to see the other one, so that I may compare them side by side."

He withdraws the first one without comment and hands it to me. At once, I can see that both notes were written by the same hand. The curly embellishments that decorate the Ts and Rs are identical.

Dropping the slips into my lap, I look at Mr. Holcroft with exasperation and say, "Plainly, please, because the small amount of intelligence I do possess is inadequate for me to comprehend your game: Why are you freely providing me with this information? Previously, you hid it from me and insisted on handling the search for Mr. Davies on your own. Now a man has been brutally stabbed to death and you are willing to let me participate. It does not make sense."

Mr. Holcroft agrees that his behavior is baffling and admits that he is confused by it as well. "I assure you, it goes against every instinct I possess to support you in this madness. And it is madness indeed and I cannot fathom why a gently bred woman in your situation would be so determined in the pursuit of your own destruction. You possess all the necessary attributes to succeed in society and attain a good marriage: a respectable family, an engaging personality, a pretty face. With these qualifications you could have a comfortable life with a man of modest expectations and unexceptional intelligence and yet you persist in acting against your own best interest. Since encountering you on the pavement in front of Lyon's Inn this morning, I have made every effort to protect you from yourself, and yet here we are, in a hackney cab, our clothes stained with fresh blood. The scene of Roberts's death was horrifying in many respects, not the least of which is what it augurs for your safety. I believe your life is in peril and will continue to be in peril as long as you look for Davies. The fact that you are unwilling to allow me to handle the matter for you indicates that there is more to this story than you have deigned to tell me. Although I question the wisdom of that decision, I cannot force you to disclose private information you are averse to sharing. With these factors in mind, I have three choices: I can inform your parents so that they may constrain your movements appropriately, I can wash my hands of the whole mad thing, or I can assist you in your pursuit. None of these options appeal to me, for they all feel wrong for different reasons. As such, I have decided that the least ungentlemanly thing to do is to help, and so that is what I am doing, Miss Hyde-Clare—helping you. I am surprised that it feels so unfamiliar to you because I have been doing it for several hours now."

It is an astonishing speech, and I am astonished by it.

I know, yes, that my prospects on the Marriage Mart are wholly beside the point, but I would be a very unnatural girl indeed if I did not pause to take *some* delight in having them affirmed by a gentleman who has no romantic interest in me. I cannot question the validity of the assessment.

It is difficult, day after day, to be in the company of Incomparables like Miss Petworth and Lady Victoria and not feel the boundaries of one's potential. Beauty is everything, and lacking it makes one feel a little hollow inside.

Here, I am sure, discerning readers will point to my cousin's success with the duke as proof that beauty is not in fact everything. But let us be honest, if only in these pages, and admit that Bea's relationship with Kesgrave is like a fairy story. It exists outside the natural order, unbound by the laws governing ordinary humans.

It is exactly as Cicero said: *Exceptio probat regulam in casibus non exceptis.*

The exception confirms the rule in cases not excepted.

We are all among the cases not excepted.

And yet for all her plainness, Bea is not hollow.

No, she is filled with wondrous things like courage and intelligence, ingenuity and daring.

For years, I thought beauty was the only quality that mattered. Until that dreadful house party in the Lake District, I believed only beautiful people had power. And then Bea emerged from that ramshackle hut in a field where she had been trapped—face bruised and bleeding, dress torn, hands thoroughly scratched and cut from removing planks of wood one by one—and calmly explained how she had figured out who had killed the spice trader.

All of a sudden there was another type of power.

Do I desire it?

If it bears any resemblance to the lovely sensation of freeing Bea and Kesgrave from the theater cellar, then I think I want it very much.

But, yes, yes, this is all a great diversion from the more pressing issue at hand and I return my attention to Mr. Holcroft's offer, for which I am grateful. Finding the villain who ran over Mr. Davies with his carriage has proved to be far more complicated than I anticipated, and having a man who keeps a level head while inspecting a bloody corpse nearby seems prudent.

Do I *suspect* Mr. Holcroft is angling for another outcome?

Absolutely, yes.

In detailing his struggle to arrive at the course of action most closely aligned with his rigid code of honor, he is hoping to shame me into providing him with a more palatable option: letting the matter rest.

Will I?

No.

Do I want to?

That is a more difficult question to answer.

Readily, I will concede that my decision to pursue Mr. Davies's killer lacked a proper understanding of all that entailed—*all* being, of course, the blood on my dress.

I am certain Bea never got blood on her dress.

Some char, yes, at the Larkwell ball when she confronted Lord Taunton and quite a lot of dirt in the Lake District freeing herself from that miserable shack. But not blood. Never blood.

If she could see me now, she would be appalled—and not just because of the bright red blood slowly drying to rust color on the edge of my gown. No, the danger inherent in my current situation would utterly horrify her. Her desire to protect me is sincere, even after everything I have done to be a horrid cousin to her. I saw it in her eyes in the hallway at the theater on the Strand. After I had secured her release from that dreary cellar and we stood in the corridor devising a plan to confront the killer, she sent me to fetch the manager from her office. I would have argued at being unfairly fobbed off with a menial errand when I had just proved my competence, but her fear pushed me back. It was almost like a physical thing.

Her understanding of the situation, however, is deeply flawed. She is older, yes, and might bear some responsibility for my safety. But it is a remnant only, a vestige from our distant past, when she was twelve and could swim and I was six and could not.

But we have been adults for a long time now and I failed her utterly in my duty to protect her.

It was different when I was a child because I had no understanding of her position in our household. But my comprehension increased as I grew older. I saw how my parents treated her, especially Mama, and did nothing to intercede.

Worse than that, I treated her the same.

I knew it was unfair.

Oh, yes, the whole entire time I knew it was wrong to treat a member of our family like an unpaid servant. Every time I asked her to fetch my embroidery and pick up a book for me at the lending library, I felt a vague sense of disquiet.

Did I ever give voice to the feeling?

No, never.

I did the opposite, in fact, treating her with deliberate contempt, as if the unease I suffered was *her* fault.

There were reasons, it turns out, for why my parents were so horrible, and while they might mitigate the awfulness of their behavior—and I say *might* intentionally because I am not at all convinced—they do nothing to excuse mine.

And that is why I cannot step away from the investigation into Mr. Davies's murder. Finding his killer is something I can do for Bea that she cannot do for herself. I know she would like to. The expression I saw on her face in the carriage when I asked about his death was unmistakable.

But it is no longer just about Mr. Davies. Now there is Mr. Roberts to consider and my obligation to him.

My investigation might have started out as a lark because heroism is heady and I would not mind being courted by a duke. But it is not a lark now. It is deadly serious.

I am deadly serious.

Obviously, I cannot say any of this out loud. It is not only my deeply personal business but my family's as well. While I am willing to risk my own reputation on the belief in Mr. Holcroft's goodness, I would never jeopardize Bea's. The fact that she is a duchess now makes the preservation of her dignity doubly important, but even before her elevation in status, I owed her my discretion.

No, I cannot say a word about my motives or explain the depth of my commitment or allow him to proceed without me.

All I can do is accept his offer to help and thank him for extending it.

Chapter Seven

A
ttending to my bedside the next day, Mama cannot decide if she is more upset about the persistence of my stomach ailment or Bea's failure to write to her family. Much dismayed, she alternately presses her hand against my forehead and her own. Resting her palm against my skin, she bemoans my ever-fluctuating fever, which appears to jump wildly from high to very high to barely perceptible. The answer appears to depend on how tightly she has clenched her fist before making the assessment. When she applies the pressure to her own head, she laments the grave misstep of allowing Bea to marry too quickly.

Her distress is so acute, she actually lets slip her first negative word against Kesgrave. It is, to be sure, a very tepid bit of criticism, noting that it was quite remiss of him not to insist that his wife write her relatives a long, reassuring missive. Nevertheless, it is entirely unprecedented.

Hearing the thought out loud, however, horrifies her, and she raises her fingers to her lips as if to stop herself from saying anything more. What other lavish words of mild rebuke she might let fly if not restrained, I cannot imagine.

Impatiently, I look at the clock and see that it is almost eleven. In ten minutes, Holcroft's carriage will arrive in Portman Square to escort me to 5 Turnbury Street and as such I still have to extricate myself from Mama's concern. I also have to change my dress, don my bonnet and sneak out of the house.

It is unlikely I will accomplish all of this in the allotted time.

The various challenges of leaving my home are one of the reasons I wanted to pursue the information yesterday. It is simply impossible for a young lady of good standing to investigate a murder without a lot of bother. It is difficult enough if I want to take a turn around the square, having to tote along poor Annie, who hates strolling at a sedate pace. She prefers to stride forthrightly with an objective in mind (a useful tendency in the country when one is climbing up a hill but slightly vexing in the city).

"I am not a nodcock," Mama says forcefully, although no such charge has been issued. "I realize why a newly married woman would not want to devote an hour to her correspondence. She is overwhelmed by Kesgrave House, with its dozens of servants, many of whom are old family retainers, and she does not want us to see her struggling. Bea has always been so dauntingly competent, hasn't she? Even so, she must find managing a house that size unnerving. She has not been prepared for it. Oh, I do wish she would write, even if it is just a few dashed-off lines telling us all is well."

The strain of peevishness in her previous complaints is replaced by an anxious note, and I realize her increasing dismay at Bea's lack of communication is in fact genuine concern over her welfare. Having to oversee a home as large and grand as Kesgrave House is a sort of nightmare for her, and she cannot conceive of it being anything less for her niece.

Her worry for Bea is touching and unexpected, and reminds me how difficult it has been for her to adjust to my cousin's new position.

If only Bea had had the decency to marry a vicar or a gentleman farmer.

Then Mama would be nothing but delighted.

Truly, she would have welcomed him into the family as a second son and even embraced Beatrice as a daughter.

But Mama is thoroughly intimidated by grand people, and in marrying a duke, Bea has flung herself well beyond my mother's comfort level. For years she had been terrified of Bea because she feared my cousin would sink into the moral degeneracy that killed her parents, and by the time she discovered it had all been a hideous lie, it was too late: Bea was engaged to a duke and Mama had a new reason to be afraid.

I love the poor dear to pieces, but she can be remarkably silly. I think whenever she sees Bea now, she recalls every single menial task she ever assigned her, as if she had sent a *duchess* to fetch her shawl.

Her mortification is genuine if utterly excessive.

Sympathetic to her anxiety, I let out a deep breath because I know I cannot leave her in this state. Before dashing off to find Mr. Davies's killer, I must first soothe her nerves.

But my sigh unsettles her even more and she pulls back in her chair as if I am a cannon that is about to fire. "What was that? Are you having an episode? Does your stomach feel queasy? Do you need the bucket? Here, let me get you the bucket."

Jumping out of her seat, she fetches the pail at the foot of my bed, which has been expressly put there in case my queasiness becomes severe. So far my ailment has consisted of racking pain and terrible cramps, but Mama worries about the linens and insists on keeping a receptacle nearby.

I raise my hand to assure her I do not require the pail, then immediately drop it when I realize her squeamishness will allow me to keep my appointment with Holcroft, albeit several minutes late.

Gratefully, I accept the bucket and bend my head over it. Mama nods approvingly as she backs slowly toward the door.

"How about some broth?" she asks hopefully. "Shall I have Cook send up some broth for you to eat? It is gentle on the stomach, I believe."

As the last thing I want is one of the maids solicitously delivering trays to an empty room, I make a heaving noise and say, "No broth, please. I cannot bear the thought of food."

Mama flinches at the sound and cries mournfully, "Those wretched oysters! I still cannot understand why you ate them. Detestable creatures!"

Detestable creatures, yes, for the way they have lodged themselves irrevocably in her imagination. It has been a full week since I was poisoned by eating a full plate of them. *This* week my condition was caused by rotten eggs, which I take pains to remind her despite the false wave of nausea that overtakes me.

I do not know why I am compelled to maintain the accuracy of my story because they are both lies, and yet I feel I owe it to the eggs. I put *so much effort* into making them turn rotten.

Mama nods vigorously and mutters, "The eggs, yes, yes, the eggs. It is quite troubling, it not, how much food has spoiled recently. Perhaps there is something wrong with our storage. I will meet with Mrs. Emerson right now to discuss it. Unless you wish me to remain with you?" she asks reluctantly, bravely recalling her duty as a mother.

The poor dear. She tries so hard to do everything correctly.

Sincerely, I assure her that is not necessary and she relaxes with visible relief.

"Do remember to keep the bucket near," she says, her hand clutching the doorknob. "Bed sheets are so very expensive to replace."

As soon as she is gone, I jump out of bed, dash to my wardrobe and take out the walking gown I selected last night. It is an unappealing pink shade and has a tear in the sleeve from where it was caught on a branch in the park at Welldale House. It was mended by one of the maids and she did a fine job, but the rend was wide and you can still see where the material was sewn together. It was always a horrible dress, even before the beastly rip, and I wear it as infrequently as possible, which makes it ideal for today's outing. I will not mind at all if the skirt gets covered with blood.

But of course that is not going to happen. Whoever is traveling around London killing law clerks in Walter Brooke's office cannot be so entirely injudicious in his behavior that he would kill two people in two days. I understand the criminal mind can be without conscience or scruples, but it cannot also be without prudence. The more victims you leave in your wake, the more likely you are to get caught. Whatever crime the murder of Mr. Roberts was meant to conceal, killing more people only risks exposing it.

At least, that is the way it appears to me because when I contemplate having to feign a *third* stomach ailment, I imagine the deception tumbling down like a house of cards. Papa would decide to get involved or Mama would finally stand the expense of a physician or our housekeeper would defend her cold-storage practices so assiduously it would call into question the whole premise of my scheme.

Holcroft agrees it is unlikely that Brooke will harm

another one of his associates.

"A second death in so few days will require the magistrate or the Runners to take action, which is the last thing Brooke wants," he said yesterday as the hack rumbled through the streets of London. "He killed Roberts to keep him from revealing information that is highly damaging to his organization, so drawing further attention to it runs counter to his goal. Silencing Roberts also serves as a somber warning to anyone else who might consider speaking to us. I think we can assume that that message has been successfully delivered, but we will find out tomorrow when we go to the address."

Alert to a trick, I instantly stiffened at the mention of a delay. "Tomorrow? We must go now. A man is lying dead on the floor of the Western Exchange. There is no time to lose."

Holcroft shook his head, looked down at his fawn-colored trousers, which were splattered with blood, and said that he did not think he would make a favorable impression. "Neither would you, Miss Hyde-Clare."

It was true, of course, for the stains on my dress were a great deal worse because the blood had quite soaked the hem. Obviously, we could not make calls, social or otherwise, dressed as we were, and stopping home briefly to change was not a viable option for me, especially so late in the afternoon.

I had no choice but to agree to the delay.

Nevertheless, I eyed him suspiciously. As reasonable as his argument was, it still provided him with an opportunity to pursue the matter without me. He had no officious family members or restrictive social expectations to constrain his movements. "You promise you will not visit the address after you change your clothes? Or tomorrow morning before our agreed-upon time? You *will* wait for me?"

At once, he assumed an air of deep grievance. His shoulders straightened against the back of the bench, and his lips twisted into a severe frown. "I won't pretend I am not hurt by your lack of trust in me. I do not believe I have done anything to earn it. Our history is brief, I agree, but from the moment we met this morning on the pavement in front of Lyon's Inn, I have been nothing but supportive of your cause. That you would doubt me now..."

He let his speech trail off as if the thought was too painful to contemplate. Then rallying, he said, "Yes, Miss Hyde-Clare, I *will* wait for you. I trust you will also abide by our agreement and not arrange to make the call on your own. You have shown yourself to be quite adept at deception."

I colored slightly at the observation because it is true. I have indeed discovered a talent for lies and misdirection. It is a shocking revelation, for I am a young woman who was raised to be honest, thoughtful and kind. Mama would be appalled if she knew how easily and convincingly I toppled Holcroft to the ground to sneak a look at the missive he had been given.

And yet it was my mother who taught me that the only proper response to an objectionable statement is a coy fluttering of one's eyelashes and perhaps a giggle. I should not proffer a differing point of view or explain why a gentleman's observation might be distasteful.

It is unbecoming to show judgment, Mama says. It is presumptuous to form your own opinions. "A young lady is agreeable," she insists, "and she agrees."

Rigorously, I have complied with this stricture, fluttering and giggling regardless of the provocation, even maintaining a delighted expression when Lord Northam dismissed *Pride and Prejudice* as a "silly nugget."

Yes, even *then*.

And *then* he compounded the offense by lavishly praising the perfection of *Childe Harold's Pilgrimage,* which is the single most tedious poem I have ever read. All that moody brooding and misplaced defiance!

I will tell you what is a silly nugget—having your every desire fulfilled and then composing three cantos in homage to your dissatisfaction.

Life is difficult, my lord. Yes, we understand.

Given how well I have mastered the lessons Mama has taught me, it is actually not at all shocking that I can skillfully lie and misdirect.

Nothing prepares one for conducting a secret murder investigation better than a London season.

Realizing that my talent for deception had been deliberately cultivated for the comfort of gentlemen like Holcroft reconciled me to the situation and I lifted my gaze until it met his directly. "You are angling for an apology that is not forthcoming. I am not sorry for knocking you down in the corridor at Lyon's Inn. You had no intention of showing me the note from Mr. Roberts."

"I do not angle for anything," he said mildly, a slight smile hovering over his lips as if the idea amused him. "I was merely pointing out that if anyone in this carriage has demonstrated they are unworthy of trust, it is not I. I am sorry if my honesty offends you."

I shook my head firmly and assured him I took no affront. For one thing, he spoke only the truth. I had lied to him on several occasions, some of which he was ignorant of even now. For another, I assumed he was quite put out that someone like me, whom he considered to be of little substance, had managed to deceive him.

He was probably mortified.

Having both promised to keep our word, we agreed to meet at eleven on the eastern edge of the square. As that is half a block away and I am only now donning my gown, I am sure to be several minutes late.

How long will Holcroft wait before deciding his pledge to me has been forfeited?

Securing the last few buttons without Annie's help is such a bother, and I contort myself into strange positions to accomplish the task. Then I slip on my ugly bonnet and leave my room.

Exiting the house unseen is its own small ordeal, and several times I have to dart into doorways to hide from either my family or the servants. It would be so much easier if Bea had devised some sort of ladder system that allowed one to climb out of an upper-floor window into the mews behind the house.

Eventually, I make it outside.

To my relief, Holcroft's carriage is still in the designated spot when I arrive. Although I expect at least some complaint about being made to wait for twenty minutes, he displays no impatience as he bids me good day.

His good humor is more rebuke than any display of irritation, and it compels me to offer an apology.

Brusquely, he assures me it is not necessary. "Knowing the lengths to which you must go to attain your freedom, I am surprised you are here at all."

It is a revealing statement, and I wonder if the reason he was so sanguine about our bargain is he assumed I would not be able to hold up my end.

If so, he grossly underestimates both my determination and Mama's discomfort with illness.

Next to him on the cushion is a copy of the *London Morning Gazette,* an indication of how he passed the time while waiting, and I ask him if there is any interesting news to report. It is a disingenuous question because I know the news is always tiresome, but Holcroft seems like the sort of gentleman who has lots of thoughtful opinions about current events on which he would enthusiastically hold forth.

Obviously, I would rather not be subjected to a lecture on the income tax or an expedition to a far-off river. I cannot imagine anything more monotonous than a discussion of the flora and fauna of the Congo. Yes, yes, different places have different plants and animals.

How very fascinating.

(Bea, in fact, would find it utterly engrossing.)

Nevertheless, I know what is required of every situation, and that is conversation. The irregularity of the circumstance is no excuse for an awkward silence.

Holcroft, also aware of the proprieties, responds with a brief account of the newspaper's contents. To his credit, he does not linger on any particular topic, and I endure an account of parliamentary debate with equanimity. Subsidiary silver coinage almost sounds interesting from the way he describes it.

When he finishes, he says, "I am surprised you did not ask your cousin for assistance in locating Mr. Davies."

Gasp!

The comment is so shocking, I can only stare at Holcroft as if he just suggested I consult on the matter with Prinny himself. I cannot imagine anything more preposterous than asking a newly married young woman to spend the *first days* of her marriage searching for the man who killed her *former lover*.

But Holcroft knows nothing of the relationship.

Of course he does not.

Oblivious to my response, he continues, "She appears to have a remarkable talent for solving mysteries. I was present at Lord Stirling's ball when she confronted Lord Wem about his treatment of her parents. A more shocking display I have yet to see. And then to figure out who chopped off the head of the chef in a neighboring house, it is extraordinary. I am sure she could advise you on the matter of the law clerk."

I nod because it is true, all of it. Bea does have a remark-able talent for—

Wait a minute. Did he say *chopped off the head?*

Further astounded, I gape at him now, my jaw dropping a full inch. "I'm sorry—what?"

Holcroft points to the newspaper and explains that there's an item reporting on the Duchess of Kesgrave's recent activities. "According to an anonymous source cited in Mr. Twaddle-Thum's column, she offered her services to the owners of the establishment as an investigator. The victim was Auguste Alphonse Réjane."

He says the name with an air of expectation, as if I should recognize it, which is baffling because no lady of quality would claim an acquaintance with a Berkeley Square cook.

Does he think *La Belle Assemblée* publishes interviews with worthy members of the servants' hall?

Nevertheless, this strange assumption is not the staggering part of his speech. No, what is utterly confounding is the fact that Bea, newly married to the divine Kesgrave, is still out hunting for corpses.

Not just hunting for corpses, *finding* them.

What did she do this time?

Knock on the neighbor's door, bid the residents good day, lament their misfortune in having a decapitation on the premises and then demand to examine the body?

The headless body.

Good God!

What can Kesgrave be about, permitting such madness?

At once, I recall the scene I encountered when I freed them from that horrid basement room in the Particular. Despite the direness of their situation, Kesgrave was ardently returning Bea's affection on the floor strewn with rat droppings.

Clearly, he could no more be relied upon to keep a level head than she.

Notwithstanding the alarming implications for both of

their safety, it does augur well for their happiness together.

They are a matched set.

While I consider Bea's troubling behavior, Holcroft rambles at length about the importance of the victim: *la grande cuisine,* Napoleon, *croquantes.* "Only a fraction of M. Réjane's many accomplishments are mentioned here because the far more salacious aspect is your cousin's interest. And the duke's, of course. His involvement does not escape the writer's notice. There is some question as to his sanity, but it is not clear if he means in following your cousin's lead or taking her as wife in the first place."

As he describes the substance of the article, I am overcome by a wave of apprehension as I realize Mama will see it. Papa reads the *London Morning Gazette* every day and will not be able to miss an article about his own niece.

What will she do when she sees it?

Wring her hands in anxiety, yes.

Let out a strangled cry of distress, yes.

Rush to my room to tell me all about it, yes.

Oh, no.

It is a dismaying thought, and my unease grows as I try to imagine what Mama would do if she finds me gone. For the first several minutes she would ramble uncontrollably in a panic, but once she calmed down enough to communicate sensibly, she would insist Papa summon the Runners or the magistrate. Inevitably, she would assume I had been kidnapped by murderers or thieves.

No, murderers *and* thieves.

Reasonably, Papa would point out that there is no evidence to support this supposition and then they would wrangle for several minutes over what constitutes proof of abduction.

My panic subsides as I picture the scene between my parents because I realize Papa would never tell Mama about the *Gazette* item. He knows it would only increase her displeasure. Bea is too busy to compose a satisfying letter reassuring her family of her continued good health but has plenty of time to interview servants about a beheaded chef?

Indeed, yes, Mama's complaining would increase fivefold.

Having listened to it for almost a week, Papa will likely decide it is better to allow someone else to break the news. Mrs. Ralston, for example. She is a determined gossip who delights in speculating about other people's lives and nothing would give her more pleasure than updating Mama on Bea's movements.

As devoted to scandalmongering as she is, even Mrs. Ralston knows it is bad *ton* to dash to someone's house with one's tongue hanging out. She will wait a respectable interval —from several hours to a full day—before paying a call on Mrs. Hyde-Clare to discuss the shocking development.

And to be clear: It is a *very* shocking development.

One might excuse an investigative spinster because her life is so small and miserly and lacking anything resembling excitement so if she has to search up dead bodies to make it interesting, then who really cares because she is a spinster.

But an investigative duchess!

There is no justification for that.

Only the opposite, in fact, because *being* a duchess should be enough to fulfill anyone's requirements. If it is not sufficient for Bea, then it is an indictment of her, not her situation.

Goodness gracious, does she *want* to be rejected by society?

Is that her goal?

"I, however, think your cousin is a charming woman," Holcroft says.

Having paid scant attention to his words for several minutes, I am not sure what he is talking about. His tone implies that he disagrees with a negative opinion of Bea, which I appreciate. "I had not realized you knew her."

He draws his brows quizzically and reminds me that he just explained that they had never met. "But I admire her audacity and intelligence."

I nod as if suddenly recalling something, although of course I do not, as I was too busy woolgathering. "Right, yes, of course. I admire her audacity and intelligence as well."

"And that is why I am surprised you did not apply to her for help finding Davies," he says again, returning to his original point. "She knows how to go about it and is presumably a friend of his family as well. I am right in my understanding that you and she grew up together as sisters?"

It is a mundane statement based on widely known information, and yet it causes my breath to hitch slightly.

As sisters.

It is not merely that nobody has ever said those words to me but also that I myself have never thought them. Bea was always the poor relation to be treated with indifferent kindness.

Even now, she is the dear cousin whom my family has wronged.

One of the carriage wheels dips into a hole in the street, knocking me to the side, and I reach for the leather strap to steady myself. "She is the logical choice, I agree. But it did not seem right to request a favor from a newly married woman. Bea requires time to settle into her new position."

"She appears to be settling into her new position by treating it like her old one," he says with amusement.

Although I am almost positive he does not intend anything malicious in this comment, I am just defensive enough of my plain cousin to find the insult. It is so easy to criticize other people for failing to do well the things we do not have to do at all. Which is to say: I would like to see how

easily he adjusted to being a duchess after more than half a
decade as a timid spinster. I am confident he would bring
along a few entrenched habits as well.

Before I can dress him down, however, the carriage stops
at 5 Turnbury Street and Holcroft announces that we have
arrived.

Then he gives me a measuring look and says, "Are you
ready, Miss Hyde-Clare?"

Well, I *was* ready, yes, until he asked me with that porten-
tous note in his voice. *Now* I am anxious about what we
might discover.

As terrible as it was to come upon Mr. Roberts's body
unexpectedly, it is still, I am convinced, the better way to
discover a corpse. The other option is to open a door or turn
a corner knowing you will step into a horribly ghastly scene.

Is that truly what Holcroft thinks is about to happen?

It does not seem fair because yesterday he gave me the
impression that he thought finding another dead body was
the last thing that would happen at this address.

Did his opinion change or my understanding of it?

As the answer has no bearing on the situation, I resolutely
push the question aside and say, "Yes, I am ready."

He nods abruptly, then climbs out of the carriage before
helping me down.

Although nearby St. James is as bustling as ever, Turnbury
Street is peaceful and tidy, with brown brick buildings lining
the short lane. Number 5 is a two-story building with a wine
merchant on the ground floor and an entrance through an
archway leading to a small residential enclosure.

If Turnbury is quiet, then this courtyard is silent.

The building's familiar facade of Portland stone bears no
resemblance to the ramshackle menace of Lyon's Inn, and yet,
somehow, I feel more apprehensive contemplating it. It is a
strange reaction considering I am in the presence of

Holcroft. I might not desire his company on the dance floor, but I certainly consider him a reliable ally in the pursuit of a killer.

Whatever we find behind the door at number 5, I am confident Holcroft can handle it.

Mostly confident.

Reasonably confident.

Confident enough.

Unaware of my shifting opinion, Holcroft knocks firmly on the door.

For several long seconds there is nothing, no sound, and I wonder if we have come all this way for nothing. Despite my anxiety about who or what we may encounter, I feel only disappointment at the prospect of an empty house. It is so difficult for me to leave my own residence, and I wonder if I will be able to sneak out to make a second attempt later in the day. Escaping Portman Square for a third time in as many days seems—

Wait. Was that something?

My eyes dart to Holcroft, whose posture stiffens in expectation.

Yes, it was a noise. A slight scraping sound.

His eyes meet mine as he raises his hand to knock again.

Another scrape.

Holcroft tilts his head, and I wonder if we should call out a greeting.

The knob turns, and slowly, very slowly, the door opens, first a crack, then wider and wider until it is fully ajar. Standing there, greeting us with a ferocious frown, is a tall man with flowing brown hair and thick shoulders. He has a deep dimple in his narrow chin and disapproving brown eyes. In his hands he holds a shotgun, and with the weak sunlight glinting off its long barrel he says with whispered malevolence, "I have been waiting for you."

Chapter Eight

Nothing stops.

It does not happen again, the bizarre sensation at the Western Exchange in which it appeared as though time itself had slowed to a standstill. Everything remains at normal speed: Holcroft's movements, the stranger's eye blinks, my own breathing.

If anything, time seems to speed up.

So swiftly I hardly know it is happening, Holcroft sweeps me behind him, determined to shield my body with his own. My thoughts fly, too, darting from one idea to another, trying to calculate the likelihood that this man intends to kill us.

Is he the assassin?

I evaluate factors and run the equation in my head.

It can be true only one of two ways.

One: He left the address in the dead clerk's pocket to lead us into a trap so that he may kill us discreetly.

Two: He found the note himself, read it, returned it to its place, rushed to Turnbury Street, killed or held prisoner the person or persons who live here and waited an indeterminate amount of time for us to arrive so he could kill us discreetly.

Both scenarios are elaborate, and the assassin Holcroft described was the opposite of elaborate. The man who cleanly and confidently drove the knife into Mr. Roberts's side has no use for intricate plans that rely on factors wildly out of his control.

If that man wanted to kill us, he could have done it far more efficiently than designing a complicated scheme and waiting to see if we fell in line with it.

Furthermore, his eyelashes are aflutter.

He is either smothering an opinion about *Childe Harold's Pilgrimage* or he is terrified of something.

As nobody has made a single remark against Lord Byron's tedious story, that can only mean...

"No, you haven't," I say.

It has been only a few seconds, barely enough time for Holcroft to step in front of me. Now he stiffens as I speak.

I ignore him and keep my eyes focused on the man with the shotgun.

"You have not been waiting for us," I continue, my voice soft and slow so as not to distress him further or cause him to startle. "We had nothing to do with Mr. Roberts's murder. He had arranged to meet us at the Western Exchange, and by the time we arrived at the appointed hour, he was already dead. We are not here to hurt you. We are here to discover why Mr. Roberts was killed."

Have I jumped to several conclusions based on flimsy evidence?

Yes, without question.

But I am right. I know I am.

The gun does not move. It remains firmly lodged on the man's shoulder.

Holcroft, apparently agreeing with my assessment of the situation or arriving at his own, lifts his hands gingerly, as if to prove they are empty. "It is true. We mean you no harm. We found this address on Mr. Roberts's body. My name is Holcroft, Sebastian Holcroft, and this is Miss Hyde-Clare. We can explain our interest in the matter if you would kindly lower the gun and allow us to enter."

Confusion flickers across the man's face as he runs his own calculation. The gun still does not lower, but his grasp on it loosens slightly. "Your calling card," he says. "I would like to see it."

A reasonable suggestion, to be sure.

What assassin goes about London carrying calling cards?

A truly devious one, I suppose. Actually, it is not an outlandish idea at all, for it would be quite helpful to possess a variety of cards with several different names that you could distribute based on your needs.

Keeping one hand firmly in front of him, Holcroft reaches carefully into his pocket and withdraws a silver case. Silently, he takes out a neat white card and passes it to the gentleman with the weapon.

Satisfied by what he sees, the man slides the shotgun from his shoulder and says, "I am Chambers, Leonard Chambers."

"The wine merchant," I say.

He nods. "We've been in business here since 1698. But let us not talk here. Come in, do, please. I apologize for the greeting. I have been on edge ever since I heard what happened to Mr. Gorman. That was his actual name: William Gorman. I hired him."

Mr. Chambers steps aside to allow us to enter, and I notice that without the gun perched menacingly on his shoulder, he is younger than he originally appeared. I would place him somewhere in the middle twenties.

He apologizes again as he leads us through the narrow hallway to a comfortable parlor with modest furnishings and several imposing portraits. The most striking is of a rotund man dressed all in black glaring fiercely from atop a horse with a large spotted hound at his side.

"That is my great-great-great grandfather Henry Chambers," he says, noting the direction of my gaze. "He founded the company."

He insists that I take a seat, then goes to the doorway and calls loudly for the housekeeper. Blushing brightly, he apologizes for yelling and explains that he instructed the servants to hide when he heard the knock on the door and is not sure where they are.

"I did not want anyone to get hurt," he says just as a matronly woman in a mob cap appears. Her brow furrows in confusion as she observes our presence, but she nods readily at his request for tea and immediately leaves to fulfill it. "As you deduced, Miss Hyde-Clare, I thought the pair of you had come to finish off the job started yesterday with the murder of Mr. Gorman. I apologize for the misunderstanding."

"That is not at all necessary, Mr. Chambers," I say as I sit down on the settee, which is upholstered in a lovely embroidered gold. "I thought you were the assassin as well."

"Understandable given your reception," he says understandingly. "I have been quite unsettled."

"That is understandable too," Holcroft offers as he assumes a commodious armchair adjacent to the settee. "As you have generously invited us into your home at some risk to yourself, I will begin by telling you precisely how we arrived here."

Briefly, he details my family's relationship to Mr. Davies, our interest in Brooke's firm and how it was that we arrived at the Western Exchange just minutes after Mr. Gorman had been fatally stabbed.

"It is my fault," I say in the silence that follows this explanation. "If I had not insisted on looking for Mr. Davies, then your associate would still be alive. I am so very sorry."

But Mr. Chambers refuses to allow me to accept any blame. "You were perfectly justified in starting that search, and I hope you achieve some measure of success in your goal even if it is not the resolution you are hoping for. In this case, however, the fault is all mine because I hired him to investigate Mr. Brooke. I suspected Mr. Brooke might be dangerous from my own dealings with him, but I paid that no regard."

"Chambers and Chambers," Holcroft murmurs softly. "I had almost forgotten."

Our host is not at all surprised by his knowledge, but noting my lack of comprehension explains. "My grandfather died with two wills. The first was written in the middle of the last century after the birth of his twin sons. His wife died soon after, and he was inconsolable. He vowed never to remarry, but then he met my grandmother and his resolve weakened. They had three children together: a son, who is my father, and two daughters. It is not clear why he did not update his will until the very end of his life. The family steward insists he simply forgot, but my father said he thought it was superstition. If he drew up a will creating provisions for his wife, his wife would soon die, making those provisions unnecessary. Regardless, he did not have a new will written up until after my grandmother died. That document was found in the pocket of his greatcoat. It was sealed but not signed because he had forgotten to bring his spectacles when he went to the solicitor to execute it. He died a few days later."

"Your father and his sisters were included in the second will?" I say.

"Yes," he says, then pauses as the door opens to admit the housekeeper with a tea tray. She lays it down on the low table in the middle of the rug, dips her head politely and leaves. After she is gone, he continues. "My uncles refused to honor the second will, whose intentions are clear, forcing my father to sue for ownership of the wine firm in the Chancery Court."

"The case has been ongoing for many years," Holcroft says.

"Almost ten," Mr. Chambers confirms as he leans over the table to pour a cup of tea, which he offers to me. "My father knew the limitations of the court and understood that the process would not be swift. All rulings must go through the Lord Chancellor, a man whose manifold responsibilities are not limited to the court. He has duties he must perform within the House of Lords as well. So my father knew to expect delays. But what he experienced...." He trails off and sighs heavily. "It was not just the amount of time it took but also the expense. Everything incurred a cost: filings, appearances, documents. It took its toll financially as well as emotionally. My father could not bear the twin burdens of expectation and disappointment. At every juncture, his solicitor insisted the matter was near resolution and then there would be an upset. He died six months ago, ostensibly from apoplexy, but I think it was really a broken heart."

"Eldon is infamous for his procrastination," Holcroft says. "They speculate that his backlog is several years' worth of cases."

This information is not news to Mr. Chambers, and he nods in agreement. "That is why my father hired Mr. Brooke at the onset of this ordeal. He is known to have relationships with several of the masters and can ensure that a case will be resolved with relative speed. My father entered the Court of Chancery system with reasonable expectations, and yet time and again he was ambushed by delays and costs. He was buoyant about a year ago because he truly thought the case was on the verge of being settled and then evidence emerged that a second cousin had married his housekeeper in secret, causing yet another delay."

"But that marriage was proved false, was it not?" Holcroft says.

Surprised by his familiarity with the particulars of the suit, Mr. Chambers nods. "The parish register contained no such union and the marriage lines were deemed to be a forgery, which caused yet another delay."

"A costly delay, I would imagine," Holcroft replies.

Mr. Chambers laughs without humor. "All delays are costly. My father could not afford to continue much longer without selling this house to my uncles."

"How do you own the house?" Holcroft asks. "Was it not attached to the business?"

"My grandfather deeded the property to my grandmother soon after my father was born. It was a way of ensuring her welfare without actually making a will. If only he had not been so bloody superstitious!" he says, then immediately apologizes for his unseemly language.

I assure him it is not necessary, as it is clearly a frustrating situation. Then I ask him why he hired Mr. Gorman. "What did you hope to prove?"

His own frown tightens at the question. "That Mr. Brooke was soaking my father for every coin he possessed. Mr. Gorman was a former Runner and had some experience with corruption within the courts. I have no idea *how* Mr. Brooke was able to control the process, but I *know* that he did. Every time my father was ready to give up, he knew how to deliver him a win, and every time it seemed as though it would finally be resolved, he would somehow manage to produce a setback. Advance or recede, it cost my father money. The operation is too sophisticated to be the work of one man. Mr. Brooke has a master or a clerk or several in his pay, and I hired Mr. Gorman to find out who it is. I can only assume he was killed because he was getting close to the truth."

Yes, he was *getting* close to the truth, a truth that Mr. Davies undoubtedly uncovered before him. Mr. Brooke's corruption must run deep if it requires so many deaths to protect it.

While I contemplate this maudlin idea, Holcroft asks if our host knows what his associate had discovered. "Did he submit a progress report or any document outlining his preliminary conclusions?"

Mr. Chambers shakes his head and reveals he did not. "The last communication I had from him assured me that he was making headway in earning Mr. Brooke's trust. His clerk had begun to let slip a few incriminating details about minor corruptions and he felt confident he would know more soon."

"Do you still have the note?" Holcroft asks.

"I do, yes, it is in my study," he says, rising to his feet. "I shall retrieve it momentarily."

As soon as he steps out of the room, I turn to Holcroft and say with a mix of excitement and surprise, "Mr. Gorman was a spy!"

Holcroft, his response more measured, calmly replies, "It appears so. But I am at a loss to understand what this has to do with your childhood friend. Obviously, Davies is connected in some way because Gorman handed me the note after we inquired about him. But why would they lie about not knowing him? It does not make sense. I wonder..."

He does not finish the thought, however, and trails off.

"You wonder...?" I prompt.

"Miss Hyde-Clare, I have no wish to cause you or your family any pain, but it seems to me the most likely explanation for the irregularity is Davies does not wish to be found," he says gently. "If he is involved in Brooke's business, then he might be too ashamed to confront his parents. He may have instructed his associates to deny any knowledge of him."

I know it is patently unfair to blame Holcroft for drawing

conclusions based on incomplete information, but I am still deeply offended by the assumption.

Poor Mr. Davies died a hero.

A hero!

And Holcroft is impugning his honor.

He was a decent human being—husband, father, object of Bea's affection—and as such deserves the benefit of the doubt. Furthermore, I have personally vouched for him. That alone should make him above reproach, but there is more evidence still. The fact is, we have discovered nothing in the course of our investigation to discredit Mr. Davies. Indeed, not a single piece of information about him has emerged.

I do not believe for a moment that Mr. Gorman intended to share information about Mr. Davies's villainy. Instead, he was going to tell us something about his murder.

Before I can mount a spirited defense of my supposed childhood friend, Mr. Chambers returns with a small stack of notes. "Our entire correspondence," he explains as he places them on the table next to the tray.

Holcroft picks up the top letter and reads it aloud. "You may be assured that my investigation is progressing apace. I am currently planning a maneuver that will gain me vital information. Presently, I will be able to provide you with the evidence you require."

Returning it to the table, he takes the next sheet of paper and observes that it is equally hopeful and vague. "Every day I grow closer to the truth. Having earned the trust of Mr. Altick (whom I believe you have previously met during dealings on your father's behalf—he has light brown hair and a deferential affect), I am sure to have the proof you need shortly."

Curious, I reach for the letter on the bottom of the stack and read it: "It is still early days, but I have successfully infiltrated the office and believe I will have something to report soon. Have no fear that I will let you down."

The Ts and Rs have the familiar curlicues, and his signature is equally coiled and florid. Below his name, written in neat letters, is his address. He lived in Kirby Street.

"Do you know what he meant by *maneuver*?" Holcroft asks.

Mr. Chambers purses his lips and says he does not. "But I never questioned him on his methods. I'm afraid the whole subject was too upsetting for me to think about so I avoided it as much as possible. Allowing the matter to drop felt like a betrayal of my father, and yet I could not see any other course. I simply cannot afford to pursue it. Even if I can prove criminal behavior on the part of Brooke's, that will not solve the problems endemic to the system. It will get only the satisfaction of seeing him imprisoned in Newgate."

Although Mr. Chambers assures us there is little to be gleaned from the correspondence, Holcroft and I read them all just to make sure. Then I ask our host how he can be certain his investigator was not swindling him as well.

He sighs heavily and admits that he cannot. "My faith in humanity has been well shaken by the experience with the Court of Chancery and Mr. Brooke. Hence my greeting you with a gun. But Mr. Gorman came highly recommended by a friend of mine from university whom I consider to be an impeccable source. If I believed Marcus decided to gammon me for a few extra shillings by arranging a fake investigation, then I would follow my father to an early grave."

On this disheartening answer, Holcroft announces it is time we leave. "I fear we have already taken up too much of your time, and it is inconsiderate of us to ask you to talk about something that you find so upsetting."

"Yes," I say firmly, echoing his sentiment. "It was quite thoughtless. I do hope you can forgive us."

Smiling faintly, Mr. Chambers insists it was a necessary evil. "There is nothing to be gained from hiding from the truth."

With a final glance at the imposing figures on the walls, I rise to my feet and follow our host to the front door. He graciously wishes me the best of luck in my search for Mr. Davies, whom he calls "my young man." It is clear he has mistaken my search for a romantic quest as well.

Next, he shakes Holcroft's hand and thanks him for his interest. "I should not be surprised by it."

The comment is strange because, yes, he *should* be surprised by it. There is no reason to expect a gentleman whom he has never met before to appear suddenly at his door to ask questions about an associate he hired to look into a deeply personal matter and who was violently attacked in a public shopping emporium the day before.

It is a highly improbable event.

My interest is also shocking because young ladies in my situation do not go haring around London investigating suspicious deaths. We are denied the privilege of curiosity by decorum and expectation.

It is so astonishing, of course, that no comment is required.

Mr. Chambers closes the door firmly behind us, and I hear the scratching sound that indicates he is engaging the lock. Although we turned out to be allies in his struggle for truth, he has not ruled out the possibility of Mr. Gorman's killer appearing at his door.

As we return to the carriage, I contemplate how to convince Mr. Holcroft of what our next step must be. Although Mr. Gorman's missives to his employer were brief, I cannot believe his records are as incomplete. A man with his pristine handwriting, who makes the effort time and again to ensure his Ts and Rs are properly curled, must have kept copious notes. Logically, the only place they could be is in his rooms.

I do not expect Holcroft to agree with my conclusion. If I cite handwriting as proof, he will almost certainly roll his eyes and scoff. Men find it so easy to dismiss little things of great significance. Furthermore, there is probably a rule among the many in his rigid code of honor that prohibits searching another man's belongings.

Despite his pledge to me, he will not agree with my idea.

No, he will require persuading, and the best way to do that is to encourage him to think it is his idea, not mine.

How to do that?

Ah, yes, that *is* the question.

All the guidance Mama has given to earn a suitor's goodwill requires me to remain silent and look pretty.

Obviously, that will not work here.

The trick, I suppose, is to talk around the objective. I should make comments that lead unambiguously to the conclusion I desire.

As we climb into the carriage and take a seat, I try to think of a statement that would serve this purpose. Perhaps something like: How strange that Mr. Gorman's note-taking was so cursory. I would think a man who writes with such precision and care...

No, I have already resolved not to mention his handwriting. I need another trait to support my assumption.

What are my options? Mr. Chambers *did* mention that Mr. Gorman came highly recommended by a trusted source. I could start by saying—

"I have directed my driver to take us to Kirby Street," Holcroft announces, startling me out of my thoughts.

Too distracted to realize the carriage is moving, I lurch slightly to the right as we turn the corner onto St. James.

"You believe searching Mr. Gorman's rooms is the best course of action?" I ask, recognizing the address.

Although I am in fact expressing my surprise, it sounds as though I am questioning his wisdom.

Somewhat defensively, he says, "If he was hired to gather evidence, then the evidence must be gathered somewhere. It is possible that he kept his records in another location, but I do believe his rooms are the logical place to begin."

He has made no effort to seek my agreement, but I give it freely. "That is quite logical," I say admiringly as I turn my head toward the window so he cannot see my smile of satisfaction.

Verily, I am vexed that Mama's advice to remain silent and look pretty has yielded results, but I am more pleased to be getting my way.

Chapter Nine

I do not have to be in William Gorman's rooms for more than one minute to realize that basing judgments of character on a person's handwriting is a faulty mechanism.

Far from living in an environment as neat and precise as his handwriting, the former Runner resided in filth and chaos. His lodgings are spacious, comprising three respectably sized rooms that offer separate areas for cooking, sleeping and lounging in repose. The parlor, which shares a space with a dining table, contains a settee upholstered in a red fabric that has been worn thin from years of use. Crumbs of bread cover the cushions, offering a feast for vermin, which the mice who also call the rooms home have not been shy in accepting. Their droppings litter many of the surfaces.

The kitchen is in slightly better condition if for no other reason than it contains less furniture to be defiled. Several bowls are piled on top of each other in a bucket, however, and none had been cleaned before being deposited. Consequently, they emit a stench that is sour and threatens to actually cause the nausea with which Mama believes I am suffering quietly in my room.

Holcroft is equally appalled and says that the scene is unfit for my gentle presence. "But I cannot suggest you wait in the hallway, as that is hardly more suitable. Perhaps you should stay by the door."

It is true that the situation in the corridor is not an improvement. Whereas in Mr. Gorman's rooms there are traces of mice, out in the hallway are actual vermin. I might have spotted the long sweep of a rat's tail entering a hole in the wall, and I am grateful it disappeared before I could draw a firm conclusion.

As unpleasant as it is, the disrepair of the building has proved advantageous to us because all it required for Holcroft to gain entry was to shove lightly on the door. There was a slight crack as the wood frame splintered and then it was open.

I am not sure how destroying property to break into a dead man's lodging conforms to his code of honor, but I assume the ease with which it was accomplished creates a loophole.

Although I appreciate Holcroft's concern, I have no intention of hovering anxiously by the entrance. In general, mice are timid creatures and the stamping of four feet is twice as likely to keep them hidden as the clomping of two.

Putting that theory into practice, I take heavy steps across the floor to the bedroom, leaving the malodorous kitchen for my companion's inspection. It requires a significant amount of effort to stomp noisily in silk slippers, and I resolve to wear sturdy riding boots the next time I search the Hatton Garden rooms of a man with pristine handwriting.

Like the kitchen, the bedroom is sparse, with only a few pieces of furniture. The bed is narrow and pressed against a wall with a grimy window overlooking a dark alley. The linens are stained. On the floor, a rug of indeterminate color peeks out from beneath an assortment of discarded clothes. An armchair in the corner appears to serve the same function as a clothespress, storing the items either not currently in use or on the floor.

I am hesitant to move anything for fear of what might crawl out or scurry away.

And yet if I am going to cringe helplessly like the heroine of a gothic novel, I might as well station myself by the door as Holcroft proposed.

Cautiously, I slide my foot underneath a pair of trousers and kick them to the side. My effort reveals another pair of trousers. Removing them, I discover a dark-colored waistcoat and muslin shirt.

Mr. Gorman's disregard for the welfare of his clothes is shocking to me. Neglect is a luxury available only to those wealthy enough to employ a valet to follow after them straightening up. He cannot possibly have had the funds necessary to endlessly replace the items he destroyed through carelessness or laziness.

Using my foot, I clear a path to the armchair, which is covered in the same rough red fabric as the settee. A cravat has been tossed haphazardly over a dark blue topcoat that rests at a precarious angle on the back of the chair. The cushion is buried under several pairs of stockings, buff-colored breeches, and another shirt. The pile of clothes is curiously high, indicating that there is something larger beneath it.

Ah, now that is intriguing.

Perhaps Mr. Gorman's excessive untidiness is merely a diabolically clever scheme to deter intruders from scrutinizing his belongings properly. If so, it is certainly fulfilling its purpose because the last thing I want to do is to touch *anything* on that chair with my hands. Unfortunately, the seat is too high for me to use my foot, and I refuse to summon Holcroft to do it for me. No doubt he would smirk at my squeamishness and advise me again to wait by the door.

I need another option.

Thoughtfully, I examine the room for something I can use to scatter the items. There are few prospects: a candleholder with a half-burned tallow, a slim volume of poetry, a broken nib.

A hanger would be ideal.

If only Mr. Gorman had a proper wardrobe.

Perhaps the rod holding up the dingy curtains?

Viable, to be sure, but difficult to detach from its holder. It might be easier to simply overcome my aversion.

Thoughtfully, I step gingerly around the mess on the floor to get a better look at the pole. As I round the foot of the bed, a glint of gold catches my eye. Intrigued, I bend down to examine it more closely. Hooked on one side, it is a brass shoehorn.

Aha!

I reach to pick it up, but it is stuck between the floorboard and the wall. I tug firmly. It remains tightly wedged.

Maybe removing the curtain rod would be easier.

No, that would bring me too close in contact with the curtains, which appear not to have been washed in years.

All right, then, one more try, I think, pulling with all my strength.

The shoehorn lifts free.

Huzzah!

But the floorboard comes up too, and appalled by this small act of vandalism, I look around to make sure nobody has witnessed it.

"Flora, you ninnyhammer," I mutter as I pick up the

narrow board to return it to its place. But it does not slip back in as easily as it slid out, and I realize something is blocking it. With a hefty sigh, I lower myself to the floor and look into the hole to figure out what is causing the problem, wondering why I care. It is not as though the owner of the rooms is going to present a bill for damages to my parents.

I shift slightly to allow more light from the window to illuminate the hole and tilt my head down. I fully expect to find something horrible like a nest of mice and am startled to see a notebook.

Moved again by an odd compulsion to secrecy, I sweep my eyes over my shoulder *again* to make sure my actions are still unobserved and remove the book from its hiding spot. It is not dusty, which means that it was placed there quite recently.

I open to the first page and am immediately greeted with an assortment of familiar curlicues and embellishments. The initial paragraph is dense and concise, outlining the assignment he had accepted from Mr. Chambers and how he intended to pursue it. He details the credentials he will need to get a position in Brooke's office and even lists the name of two clerks who he knew could provide him with convincing references.

Wonderful Mr. Gorman, keeping copious notes *exactly* as I speculated.

Skipping ahead a few pages, I find his interview with Brooke, a cursory event that took all of ten minutes. His primary concern was discovering the clerk's familiarity with procedural minutiae of the Chancery Court. Once he was satisfied by his knowledge, he offered him the position at a salary that was just below meager.

Mr. Gorman grumbled about the income for several paragraphs.

It seems like an indulgent digression to complain about

the compensation he was collecting only in the service of another employer, but in fact his conclusion is highly relevant: By providing a miserly wage, Brooke was inducing his clerks to take on less savory responsibilities for additional remuneration.

"Few forces are as corruptive as deprivation," he wrote.

Curious to see where his investigation had led him, I turn to the last entry and find a schedule listing the actions of...I flip to an earlier page...Brooke and various members of his household. Also included in his notes is a drawing of Brooke's residence, with an X on the room identified as the study.

Seeking an explanation for what treasure the mark indicates, I peruse the previous page, which details Mr. Gorman's efforts to find evidence of Brooke's criminality. After repeated inspections of the Lyon's Inn rooms revealed nothing untoward, let alone transgressive, he decided the proof of Brooke's misdeeds must be kept in his private residence.

Ergo, a meticulously planned mission to break into the lawyer's home and steal the documents from his study.

And meticulous it is, with the daily movements of each member of the small household recorded in a timetable. Having assessed the situation from every angle, Mr. Gorman had concluded that the most opportune time to attempt an incursion is two o'clock in the afternoon on Tuesdays or Fridays, when the house is least occupied.

To wit: At one-thirty the maid of all work leaves the house with her basket to purchase vegetables at Covent Garden. A few minutes later, the kitchen boy, availing himself of the lack of supervision, sneaks out the back door to play dice with the fruit seller down the street. At two fifteen, the valet, confident that neither will return unexpectedly, pours himself a generous glass of his master's finest port and settles comfortably in the front parlor with a gothic novel. He enjoys this idyllic repose for seventy-five minutes before resuming his chores. When the maid of all work returns from her shopping a short while later, she finds him polishing the silver or ironing a cravat. The kitchen boy is at the basin, still scrubbing the pots from breakfast.

"Aside from a reverence for cleanliness that I did not know I possess, I have discovered nothing of interest in the kitchen," Holcroft calls from the other room. "I am searching the bookshelf now."

Thoroughly engrossed, I acknowledge this information with an absent nod, which of course he cannot see, and continue reading.

Mr. Gorman proposes entering the house boldly through the front door, which would be unlocked in the middle of the day, and proceeding directly to the study.

Did walking past the parlor present a risk?

Yes, he determined, but a minor one.

The valet's level of absorption in his book was so acute that nothing less than a gong struck forcefully with a hammer disturbed him—a conclusion Mr. Gorman reached after performing a series of experiments under the parlor window. Tapping on the glass, ringing a cowbell and blowing a bugle had no effect on his concentration.

I do not know what the front of Brooke's home in Calvert Street looks like, but I am fairly certain it does not have a dense assortment of shrubbery concealing part of the first floor. Most townhouses in London abut the pavement. As a result, Mr. Gorman must have presented an absurd picture to passersby, with his large bag of instruments.

Or did he perform his experiments on various days?

Making one sound at a time would certainly draw less attention than making four in rapid succession. *And* it would improve the validity of the results because noise has a cumulative effect, doesn't it? The light tapping would interrupt your thoughts just enough that you are more inclined to notice the cowbell and by the time you hear the gong, you are fully alert.

To get a true assessment of the valet's responsiveness you would *have* to run your experiment over the course of several days.

His susceptibility would also depend on the book he was reading and where he was in the narrative. If he was in the middle of one of the interminable descriptions of the Sinai landscape in *The Legend of the Saracen* (yes, thank you, Mr. Crowley, there is such a lot of sand in the desert, I perceive that now), then disturbing his concentration would require very little effort. *But* if it was the part of the story where Miriam is seconds away from being kidnapped by the dastardly Comte de Rochambeau, who is masquerading as a Bedouin, and Sir Percival is racing to save her before it is too late, it would be considerably more challenging to pull his focus away.

Indeed, Mama had to call my name several times while I was reading precisely that passage to remind me to change for—

"Did you find something?"

Startled, I look up to see Holcroft regarding me with interest from the doorway. His view is partially obstructed by the bed, the length of which is between us, and as a result he does not see the book on my lap.

Am I tempted to hide it from him and withhold vital information the way he withheld Mr. Gorman's note from me?

No, not at all.

Not even for a minute.

I am too eager to show off my ingeniousness in discovering it.

He never would have. Without thinking twice about it, Holcroft would have moved the clothing on the chair with *his bare hands*.

To test this theory, I point to the lump that has aroused my curiosity and ask him what he thinks it could be.

Easily, he strides to the chair and lifts the assortment of clothes to reveal a pair of shoes.

After all that I have seen in the past half hour, somehow Mr. Gorman's utter lack of regard for the sanctity of his own possessions is still shocking.

His poor mother, I think for the second time in as many days.

Without question, there is *nothing* more tragic than Mr. Gorman's violent murder at the hands of a ruthless assassin. It is a horrendous act, and the person who committed it *must* be brought to justice.

That said, there is something horrifying in a different way about the exposure of one's slovenliness to a pair of strangers. I do not doubt for a moment that Mrs. Gorman taught her son better than to leave his shoes on a seat cushion, and to have that lesson scorned so blatantly would humiliate any mother.

With little concern for Mrs. Gorman's dignity or mortification, Holcroft returns the clothing to the chair and gestures to the book I am holding. "That looks promising."

I dip my head in acknowledgment and consider how to respond. Obviously, I want to excitedly proclaim that I hold in my hands a Very Important Document and then giddily explain my ingenuity in finding it. Mr. Gorman's notes are by far the most astounding discovery I have ever made in my life, and I want to bask in Holcroft's astonishment.

Will his jaw drop?

Will his eyes pop?

Will he stare uncomprehendingly at the overwhelming improbability of someone with my small amount of intelligence locating an item of profound consequence?

I dearly hope so.

But appearing to enjoy my own cleverness is the opposite of being clever. Genuinely clever people do not draw attention to their accomplishments. When Bea deduced which poison had killed Mr. Wilson based on knowledge she had gleaned from various books, she did not trumpet it to the world. No, she merely took the information and proceeded to identify how the lethal dose was administered.

Struggling for a likewise understated reply, I swallow the smile that rises to my lips and say with studied calm, "It is Mr. Gorman's notebook, where he obligingly recorded all of his thoughts."

Surprise flickers across his face as his eyes meet mine. It is so fleeting, I almost think I imagined it. But it was there and I saw it.

Delighted by the response, I add that I found it under the floorboard. I titled my head down to indicate where but otherwise show no reaction. My tone is matter-of-fact, almost indifferent, but inside I am screaming: Ask me how! Ask me how!

Holcroft, fishy-breath, chivalric-code adherent that he is, shows no interest in how I made this remarkable discovery. He merely nods his head and asks if he may look at it.

Yes, of course, he must examine the contents for himself. Clearly, I cannot be relied upon to assess its value accurately.

Seething silently, I school my features into an expression of bland indifference and hand him the tome. He flips randomly through the book, turning from the beginning to the end to the middle and then back to the beginning. He does not say anything, but I can see the moment he realizes it is a document of some significance.

"You found this under the floorboard?" he asks mildly.

How cool he sounds—as if he is determined to appear unimpressed.

"Yes," I reply before indicating which floorboard in particular I found it hiding beneath. As just the one plank has been removed, it is an entirely superfluous gesture. The only reason to make it is to draw attention to the precision of my search. I did not dislodge half a dozen floorboards on the sneaking suspicion something might be underneath one. No, as the evidence indicates, I knew exactly where to look and what I was looking for.

When Holcroft does not respond with due appreciation, I say, "I used the shoehorn as a lever to raise the beam."

This explanation is entirely true. Just because I had not intended to use the shoehorn as a lever to raise the beam when I reached for it does not make the action any less valid.

"Something about the floorboard caught my eye," I add.

Also true!

Holcroft shakes his head as if confused and lowers himself to get a better view of the compartment I have uncovered. After a long moment of consideration, he says, "You are to be commended, Miss Hyde-Clare. I cannot conceive how you found it and know for a fact I would not have been half as astute as to notice something awry."

I have to bite my bottom lip to keep from grinning. The admiration in his voice is perfect. It is all that any young lady in her second season could wish for. Indeed, if he had spoken about the weather with the same warmth when we danced, I would have succumbed to infatuation by the time he returned me to Mama.

Remaining firmly in control, I nod solemnly and say with deliberate understatement, "I thought it might be helpful."

Now Holcroft grins. "Helpful, yes, that is certainly one way to describe its value."

"You will see when you get to the end that Mr. Gorman was planning to break into Brooke's home," I say. "He was convinced the evidence he needed to prove his guilt was stored in his private study. He reached this conclusion after an exhaustive search of the Lyon's Inn office. He was meticulous in his research and determined that the optimal time to make the attempt is today at two-thirty."

The words are out of my mouth before I even consider them.

Optimal time?

Two-thirty?

It sounds as though I am intimating that Holcroft and I should follow the scheme Mr. Gorman laid out.

Is that my intention?

Is that *actually* what I want to do?

It is madness, surely, to cross the line between poking around in a man's private business and violating the sanctity of his home. The former might appear to be in poor taste, but it is really not that far removed from gossiping, which is the favorite pastime of half of London. When Mrs. Ralston came to dinner a few weeks ago and quizzed Bea on her engagement to Kesgrave, it was little different from my visiting Brooke's office and asking his clerk questions about Mr. Davies.

But boldly entering a residence from which no invitation has been issued and brazenly opening desk drawers and file cabinets is unlawful. In trying to prove Brooke's lack of morality, I would be demonstrating my own.

I cannot even *begin* to imagine what would happen to me if I were caught.

Scandal, yes.

Disgrace, absolutely.

Banishment to a distant corner of the Empire, without question.

Mama would be so heartbroken she would vow never to speak to me again. But she would have too much to say on the matter to remain silent and would work herself into such a lather of anxiety and apprehension.

The poor dear, she would be beyond herself with distress!

And Papa—he would be disappointed and confused. Ordinarily, I would not consider my father's reaction to anything because he is a distant figure at the breakfast table who sometimes lowers his newspaper to make a cutting remark about me or my brother. (To be fair, Russell usually deserves the criticism because if there *is* anyone in our family who is truly a ninnyhammer, it is he.) But Papa has been different of late. A little more than a week ago, he came into the drawing room and *chatted* with me and Bea.

And the topic was utterly frivolous.

Fashion, I believe.

But he graciously insisted it was worthy of serious consideration.

In the wake of his unexpected interest, I find myself suddenly reluctant to cause my father disappointment and confusion.

Even as I contemplate the disastrous consequences of breaking into Brooke's office, I know it is immaterial to the conversation. Mr. Holcroft would never consent to such a plan.

Indeed, he is too engrossed in Mr. Gorman's notes to even dismiss my suggestion. "His argument is convincing," he murmurs, turning the page.

As I do not know to which argument this comment refers, I make no reply and wonder how much longer we will remain in this filthy room, with its dirty linens and thought-lessly discarded clothing. It is possible that Mr. Gorman had other secret compartments hiding other useful notebooks, but if that is true, then the onus to locate them falls on Holcroft. I have already made my fair share of significant discoveries.

That said, I suppose I *could* walk the floor looking for loose boards. If one rattles, I can always use the shoehorn as the lever I have already described it to be. But to gain access to the whole floor, I would have to methodically clear a path, kicking clothing to one side and then the next. It is a simple enough thing and yet it will bring me into so much contact with—

"I concur," Holcroft says firmly as he snaps the book shut.

Since I have been paying scant attention to him, I have no idea with what he is agreeing. Hopefully, that it is time to leave.

Observing my perplexed expression, he explains. "I concur with your assessment of Gorman's notes. They *are* helpful. His reasoning is sound and persuasive. As you noted, the optimal time to find the evidence is before us, so I suggest we be on our way. We have plenty of time, as it is only one forty-five now and it should not take us more than twenty minutes to get to Clerkenwell. London traffic, however, is unreliable and one can never be too cautious."

Dumbfounded, I stare at him, incapable of compre-hending what I heard. It *seems* as though he just announced that we are going to follow through on Mr. Gorman's plan to retrieve documents from the lawyer's home.

We are going to illegally *enter* Brooke's home and illicitly *rifle* through his possessions and unlawfully *pilfer* his documents.

And yet his concern is that we *arrive* safely in time.

He cannot be sincere.

Holcroft, with his rigid code of honor and conversation about the weather, would never indulge in such an impetuous act. His comment about caution was meant to mock me. He is displaying his ardent contempt for my proposal.

To be fair, I will admit that the concern is not entirely undeserved. Rushing headlong into a reckless scrape does nothing to advance our cause and risks undermining it altogether. If we are caught, I would be utterly ruined and Mr. Davies's killer would still be unpunished, to say nothing of the assassin who murdered Mr. Gorman almost before our own eyes.

The pursuit of justice demands caution and forethought!

Ah, but is not Mr. Gorman's plan *all* caution and forethought?

He spent weeks painstakingly gathering information in order to devise a plan so nuanced he knew exactly how much noise the valet could withstand before looking up from his book.

Mr. Gorman's plan is not so much a scheme as a schematic that a carpenter follows when constructing a new building. Every wood beam is accounted for.

Why shouldn't we follow the diagram?

Scandal, I remind myself. Disgrace. Banishment.

Well, yes, these outcomes are too serious to scoff at. Ruination cannot be courted on a whim.

But the lives of two brave men have been lost.

What is the preservation of one's reputation against the unmitigated tragedy of death?

Clearly, I have no choice but to respond earnestly to Holcroft's mocking comments and agree that there is no time to lose. "As you said, we cannot rely on London traffic to comply with our schedule. Let us be off."

Although I spin purposely on my heels to stride to the

door, I expect my movements to be halted by his vociferous objections.

No, Miss Hyde-Clare, I cannot permit it, for I would suffer the torments of the damned if I betrayed my beliefs by allowing you to go through with this lunacy. Those are not the actions befitting a man of honor such as I!

But Holcroft does not protest.

He follows me out of the room and through the lounge to the front door. I pause with my hand on the knob and turn to face him. Plainly, so there can be no misunderstanding, I state our intentions. "We are going now to Brooke's residence to steal the evidence from his study."

He nods in agreement. "Yes."

And yet somehow I remain unconvinced that I am communicating clearly. "We are going to Brooke's residence to perform an illegal act with potentially disastrous consequence for the both of us."

Solemnly, he says, "I find your understanding of the prevailing state of affairs reassuring."

But for all the gravity in his bearing, I perceive a hint of laughter lurking in his eyes.

He thinks the situation is amusing.

My determination to do right by the pair of dead law clerks is a source of humor to him.

He is a vile creature.

That one realization is followed immediately by another: He expects *me* to put a halt to the proceedings. He does not believe for one moment that I have the spine to go through with it.

Does he really think I am so hen-hearted as to value my own safety over the deliverance of justice?

Actually, no.

He merely thinks I am silly.

"As I do yours," I say, opening the door and stepping into

the hallway. Its level of cleanliness is little better than Mr. Gorman's rooms, but I am grateful to be free of the sour smell, which had begun to make me queasy.

Or perhaps the sensation in my stomach is apprehension over what we are about to do.

Chapter Ten

alter Brooke's door is painted a rich bottle green. In the center, about one-third of the way down, is a brass knocker in the shape of a lion's head. A ring is gripped tightly in its mouth.

Inconceivably, this is where we are—on the threshold of Brooke's home contemplating the color of his door and the shape of his knocker.

I cannot say for sure how we got here.

Even though I was with Holcroft every step of the journey, from the moment we climbed into his carriage in Kirby Street and descended from it in Calvert, I feel as if I missed something vital. At some point he had to have turned to me and said with frank disapproval, "You must know, Miss Hyde-Clare, that although I am pretending to go along with your objectively crackbrained idea to invade Brooke's house, I actually have no intention of allowing you to risk yourself so rashly. Recall your marriage prospects, young lady!"

But no, nothing like that crossed his lips.

Instead, he inquired about my mother.

There, in the carriage, on the way to engage in a wildly

dangerous activity, he asked how Mama was holding up under the strain of her daughter's terrible illness. "It must be a source of anxiety for her."

It was, I thought, entirely in character for him to make banal conversation when something much grander is in the offing.

Recalling the exchange now, however, I realize that he was not genuinely interested in my mother's welfare. He was trying to exert subtle pressure by reminding me of my filial duty.

His refusal to state forthrightly what he is so clearly thinking makes me wonder if this is all a game to him. Is he toying with my expectations? Perhaps I am a diverting chess piece he enjoys moving around the board.

Or maybe his motive is slightly more nefarious and he seeks to prove something to me about myself—about my own lack of courage. He is confident he will not have to end this madness because he believes I will do it for him.

He thinks that I am silently cowering in fear.

Do I feel some unease about what we are on the verge of doing?

Well, yes, of course, I do. I am, after all, a young lady reared from childhood not to ask intrusive questions and now I am literally intruding on a man's property.

With very little effort at all, I can picture the valet striding into the study and discovering me with my hand in the top drawer of his employer's desk. Easily, I can hear his shout of alarm and almost feel his fingers closing around my wrist as he stops me from running away.

But I will not permit fear to dissuade me, not when it has no firm basis. If I doubted the accuracy of Mr. Gorman's notes, then I would yield to the vague sense of alarm I feel.

So far, however, they have been correct. Peering through the window a few moments ago, we observed the valet comfortably ensconced in an overstuffed armchair with a glass of port at his elbow and a thick book on his lap. He looked content and oblivious.

As his movements comply with Mr. Gorman's research, I feel it is reasonable to conclude that nothing remarkable happened during the day to upset the schedule. As such, we can safely assume that the other members of the household have also followed their typical routine: The housekeeper is abroad buying apples, and the kitchen boy is throwing dice several blocks away.

The moment has arrived.

Collige virgo rosas.

I wrap my hand around the doorknob and glance at Holcroft, unable to believe he is actually going to allow me to turn the handle.

He looks back at me with mild amusement, still entertained by the game.

But it is not chess anymore, is it?

No, it is something far more dangerous.

Now it is as though we are daring each other to test our bravery, both of us standing at the edge of a cliff inching forward and waiting to see who pulls back first.

Somehow, he is still convinced it will be me even though my toes are several inches over the abyss.

Confidently, I turn the knob and push the door open.

It creeks!

The noise is slight, barely a peep, little more than a mouse protesting the abuse of its tail by a human shoe, and yet it echoes in my ears as loudly as a grandfather clock chiming midnight.

Aghast, I freeze.

Bizarrely, the image of Madame Bélanger's red gown flits through my head as my heart races painfully and my breath hitches.

Why that dress—that lovely, gorgeous, beautiful dress?

I cannot say, and yet I know it is the last thing I can remember wanting before I embarked on this hunt for Mr. Davies's killer. Effortlessly, I recall seeing it in the window of the French modiste's shop and thinking fleetingly that the woman who wore such a splendid garment could have no problems.

My hesitation breaks Holcroft's resolve and he clutches my elbow as he draws me toward the street. "Let us go."

I shake my head at the soft-spoken command and, taking a deep breath that sounds as loud to me as the door itself, step into the hallway. It is yellow, more of a warm shade of primrose than a bright canary, with wide-plank floors painted white.

At once, I call up Mr. Gorman's drawing of the home and superimpose it on the corridor. The office is two doors up on the right. To the left, barely three feet from where I am standing, is the entrance to the front parlor.

Horrifyingly, the door is ajar.

Nowhere in Mr. Gorman's notes does it mention the door to the parlor being open.

I take a step back and bump into Holcroft, who has entered the house behind me and silently shut the front door. Although I hear a panicked screech inside my head, I know I have not made a sound.

Carefully, I take a very gentle step forward, my movements exaggerated as if I am performing in some pantomime.

Nothing happens.

Relieved, I do it again—lifting my leg high, dropping it firmly, looking to my left and my right to make sure nobody is watching.

It is only six steps to the parlor, and far too soon for my comfort I am there, at the edge of the doorway, knowing I have to peer into the room and terrified I will find myself staring directly into the gaze of Brooke's valet.

Ordering myself to trust Mr. Gorman, whose research clearly indicated that the servant would be too engrossed in his book to notice intruders, I tilt my head to the side to peer into the room.

It takes me a moment to locate him because the large chair almost envelops him entirely, and in the interval my heart beats so frantically I fear it might actually explode from exertion.

But there is his elbow, poking out just a little from the corner of the chair.

My head swimming with relief, I swoosh past the opening, scurry down the hallway and enter the study in one breathless rush.

Holcroft is two steps behind.

As he closes the door, I examine the room. It is modest in size, with a window that overlooks a small garden and is swathed in voluminous curtains in a rich fabric. Positioned in the faint shard of light filtering through the glass is a large cherrywood desk. Green wallpaper decorated with a delicate floral pattern sheathes the walls, and a trio of armchairs form a little enclave around a low table with scalloped edges and a glass top.

It is a welcoming space, which is not at all surprising given the comforts of his Lyon's Inn office. Brooke might be a dyed-in-the-wool villain, but he understands elegance and taste.

Having made a cursory inspection, I turn to Holcroft to discuss the challenges of a more thorough search. The lack of light is a significant barrier, but I question the wisdom of lighting one of the candelabras in the room. Mr. Gorman had the sense to test the valet for his susceptibility to noise, but what about his sensitivity to smell? Is it so highly refined he might notice the scent of burning candle all the way down the hallway?

Before I can voice this concern, Holcroft reaches into the pocket of his greatcoat and retrieves two candles. He asks me to hold one while he lights the other.

Taken aback, I comply.

Perceiving my surprise, he says, "I thought it would be prudent that we not use Brooke's own candles, so I took two from Gorman's rooms. It is highly unlikely anyone would notice that the wax has burned slightly more, but we do not know how meticulous his staff are with trimming the wicks."

It is impossible to articulate how this revelation makes me feel. All at once, I am confused, delighted, giddy, relieved, anxious and annoyed. The emotions, all swirled together like milk in a cup of tea, cause my heart to pound again but differently, and although I know there is something significant in the difference, I cannot begin to figure it out.

No, all I can think is: two candles.

He took two candles.

Two candles.

Overwhelmed, I strive to appear unaffected and, unable to think of anything original to say, repeat his own words back to him. "One can never be too cautious."

Holcroft grins at me, and I realize it is the first time I have ever seen him smile with genuine amusement. And in that instant, as if by the wave of a fairy's wand, my swirl of emotion dissipates and I feel only calm.

The fact that he brought the candles (two!) indicates that he knows what he is doing, and despite my fear that we have embarked on a reckless escapade, it is in reality a well-planned enterprise.

"No, one cannot, Miss Hyde-Clare," he says as he hands me a lighted candle. "Now do tell me how you would like to proceed with the search."

Prior to the unveiling of the candle, I would have taken this remark as further mockery. Now I know he is sincerely deferring to my preference.

Since the desk has two sets of drawers, I suggest he take the trio on the right side of the chair. He nods, and I devote myself to sorting through the papers and files on the left.

According to Mr. Gorman's notes, there are a variety of documents that would plainly reveal the lawyer's corruption: contracts, letters, ledgers. The one he was most confident of finding in Brooke's study was the last because a criminal has to keep track of his transactions just like any other man of business.

Although I understand the value of staying abreast of one's dealings, making a record of all the bribes one offers and the monies one extorts still strikes me as excessively foolish. Anytime I have done something slightly underhanded, such as pocketing a few shillings from the gilded box in Russell's bedchamber (he was only going to lose the coins in some useless bet with Mr. Muspole, anyway), I immediately erase it from memory.

But I suppose it is different if you are a villain continually engaged in villainous activities. Neglecting to keep track might cause you to under-extort or over-bribe, two situations that must be abhorrent to the criminal mind. How demoralizing to surrender all one's scruples in the pursuit of wealth and then fail to optimize one's profits.

Knowing what I am looking for, however, does not make finding it any easier. The two drawers I reserved for myself are filled with documents pertaining to the management of the house. The only ledger I encounter details domestic expenses such as tallows, coal, and lye. Last month, Brooke spent three pounds on butter.

Closing the bottom drawer, I look at Holcroft, who is engrossed in a letter.

"Something interesting?"

He shakes his head. "A missive from his mother, who lives in Shropshire. It appears they are having problems with the coke blast furnace at the foundry. She goes on for several paragraphs about the difficulty."

As I can imagine few things more tedious than the mis-workings of a mechanical device, I am relieved I gave him the less interesting drawers. Although the price of candles hardly makes for a scintillating read, it is always interesting to see how other people live.

His ice cream expenditure, for example. Mama would never spend such an extravagant amount on an item that literally melts in the bright light of day.

"The top drawer is all correspondence," Holcroft adds. "There are two dozen letters from his mother. Presumably, they are much of the same. He has a sister with four children, also in Shropshire, and her reports are filled with complaints about their mother and her children's lessons. There are also brief notes from the manager of the foundry and messages from a neighbor complaining about the smell of the forge. I will quickly review the other letters from his mother to reassure myself that they do not contain useful information, then examine the second drawer. Am I correct in assuming you found nothing of consequence?"

"Household expenses, staff salaries, stabling costs," I say, peering around the room for something else to search.

The bookshelves, yes, obviously.

Pressing an item between the pages of a heavy tome is a time-honored way of preserving a keepsake or hiding a secret document.

In *The Dark Skies of Terlano,* Priscilla hides the proof of her parentage in her wicked uncle's Bible because she knows it is the one place in the castle he would never think to look.

And she *discovers* the deed to the property where her

mother was supposedly buried in a safe tucked behind a large portrait.

Brooke's study has few pictures. There's an artful assemblage of eight miniatures on the wall next to the window, and a large painting of a woman in a red headdress playing the harp over the fireplace.

The assortment cannot be considered because each canvas is too small to conceal anything, but the turbaned musician seems like a reasonable prospect. Could a safe be hidden behind her placid expression?

Possibly.

The painting is certainly large enough to cloak a strongbox. Ah, but its placement above the mantel—that is not ideal. I have never sited or constructed a secret compartment, so perhaps there are factors to consider of which I know nothing. But I would think you would want to locate it in a spot that is easy to reach. Presumably, if you have *one* thing to hide you have *many* things to hide, so having to fetch the stool and climb up it several times a week would get tiresome. Furthermore, the portrait is big and cumbersome and cannot be moved without a great deal of bother.

Patently, it is not concealing anything.

I sigh heavily, disappointed to let go of an encouraging prospect.

But still—the bookshelves!

Unlike the leather-bound tomes in Brooke's office, which were all volumes devoted to the law and statutes, the collection in his study comprises mostly novels. Examining each book, I dutifully flip through the complete works of Aristotle, Shakespeare and Chaucer; *The Divine Comedy* and *Don Quixote*; and several editions of *Beowulf*.

It is a remarkable little library because somehow it contains all the Important Books my governess tried to cajole me into reading. The prizes to be earned if I just picked up *The Faerie Queene* or *Candide*!

And I did not even have to finish reading it.

All Miss Higglestone wanted was for me to peruse the first few pages and give it fair consideration.

At least, that is what she *said* she wanted.

In practice, she was never satisfied with my judgments and always insisted I continue past the boring bits until the story became interesting.

Naturally, I refused because it does not seem fair to me that I, the reader, should have to do *all* the hard work. By rights, some of that burden should fall on the author, who could have exerted himself to produce an engrossing tale from the very beginning.

Poor Higgy, how she did despair of me.

To spare her the desolation of utter failure, I made an effort to learn the harp, algebra and drawing. A seemingly random assortment of subjects, I know, but they had in fact one thing in common: Bea could not master them.

Did I arrange my entire education in opposition to my cousin's?

Not at all.

I considered Russell's weaknesses as well. He was always hopeless at Latin.

If Higgy did not like how selective I was in my interests, she had only herself to blame. The lovely dear had the unfortunate habit of prattling on about their accomplishments, especially Bea's.

Of course my cousin excelled in her studies. What other distractions did she have? Certainly not friends, and being in the schoolroom was a particularly effective way to avoid Mama, who was intimidated by Miss Higglestone's imposing stature. I always wondered why she agreed to hire a woman who towered over her at six feet tall. She has never been comfortable with things that veer from what she describes as the natural order.

Recalling Mama's flabbergasted expression when Higgy said she was considered petite in her family, I take the last book off the shelf and give it a rigorous shake.

No concealed documents fall out.

Devil it.

Ah, but that would have been too easy. A crafty villain such as Brooke would not hide damning information in an obvious place. It would be somewhere clever and sneaky, like Mr. Gorman's floorboard compartment.

Actually, Mr. Gorman's floorboard compartment was not even *that* clever and sneaky because Penelope in *The Dark History of Lord Bright* dislodged one of the planks underneath her bed to hide her mother's suicide letter (which turned out to have been written by her evil stepbrother, a shocking development that was readily apparent to me from page twenty-five).

A truly cunning spot would be a little less common.

Thoughtfully, I take a step back from the bookshelves and consider the remaining options. They are limited to the trio of armchairs, the low table and a shelf containing a few decorative objectives.

The table is beyond consideration because it is made entirely of glass and brass, with a frame that is delicate and narrow. The armchairs are slightly more possible in theory but highly unlikely in practice. Although a cushion stuffed with ledgers and paper might appear perfectly ordinary, the moment a visitor sat down they would notice something amiss. Even the shelf is dubious, with its marble bust, stuffed grouse, porcelain urn and silver candlesticks.

Nevertheless, it is the best of what is on offer and I walk over to take a closer look, raising my candle higher to illuminate the shadowy crevices. The light falls gently on the bust, giving the young girl's youthful features a delicate luster, but it sharpens the hollows of the gargoyle and the creature takes on a nightmarish cast. Its wings, coved and stretched, loom over its porcine head as if they are about to spread and take flight. The ugly statue is out of place among the pretty *objets* on display—the urn with its lovely depiction of pink peonies and yellow roses, the elegant candlesticks gleaming in the flicker of the taper.

"There is nothing here," Holcroft announces.

Startled, I jump slightly at the sound of his voice and realize belatedly that he is standing next to me. Briefly, I dart my eyes toward him, observing the discouraged expression on his appealing face before returning my eyes to the strange assortment of items. I do not know why I am so fascinated by the gargoyle, but I am. Its ugliness is vaguely transfixing.

"As confident as I am in the accuracy of Gorman's conclusions, I believe he was wrong to assume the evidence must be in the study," he says. "It is clearly not here. My next best guess is his bedchamber or dressing room."

I agree that both prospects are more likely because if I had damning proof of my own nefarious deeds, I would hide it as far away from the front door as possible. We do not get many visitors at Portman Square and Mama's management of the household is not so lax that a guest would be allowed to roam freely among the rooms, and yet here we are, in Brooke's study, making a thorough inspection of his things.

A bedchamber on the upper-floor is much harder to penetrate.

Holcroft, his thoughts aligning with mine, makes that exact observation as he refers to the time. "We are already twenty minutes into a forty-minute window. It is not feasible to make the attempt now."

I nod absently because it is true. Mr. Gorman's schedule did not anticipate any complications. But my eyes remain focused on the gargoyle. As ugly as it is, it's not its fanged grin that holds my attention.

No, I am fascinated by its discordance.

All those lovely things and then this hideous creature.

It has to be there for a reason.

With some vague idea of discovering a treasure map with an X marking the spot where the documents are hidden or perhaps some mysterious key, I reach for the gargoyle. Maybe there is a secret compartment in its belly.

The limestone statue, which is large and dense, does not raise easily. I shift my weight, adjust my fingers and try again.

It still will not lift.

I tug harder.

The gargoyle does not move but amazingly the shelf does.

With a click, the wooden backing drops forward a half inch.

Stunned, I stare at the opening.

"Raising the statue triggers the Roentgen lock," Holcroft murmurs. "I expected a secret compartment in the desk, but every inch of space is accounted for. Installing one behind the shelf is ingenious, and you are ingenious, Miss Hyde-Clare, for discovering it."

I blush with delight.

There is an intriguing mystery before me, the revelation of what lies in darkness behind the barrier of the panel, and yet all I can do is stand there and feel pleasure at the compliment.

It is particularly enjoyable to be commended for my ingenuity by a man who had only the day before scorned my intelligence as limited.

Although I have never *sought* his admiration, I certainly *desired* it from him and the rest of the *ton*. What is the point of the London season if not to turn oneself out in the height of fashion and be admired for it?

That is why I resent Miss Petworth and her ilk so strongly —all an Incomparable has to do to be admired is exist.

It is that easy, and I defy anyone to scoff at the simplicity.

And yet I cannot help but think that this feels better. Being admired for one's accomplishments has the hard reality of solid ground. I can feel it beneath my feet.

Holcroft does not notice my distraction because he is too engrossed in the secret compartment. He brings his candle closer to the opening to get a better look but does not remove the panel. He is willing to allow me the honors.

His chivalric code, however, obligates him to remind me of the various creatures that may live in the wall and offer his own hand as sacrifice to anything that might bite or sting.

He speaks somberly, as if raising an issue of genuine concern, but even in the dim light of the candle I can see the excitement in his eyes.

Staunchly, I thank him for his gallantry but assure him I am not so missish as to allow a little thing like a mouse stand in the way of a Great Discovery.

In truth, however, I am *exactly* that amount of missish, and it requires all my resolve to lift my fingers to the panel. I press on it and it flattens unresistingly against the shelf. I hold my candle to the opening to gauge the dimensions of the space, but it is awkward to maneuver around the vase and the bust. I am simultaneously worried about breaking something and burning myself.

"Here," Holcroft says, perceiving the difficulty at once and shifting the objects to the side. Then he suggests that he provide the light.

Grateful, I hand him my candle and wait while he positions it as closely as possible to the opening. It is better but not ideal, and with the phantom sound of squeaking echoing in my ears, I stick my hand into the cavity and feel around. At once my index finger meets something pointy and sharp.

A mouse!

Gasping in horror, I pull my hand back and knock it against the wall, where I am poked again.

"Are you all right?" Holcroft asks. "Is something the matter?"

I appreciate his concern, but I do not want to be distracted by it. I wave him off. It was only a nail or a rough section of wood.

Nothing to worry about.

Concentrating, I close my eyes and try to picture the invisible space as I explore it with my fingers: studs...plaster...more nails...anoth—

No, wait, that is not another stud.

It is too soft.

And that ruffling of the edge is paper.

"Found it," I say with almost underwhelming placidity.

It is there. I can feel it. But I cannot quite get my grip around it to figure out what it is....

I raise to my tiptoes to improve my leverage.

Ah, yes, that did it.

Now I can clasp it between my thumb and index finger.

I lift it several inches, then swing my left arm around to grasp the edge with my other hand. I pull it through the opening.

It is a large envelope.

Although I expect Holcroft to reach for it immediately, he stands back and waits.

Then he compliments me *again*.

"Well done, Miss Hyde-Clare," he says approvingly. "Very well done."

Grinning widely, I hand him the envelope to inspect. It is precisely the evidence we came here to find. I know it is. One does not carve a hole in one's wall and install a Roentgen lock in a hideously ugly gargoyle to store one's perfectly benign documents.

While Holcroft examines the contents of the envelope, I return my hand to the opening and begin to feel around again. Familiar now with its textures, I do not jump when my wrist brushes the sharp nail about a third of the way down. My fingers skim paper.

Another envelope?

Maybe.

As I move my fingers around the edge, Holcroft laughs gleefully and says, "This is it."

No, not an envelope. Too thick.

Distracted, I ask, "What?"

"El Dorado," he replies cryptically.

One does not have to be a Patroness of Almack's to know that it is bad manners to use obscure foreign terms to describe a cache of documents hidden in a crevice behind a wall.

Noting my confusion, he adds, "It is all we need to prove Brooke's guilt."

"Are you sure it's *all* we need?" I ask with my own giddy laugh. "Because I am reasonably certain I just found the ledger."

"Did you?" he says, clearly delighted. "Clever girl."

"And there's at least one more envelope," I add.

His eyes sparkle as he says, "If the letters inside it are anything like—"

Holcroft breaks off and stiffens.

Without saying a word, he waves sharply to my hand, indicating that I should pull it from the wall at once.

I shake my head.

The ledger!

More envelopes!

His gesture becomes more pointed, and I remove my hand.

Confused, I watch him close the panel, which latches easily, and slide the vase back to its original spot.

Then I hear it.

The murmur of voices.

It's Brooke.

Chapter Eleven

Brooke is here.
In the house.
In the hallway.
Just outside the door!

Smoothly, Holcroft returns the bust to its place.

His movements are swift but steady.

He understands the urgency but will not give into panic, which is good because I am all panic.

Frozen in place, I can only stare at him as he restores everything to normal.

But is it normal?

Or should the vase be a half inch to the right?

"Come," Holcroft says, his voice firm with command even though it is little more than a whisper. He blows out the two candles and the room is once again faintly illuminated by the weak light from the window.

The window!

Yes, of course, we can climb through the window into the small courtyard garden, then enter the house and scurry through the kitchens to—

Holcroft grabs my arm and tugs me toward the window.

It takes my brain only a fraction of a second to realize we have the same plan.

To the garden, ho!

But even as Brooke's voice gets louder and louder and draws nearer and nearer ("I don't want to hear another damned excuse, Pearson!"), Holcroft does not throw open the sash.

Instead, he stashes me behind the curtain—heavy, green, dusty.

When I open my mouth to protest, he says, "Stay here. Don't move."

Then he arranges the drapery to make sure the tips of my shoes are not exposed and disappears, presumably to hide himself behind the other curtain.

Dumbfounded, I nod. But it is a futile gesture because I am not only in the dark, I am alone in the dark.

I have barely comprehended the reality of my situation when the door opens and Brooke enters the room, yelling at his servant to find his spectacles. "They are in the desk," he barks. "Top drawer."

He sounds exactly like a villain—grumbly and angry, authoritative and annoyed.

Do I want to peek out of the curtain just a tiny bit to see what he looks like?

No, not at all.

I am grateful for the heaviness of the velvet and the way it drapes all around me like a cocoon. Ensconced safely, I am free to create my own image based on his snarly rumble and picture a skeleton-thin man of unusual height with black eyes, a patrician nose and pale pink lips.

His appearance is so terrifying, I shudder.

Pearson, agitated by his employer's sudden arrival, replies

in a tone that is as harried as it is obsequious. "Yes, sir. Of course, sir. If you please, sir."

This display of meekness, however, fails to appease his employer, who orders his valet to hurry up. "I do not have all bloody day."

"Yes, sir," Pearson says, scurrying to the desk and drawing so near to the curtain that it flutters briefly from contact.

"Incompetents!" Brooke yells angrily. "I am bedeviled by incompetents! You are an utterly useless squab, leisurely sipping my own port without a care in the world. Damn your impertinence! And Altick, dropping Mr. Firth's *Compendium of Law* on top of my spectacles and crushing them into a dozen pieces! Slipped out of my hands, he said. The magistrate made me nervous, he said. Of all the whey-faced nonsense! I have never met such an anxious young man, always jumping at—"

Abruptly, he breaks off his tirade and says, "Do you smell that?"

At the desk, Pearson is pushing items around in the top drawer with frantic imprecision, knocking them against each other and muttering under his breath. He pauses at the query and says with obvious inattention, "Smell what, sir?"

Brooke inhales so deeply even I can hear it though the heavy velvet of the curtain. "That faint mix of wax and smoke. Surely you smell it."

Oh, no.

My breath hitches painfully as I realize Brooke suspects our presence. It is only a whiff, a faint smell in the air, but it is enough to lead to an intensive search of the room.

The sparsely decorated room.

With its meager hiding spots.

I can see it all in a single flash—Brooke whipping back the curtain and knocking me unconscious with a single blow. I collapse to the floor while Holcroft leaps out from behind his own drape to defend my honor. Brooke pulls out a gun of some sort (perhaps a dueling pistol or a rifle) from the pocket of his coat (no, wait, a rifle is too large to carry in a coat pocket) and shoots him in the chest. He collapses to the floor, and we both lie there, me greatly imperiled, him slowly bleeding to death.

Despite the horror unfolding before me, I hold myself still. I do not tremble or quake.

Any display of fear would reveal my location that much more quickly.

While I am contemplating my fate, Pearson closes the drawer and takes a deep breath.

Does he smell it too?

He must because he says quickly, almost desperately, "That was me, sir. I was in here."

It is a lie.

A bold-faced, blatant, stunning lie.

Why?

Not to protect me.

He does not know I exist, and even if he did, what concern would he have for my well-being?

I mean nothing to him.

The same applies to Mr. Holcroft.

No, the only person in the room he must truly care about is himself.

Well, yes, of course.

Self-preservation is the most logical explanation and a common, if not quite noble, reason for telling a lie. Revealing that he has no idea what may or may not have transpired during his period of leisurely repose would expose him to further charges of incompetence.

Or would it be much worse than that?

Allowing invaders to penetrate the inner sanctum of his employer's home is a far more grievous sin than malingering.

His possibly, most likely corrupt employer's home.

What does he know about Brooke that makes him so quick to lie?

Has he seen him skillfully gut an untrustworthy associate with a knife?

These thoughts race through my head as Brooke says with scathing contempt, "You? Not a full minute ago I found *you* lounging in my front parlor drinking my port and reading Mrs. Radcliffe."

The incredulity in his tone is so thick, I would wither under it. But Person is made of sterner stuff. Determined to brazen it out, he concedes the accuracy of this statement without hesitation, as if the two truths are not in direct opposition to each other. "But I was in here moments ago, sir, to pour my glass. You see, I keep the bottle in your study. It is here."

His voice grows incrementally louder as I marvel at his ability to find anywhere in the sparsely furnished room to hide—

Light assaults my eyes as the edge of the curtain is drawn back, and there he is, the valet, his eyeballs almost popping out of their sockets as he sees me pressed up against the wall.

Gasp!

Astonished, we stare at each other for one seemingly endless moment.

Once again, time sputters to a stop, and scene after scene of discovery and death plays in my head. Frantically, endlessly, quickly, resolutely.

The terror is so strong I realize the panic I felt in the Western Exchange was merely a drop in a bottomless sea.

My heart ravages my chest, beating so loudly I am sure Brooke will pull back the drape and tell me to cease that infernal pounding.

But I am not alone in my fear.

Pearson is frightened too, and I can feel his terror in the air between us. It is almost like a thread of yarn connecting us.

Inconceivably, inexplicably, like a madwoman who has lost the ability to reason, I raise a finger to my pursed lips.

Shush.

What do I expect?

I have no idea. I cannot imagine the moment that comes next.

Pearson's dark-colored eyes widen further, but he complies. He remains silent. Almost imperceptibly, he nods his head.

I think he is agreeing, but then he tilts his eyes down and I realize it's a gesture. My own gaze follows.

And there it is—the bottle. It's just to the right of my foot. If I had moved another half inch, I would have knocked it over.

What noise would it have made?

A dull thump?

A loud bang?

At any moment, I could have revealed my own position.

Somehow discovering that after the danger has passed makes my head swim with apprehension.

Oh, but the danger has not passed because I still have to figure out how to get the bottle from the right side of my body to the left.

I cannot bend down and pick it up.

Can I slide it across the floor with my foot?

The answer is immaterial because I have no choice. It is the only way to do it.

Cautiously, I lift my foot and place it on the far side of the bottle. With deliberate slowness, I push it slightly and it slides easily. I move it again, farther this time, and my luck holds. The bottle glides without tipping over.

Finally, it is there, within easy reach of the valet, and Pearson bends down to pick it up. Then he is gone and the curtain falls back into place and I am returned to darkness.

How long does the exchange take?

I cannot possibly say.

I do know, however, that it was too brief to raise Brooke's suspicion, and only a moment later he is berating Pearson for stealing his favorite vintage. "You told me Mrs. Clutsam dropped the bottle in the kitchen."

Unable to deny it, the valet says, "Yes, sir."

Brooke growls in anger and asks why he must be surrounded by incompetents. "I have a mind to sack you here and now. You and Altick are useless to me."

Pearson promptly agrees with this assessment, which strikes me as an unlikely tactic. But I also know he cannot argue with his employer.

Furthermore, he *has* shown himself to be largely useless.

Brooke makes no immediate reply, and as the valet waits to hear his fate, I wonder what will happen to me if he is actually fired. The only protection I have is Pearson's desire to keep his position. If he loses it anyway, then the best chance he has to prove his worth is exposing my presence.

Look, sir, I've captured a thief or a spy. So you see, I am not entirely without my uses.

My heart speeds up as I picture the moment of revelation. Logically, however, I know Pearson won't play that card.

He can't.

It exposes him to too much danger.

Having begun the lie, he must uphold it or risk punishment far worse than unemployment.

Obsequiously, Pearson apologizes for giving his employer a misleading account of the bottle's fate.

Brooke is not amused by the intentional understatement and rebukes his servant as he calculates how much of his salary to withhold to compensate for the loss of port and reputational harm done to Mrs. Clutsam. "And where the devil are my damned spectacles?"

"Here, sir," Pearson says. "I have them here. Now let's do retire to your dressing room to change."

"Change?" the lawyer repeats in disgust. "Why the devil would I change my clothes in the middle of the day? I am working in my own private study, not going to the club for a hand of whist. Pearson, you are a fool in addition to being useless and I *will* sack you right now if you say another word."

"Yes, sir," Pearson says. "I will pack my things at once, sir, and remove myself from your presence. But I still cannot allow you to set foot out of this house with brass spectacle frames and silver buttons. It would be a gross dereliction of duty, sir."

Brooke sputters at the audacity. "I find you in *my* armchair drinking *my* port in *my* front parlor, but allowing me to leave the house with mismatched buttons is a dereliction of duty?"

"Clashing buttons, sir," the valet clarifies.

Brooke sighs, a most unvillainous sound, and submits to the alteration, but only because he has a meeting later in the day with a man named Stanton. "And I wish to appear intimidating because he has been rebellious of late, insisting he will not defer—"

"Now, sir," Pearson says forcefully. "You must go change now."

Although the interruption is inordinately vigorous and clearly intended to preempt an indiscreet remark, Brooke notices nothing amiss and grumbles peevishly, "Where was that sense of urgency when you were looking for my damned spectacles?"

Pearson apologizes yet again for his failures. "I will allocate a special compartment to their storage so this does not happen again. Now do let us go *upstairs* for *five minutes* so that I may dress you in the appropriate waistcoat."

Brooke, unaware that this information is for my benefit, not his, takes exception to the implication that he does not know where his dressing room is or how long it will take him to change his clothes. "I am not an imbecile."

"No, you are not, sir," Pearson agrees. "You are an important and accomplished man, and I am very fortunate to be in your service. I hope that I am *still* in your service."

There is a moment of silence as Brooke considers this statement before agreeing to rehire the valet at a lower wage. "For insubordination."

Pearson, thanking him for his consideration, suggests a percentage cut that is less than what Brooke has in mind, and their voices fade as they stride down the hallway, wrangling over salary.

When the room is completely silent, I lean my head against the wall, close my eyes and sigh deeply. The relief is so pervasive and intense, I feel as though I can almost dissolve into the floor.

Suddenly, a flush of cool air sweeps across my face and I open my eyes to find Holcroft standing before me, his eyes blazing intently as he stares at me. He grips my upper arms, as if to hold me still—which is absurd because where am I going to go—and says, "Are you all right?"

This question is also absurd. He knows I am all right. He heard the entire exchange. My presence was not mentioned a single time. "Yes, I am fine."

Despite these assurances, his fingers close tightly around my arms for a second before he steps back with a nod. But his expression remains intent. "I really must insist that you reconsider the wisdom of pursuing this matter. First there was that wretched scene at the Western Exchange, and now your very person has been threatened with bodily harm. I find it insupportable."

I trust it goes without saying that I do not find it very supportable either. The image of our bodies on the floor is still fresh in my mind even though it is a fabrication born of panic. Nevertheless, I refuse to abandon the field now. We are so close to attaining justice for Brooke's victims. "We are almost there," I say hearteningly. "Recall, if you will, El Dorado. All we have to do is bring that envelope to Kesgrave and he will make sure it is delivered to the right person."

"Kesgrave?" he says, appearing confused by the name.

"The Duke of Kesgrave," I explain. "He is my cousin-in-law."

A faint smile hovers around his lips as he nods. "Yes, Miss Hyde-Clare, you have mentioned it before."

Is that a smirk?

Is he laughing at me because I am not ashamed of my illustrious relation?

It is not my fault he does not have any dukes in his family.

"Very good," I say, standing on my dignity. I will not allow him to make me feel defensive about my pride. It is a remarkable thing that the Hyde-Clares can claim any peer among their ranks, let alone a duke. "Then you know he can be trusted to reliably resolve the matter."

Something about this reasonable observation causes Holcroft to grow rigid with offense and he insists that he has his own connection to whom he will give the documents. "While I am sure Kesgrave would handle it ably, I would feel more comfortable turning it over to someone I have consulted with in the past."

Obviously, I am not going to argue over which governmental official we deliver our evidence to. Not only is it a detail too minor for me to care about; it is also wasting valuable time.

We have five minutes—probably only four now—to retrieve the rest of the evidence. I dash to the shelf and reach for the gargoyle just as Holcroft arrests my movement.

"We don't have time for that now," he says forcefully. "We must leave."

Leave without the evidence?

Additional seconds tick by as I stare at him, dumbfounded.

"Do not worry," he adds, his tone urgent. "The authorities will return to collect the rest, I promise."

"But the murders—" I begin, then break off abruptly when I realize my slip.

Murders, plural.

Holcroft does not notice. "I do not believe there will be any evidence of a murder, especially one that happened just yesterday. But Brooke is finished. He will be convicted of a crime, several no doubt. Now we must leave before he returns."

Knowing Holcroft has a better sense than I do of how long it takes a gentleman to change his waistcoat, I cast a lingering glance at the gargoyle and stride toward the door.

He is right, of course.

There will be no evidence of Mr. Gorman's murder among the cache in the wall. But Mr. Davies's was months ago, and it is possible that information about it leaked into Brooke's correspondence or notes. That means it will be gathered along with the rest of the incriminating evidence.

I have done it.

I have found the killer.

Briskly, we pass through the silent corridor and emerge outside only a few seconds later. Holcroft's carriage is waiting several dozen yards away. The moment I see it, I let out the tense breath I had been holding.

My heart is beating wildly, and I am astonished it is still so out of control now that the danger has passed.

"Are you sure you are all right?" Holcroft asks. "I could not believe it when Pearson went to your curtain to retrieve the bottle. I thought for sure he was going to pull it back to reveal you. I cannot imagine how you convinced him not to."

"He was more worried about his employer than me," I say, "presumably with good reason. But I will admit I was not expecting such a dramatic denouement."

Holcroft's expression changes, grows darker, as he reminds me that we are not done yet.

I am startled by the strange accusatory note in his voice. Darting him a confused glance, I clarify that we are *almost* done. "After we meet with your contact in the government and I am assured of his competence, *then* we will be done."

We are halfway to the carriage, but Mr. Holcroft halts suddenly and gives me a look of genuine grievance. It is so earnest that I stop as well and wonder how I have offended him. Perhaps I have not thanked him enough for his assistance? It is true that I could not have got this far in my investigation without his support.

"Mr. Holcroft," I say firmly, "please accept my utmost gratitude for your help in this matter."

My remarks, however, have the opposite of their intended effect.

Stiffly, he says, "I am insulted, Miss Hyde-Clare."

But he is also angry. His green eyes spark with it.

"I have kept my word to you," he adds. "I have stood by you. I have assisted you. I have done everything possible to advance your investigation. When you said we had to break into Brooke's study to find the evidence Gorman was convinced was there, I did not argue. I did not point out what a foolhardy and dangerous plan that was for a young lady to involve herself in. No, I displayed remarkable sangfroid and agreed without argument to bring you here. And this is the thanks I get!"

"Well, no," I say calmly, utterly baffled by the source of his displeasure. "I used considerably more words than just 'thanks.' Mama would be horrified if I were so informal and abrupt after all the help you have given me."

"You are mocking me," he says.

Now *I* stiffen with insult, for I have never mocked anyone in my whole life. Except Russell. But obviously poking fun at one's brother does not qualify as mockery. It is an obligation of siblinghood.

"I realize you did not appreciate my address during our waltz," Holcroft continues.

Our waltz?

The one from two months ago?

How did that enter the conversation?

"But that is no reason to treat me with such contempt or lie so blatantly," he says. "We both know this is not done until you find Mr. Davies."

Find Mr. Davies...?

Good lord, yes, *find* Mr. Davies.

Because Mr. Davies is missing!

Yes, yes, of course he is.

That is the fiction at the center of the entire plot.

How could I have possibly allowed a lie so integral to everything to slip my mind?

It is a *horrifying* oversight.

And yet, to be fair, it *has* been an eventful afternoon, I think, as a slight *giggle* escapes me. Then another and another and then suddenly I am laughing so hard I fear my legs will collapse underneath me.

Find Mr. Davies.

Grasping my belly for support, I tilt my head upward and discover myself staring into Holcroft's green eyes.

But it is such a green, cold and sharp, almost brutal in its intensity, nothing at all like the verdant hills of Sussex.

I stop laughing at once.

"I beg your pardon," he says frostily, and although there is offense in every rigid line of his body, he isn't offended.

No, he is hurt.

He is deeply injured by my shabby treatment, and I cannot blame him.

We have embarked on an adventure together—hidden behind curtains, inspected filthy rooms, examined dead bodies—and fellow adventurers owe each other respect.

Instinctively, I reach out my hand to touch him because at that moment, not touching him feels wrong. Then I immediately allow it to drop because touching him seems *more* wrong. "No, it's just that—"

It's just that...what?

Mr. Davies is not missing?

I have been lying to you for two days?

I do not in fact consider you worthy of my trust?

I cannot say any of that, and what purpose would it serve anyway? Mr. Davies is dead. We are never going to find him.

In ways I cannot even begin to quantify, Mr. Davies is not quite real.

Drawing a steadying breath, I say, "It's just that I am so profoundly relieved to be out of that house. When Pearson opened the curtain and looked directly into my eyes, I really thought that was it for me."

He is instantly contrite, his lovely eyes softening to that gentle green as he calls himself a brute for thinking only of himself when I have just gone through a terrifying ordeal.

Then *he* asks *me* to forgive him.

"There is nothing to forgive," I say.

It is the honest truth because he has behaved reasonably

based on the information available to him, but it *sounds* as if I am being gracious.

"You are kind," Holcroft says.

But I am not. I am the opposite of kind, and I feel a faint queasiness in the pit of my stomach as he continues to regard me with concern.

Obviously, I should just tell him the truth about Mr. Davies, but I cannot bring myself to say anything that will alter his opinion of me.

Instead, I tell him that I have decided to suspend my search for Mr. Davies. "I think it is best if I let the matter rest."

Although he is suspicious of this claim, Holcroft does not want to accuse me of lying again. After a thoughtful pause, he says, "Are you sure?"

I nod firmly, yes.

He smiles with relief and it reaches his eyes, which gleam in the sunlight. "That is good. That's very good."

Because I suddenly feel as if I could stand there all day, staring into the lush green of his eyes, I resume walking toward the carriage. "I am looking forward to discovering what is in that envelope," I say, nodding to the packet.

He hands it to me while opening the carriage door, and while he confers with his driver about our next destination, I pull out the documents.

They are letters from various clerks who work for the Chancery Court. From a cursory perusal, all appear to be updates about various legal matters and points of procedure. The page on top, for example, notifies Brooke that a marriage certificate for Elizabeth Holder and Jonathan Chambers had been discovered precisely where Brooke had indicated it would be. Accordingly, a bill of revoir would have to be filed before the case could proceed.

Perhaps it is interesting reading to someone with a familiarity with the law, but it seems dreadfully dull to me and I cannot conceive why Holcroft considers it damning.

The second letter, also from a clerk who reports to one of the masters of the court, informs Brooke that in response to the information he supplied regarding Mary Trudeau's parentage, her evidence was no longer relevant to the case. As a consequence, a bill of revoir would have to be filed before the legal matter could proceed.

Again, I perceive nothing in the document but the dry discharge of legal duties.

Holcroft, assuming the bench across from me, readily observes my confusion and says with some amusement that my lack of training in the law profession is a detriment to my investigation of it.

"Filing a bill of revoir is a procedure requiring the repetition of several administrative processes, beginning with an interrogating section, in which all the issues at stake in the case are distilled into a set of queries presented to the respondent. The interrogatories are rarely clear or concise in their wording, and the answers are mediated through a third party who has no familiarity with the issues at stake, resulting in perplexing answers that seem to bear no relevance to the case. Now the interrogatories have to be posed again because the case cannot move forward until a reasonable standard of clarity has been met. Once the evidence is deemed admissible, all suitors involved in the case must purchase several copies of the masters' reports, which are inordinately long because each new report contains all the information from the previous report. It is costly and complicated and damned near interminable."

Although the intricacies of the system escape me, Brooke's manipulation of it is easy to comprehend. "So by producing new witnesses, Brooke is creating more work for himself and the clerks by extending the legal action."

"Yes," he says with a firm nod.

"And it works the other way as well?" I ask, recalling the document that invalidated Mary Trudeau's legitimacy. "When a witness is removed from the case it also costs the suitor time and money?"

"Precisely," he replies. "Brooke has been working his fraudulent scheme from both sides—at once introducing new witnesses and discrediting them. Remember what Mr. Chambers said about his cousin's marriage lines? The records proved to be false, and it is true. The lawyer representing the plaintiff checked the parish registry and discovered the union never took place."

"Brooke," I say, "working the scheme from both sides."

"And charging his clients every step of the way," Holcroft says.

"He bribes the clerks to gain their compliance?" I ask.

"I'm sure they are happy to add or subtract as many witnesses as Brooke wants because they are getting paid twice: once by him and once by the suitor, who has to purchase the records at an absurdly inflated price. All in all, it is a tidy scheme and much more lucrative than the petty larceny Charlie described."

"You sound almost admiring," I say.

"Do I?" he asks, startled by the idea. "I do not mean to. It is just the opposite, in fact. I take a very dim view of people exploiting the vulnerable to benefit themselves. I believe strongly in the value of decency, honesty and generally equitable behavior. When I uncover duplicity, I am constrained to root it out, even if it is to my own detriment."

Having run up against his rigid code several times during our association, I am not at all surprised to discover he holds these opinions. It is one of the reasons I could not bring myself to tell him the truth about Mr. Davies. I am disconcerted, however, by the sharp downturn of his spirits.

Something about the articulation of his beliefs has made him sad.

Why does this unsettle me?

Why does his unhappiness make me feel as though sitting calmly across from him in the carriage is almost unbearable?

Compelled by something I do not understand, I smile brightly and say with beguiling affability, "Tell me about your connection and why he is better than my cousin-in-law the Duke of Kesgrave."

He responds just as he ought, with a smile, and explains that we are going to meet with Sir Dudley Grimston. "Not as illustrious as your relative, to be sure, but as the Master of the Rolls, he is a person of some import. He was a classmate of my father's at Oxford, and I referred a delicate matter to him once before. I am confident he is the right person to ensure that Brooke's corruption is brought thoroughly to light."

"But not his murder of Mr. Gorman," I say.

"No, not his murder of Gorman," he agrees. "Unfortunately, one does not get a receipt for murder."

"Well, no," I reply, "but if you do employ someone to commit your murders for you, then you would have a record of the expense, no?"

Holcroft is reluctant to encourage this line of reasoning, which he believes will not prove fruitful. "Perhaps, but the description in the ledger will not be so blatant as to say: Murder for hire, thirty pounds. And we have no proof that Brooke did not kill Gorman himself. His clerk claimed he was in court yesterday, but we did not confirm that was true. Regardless, it is likely the evidence will reveal other conspirators, and I am confident that in that process the person who plunged the knife into Gorman's body will be brought to justice."

As a resolution of a murder investigation, it is far from ideal. Bea had the satisfaction of looking directly into the eyes of the man who killed her parents and confronting the murderous actor who entombed her beneath a theater.

In place of a sweeping moment of justice and retribution, I get the vague hope that the ruthless assassin responsible for one or more brutal deaths will suffer the indignity and discomfort of our vast and confusing legal system.

It is hardly the heroic narrative I imagined for myself when I finally managed to wrest a mystery from Bea. But it *is* the best I can do, and I am not so childish that I do not recognize the value in making sure several corrupt clerks are no longer able to pervert the course of justice.

A good thing has been accomplished.

Nevertheless, I sigh.

Chapter Twelve

❦

Sir Dudley has a large gap between his two front teeth, which tip forward at a slight angle, making the space appear larger. His nose, in contrast, dips curiously inward, like a hole in the road, and his forehead protrudes at a steep slant.

With all the ups and downs, his countenance has a bit of a rolling hill quality to it like a field.

That said, it is not an unappealing visage. Except for the heavy brows, which make him seem as if he is frowning even when he is smiling, his face is sharp and interesting. His eyes are light blue, his hair is grayish blond, and his manner is warm and welcoming.

The moment we are announced by a servant who attends to both his private office and the office where his staff works, Sir Dudley stops what he is doing and declares himself delighted by the company. Immediately, he calls for tea to be served and urges us to make ourselves comfortable around a thick round table in the middle of the room. When I ask where I should put the files currently occupying one of the cushioned leather seats, he laughs with amusement and offers to take them.

"I am sorry about that," Sir Dudley says, tossing the papers onto his desk, where they scattered upon landing. "We are drowning in paper. We are *always* drowning in paper. Finding enough room for everything is the ongoing struggle of my life. But obviously you did not come here to listen to me grumble about my storage quandaries."

As Mama also suffers from the debilitating effects of limited space, I offer my earnest sympathies and note that his challenge does seem rather overwhelming. The office is large and comfortable, with a coved ceiling, gilded sconces and wood paneling, and every surface is buried under a stack of papers. Additionally, there are three desks in the room immediately outside his door, which are occupied by the various clerks who assist him in his duties.

What *are* his duties?

My understanding of the Chancery Court system is limited by my interest in it, which until now had been nonexistent. According to Holcroft, his responsibilities are at once managerial (overseeing the dozens of Chancery clerks) and archival (ensure the safekeeping of charters, patents and records of important judgments). He is also a junior judge who maintains his own court, which is subordinate to the Lord Chancellor's.

If the details *seem* thoroughly uninteresting, it is because they actually are. But I am forced to admit that Holcroft is correct. Sir Dudley Grimston is exactly the right person with whom to raise the matter.

I am sure Kesgrave could have done only a *little* better.

As I am taking a seat, one of the clerks who works in the outer office enters with a problem that requires a long, murmured conversation. After the issue is resolved, I thank

Sir Dudley for agreeing to see us without an appointment. "You are very busy."

"Oh, yes, very busy," he says with an emphatic nod of his head. But then he grins broadly, his front teeth seeming to dangle dangerously in midair, and announces he can never be too busy to spare time for Sebastian Holcroft. "Regardless of the circumstance, I am always delighted to see the son of my oldest and dearest friend. How is your father doing? It has been far too long."

Holcroft assures him his sire continues to prosper.

"Still in the country, eh?" Sir Dudley asks.

"Yes, sir," Holcroft replies with a smile. "You know he would rather have the mud of Bedfordshire on his boots than the grit of London."

Sir Dudley concedes that he knows that far too well just as another clerk enters with a query.

Again, we wait as the Master of the Rolls advises on the issue. It is difficult for me to be patient because I am anxious to discuss Brooke. We are so close to holding the vile lawyer accountable, and yet I can almost feel him slipping away with every minute that passes.

As soon as the second clerk leaves, Holcroft says, "I must apologize, Sir Dudley, for only coming to you with serious matters, but I am afraid this one is very serious indeed and we require your help in resolving it."

Sir Dudley is unmoved by these somber tones. "No matter, my boy, no matter. We all do what we must. Now tell me how I can assist you." Then he laughs as his servant enters with the tea and he asks Holcroft to hold off on his response. "Thank you, Chivers, your timing is impeccable. I was just about to expire from thirst. I think I am a bit peckish as well. Perhaps you can find us some biscuits?"

"Certainly, sir," Chivers says quietly.

"Glorious," our host says happily. "Simply glorious. Now, Miss Hyde-Clare, do allow me to pour you a cup."

His cheerfulness is infectious, and I feel some of my anxiety ease.

Everything is going to be all right.

We will share our information with Sir Dudley, he will respond with proper horror, and Brooke and his band of corrupt clerks will be brought to justice.

Holcroft, accepting a cup of tea, leans forward to explain. He begins by touching on Mr. Davies's disappearance, provides a brief description of our investigation and concludes with the disquieting discoveries we have made about several members of the Court of Chancery.

He does not mention Mr. Gorman's murder, and although I grumble quietly in surprise at the omission, I do not interrupt.

Sir Dudley's good humor diminishes the longer Holcroft speaks, and by the time he has finished explaining, there is a dumbfounded grimace on the Master of the Rolls' face.

Silently, for what feels like almost an entire minute, he gapes at Holcroft with disbelief, his gapped teeth dangling. Then his slack expression snaps sharply into anger and he says, "That is not possible."

Holcroft, seeming to understand the other man's deep unwillingness to acknowledge the truth, does not argue. He simply nods his head and waits.

Hesitantly, because the gentleman is not an old friend of *my* family, I say, "I realize that you are troubled by this news, Sir Dudley. We are, too, which is why we came directly here upon discovering it. Holcroft insisted that you were the only person he would entrust with the evidence. As serious as the matter is, it is more serious still because Brooke is also a murderer. An investigator posing as a clerk in his office was killed yesterday because he knew too much about Brooke's operation. You may have heard the news. It was at the Western Exchange."

Although my tone is as gentle as a lullaby, the words infuriate him and he announces in a voice loud enough to shake the rafters that I am mistaken. "How dare you accuse any member of my profession of murder? You go too far!"

I won't lie.

His anger is unsettling, and I shrink back in apprehension or maybe fear.

He forms a fist with his right hand and pounds the table so firmly the teacups rattle.

The yelling draws the attention of Chivers, who comes darting into the room only to hover by the table and then quickly pull back. Two of the clerks tilt their heads resolutely down, determined to show no interest. A third, unable to quell his curiosity, sidles over to the desk nearest the office's doorway and pretends to look for something among the files and papers cluttering the space.

Sir Dudley colors slightly at the ruckus he made and apologizes with a self-conscious smile. "As Sebastian can attest, I am a man of very easy temper, which I rarely lose. But what you are proposing is quite troubling for me to comprehend and acknowledge. I lashed out instinctively in anger, and that is inexcusable of me. The idea of corruption within the Chancery Court is difficult enough for me to digest and then you added a charge of murder and it was simply too much. I do hope you can forgive me."

I am nodding before he reaches the end of his apology because his response is perfectly understandable. The news we have brought him is shocking, and he has the right to be shocked. "Of course, sir. Your response is not inexplicable."

"You are being too generous with me, Miss Hyde-Clare," he says, "and I am grateful for your kind heart. Now I know you too well, Sebastian, not to realize you would never have

come here if the evidence you possess was not incontrovert-
ible. Please show me what you have, and I will take it from
there."

Without commenting, Holcroft slides the envelope across
to Sir Dudley, who looks at it for a long time. Just when I
think he is going to slide it back without opening it, he lifts
the envelope and empties the contents onto the table. He
reads the first letter. His expression reveals nothing, but the
fact that he does not drop it in disgust indicates that he
perceives its significance. He reads the next one without
commenting, then proceeds silently to the third, fourth and
fifth.

At some point during Sir Dudley's perusal, Chivers
returns with a plate piled modestly with Prince of Wales
biscuits and rolled wafers. Our host is too engrossed to
notice, but I thank the servant and take a wafer. I hold out
the plate to Holcroft, who refuses. Then I put the biscuits
down and resume waiting for Sir Dudley to render his
judgment.

That he finds the letters persuasive is evident from the
pallor on his face. As he reads, the flush of outrage drains
entirely until his cheeks are completely devoid of color.

When he is finished, he allows the last letter to drop to
the table and expels a hefty sigh. Then he rubs his hands over
his face, as if trying to scrub something away.

"I know these men," he says sadly, almost as if he is
exhausted by what he read, "and cannot believe they are such
fools." Then he sighs again before asking for the evidence of
the murder. "I do not see it here."

"No, sir," Holcroft replies. "We have not been able to find
any yet. As you can imagine, that is harder to prove than
corruption."

"But there is more," I say.

"More?" Sir Dudley echoes, almost confused by the idea.

"Yes, where we found that envelope," I explain, "there are others and a ledger too. We did not have time to retrieve them because Brooke came into his study. We had to hide and then sneak out before he discovered us. But there is more evidence, a lot more, I think, and I am hopeful we will find some proof of murder among those documents."

"If there are more documents, then there are more corrupt clerks," Sir Dudley observes.

Holcroft nods and admits that it is likely. "I imagine Brooke keeps incriminating evidence as a way to ensure compliance. It is impossible to say what you will find when you search his study," he says, then places a bracing hand on the gentleman's shoulder to offer support. "It is just a few bad apples, sir, I am sure of it. Remove those from the barrel, and this esteemed institution will continue to flourish."

Given everything I have learned about the Court of Chancery in the past two days, I am not sure *flourish* is the correct description of what the institution is currently doing.

Rot, perhaps, is the more appropriate verb.

"You are right," Sir Dudley says determinedly, "of course you are. It is not nearly as bad as it seems, and there is nothing to be gained from my descending into a sulk because something has not turned out the way I want. Thank you, my friend, for being the voice of reason."

Holcroft, who clearly considers being the voice of reason his raison d'être, acknowledges by murmuring, "Of course."

"I do not know why I am surprised that you discovered all this," Sir Dudley adds. "It is certainly your area of expertise. Now let us try not to be maudlin and think of how the Court of Chancery will be improved by your action. You said there is *more* evidence, Miss Hyde-Clare? Please tell me how I may find it so that I can instruct the authorities when they apprehend Brooke. Is it in his desk or a safe?"

"It's hidden in a secret compartment in his wall," I say.

A hint of a smile appears on Sir Dudley's lips. "Ah, yes, precisely where one *should* hide information about one's corrupt associates. How did you discover it, Sebastian?"

"Not me. I was still looking in the desk when Miss Hyde-Clare noticed something amiss on one of the shelves," Holcroft replies easily. "As I have learned during the course of this investigation, she possesses a unique ability for finding secret compartments. It's quite impressive."

Calmly, as if I am paid generous compliments every day by handsome gentlemen for whom I have developed a begrudging respect, I nod my head. We are only one day removed from his insulting my intelligence ("For God's sake, I knew you were silly but this—") and yet it feels like weeks.

"How remarkable, Miss Hyde-Clare," Sir Dudley says with admiration. "We are very fortunate, then, that you chose to search for your childhood friend. I am sorry that you have been unable to find him. When this awful business is settled, I hope you will allow me to help you look for him. If he is a law clerk in London, I am certain I will be able to locate him."

"I would like that, thank you," I say, grateful for the offer, which is generous and kind.

And futile.

So many of my efforts on Mr. Davies's behalf have been futile.

I failed not only to figure out who actually killed him but also to confront the man who is responsible for his death. At no point did I have the satisfaction of looking him in the eye and saying, I know you did this. I know you killed Mr. Davies.

At no point did I have the satisfaction of looking at him *at all*.

Our only clash was a narrow escape in his study.

It feels like nothing.

Determinedly, I remind myself of the good that has been achieved today: corrupt clerks held accountable, justice restored to its fair course.

Vindication for Mr. Chambers and perhaps a little peace.

Thinking of Brooke's victims, I ask what restitution will be made to the poor men and woman whom his scheme harmed. "In many cases, *poor* is a literal description of their financial status because they were persuaded to surrender all their funds to a perverted system."

Sir Dudley shakes his head and admits that there will be no equitable resolution for Brooke's victims. "I am afraid the court simply does not function that way. What Brooke did was morally reprehensible and bribing clerks to change the outcome of a claim is illegal. I am not denying these things, Miss Hyde-Clare. I am condemning them categorically and will work tirelessly to make sure every man responsible for this perversion is punished. But ultimately all he did was exploit weaknesses in the system itself. What you are describing—compensation for the victims—is a much larger project. It is, in fact, a reformation of the Chancery Court itself, and that is something with which I cannot help you."

As he explains the inevitable outcome, I feel my cheeks grow warm in embarrassment.

Of course there will be no restitution.

Only a child expects life to be fair.

"The clerks will lose their positions," he continues. "They will be stripped of their power and forced to pay large fines. It is unlikely any will be remanded to prison or the Tower, but the loss of money and reputation will be severe. Trust me when I tell you that is a terrible punishment for a man who is accustomed to ease and respect."

I will have to trust him, yes, because the measures he describes seem to me to be woefully inadequate. "You will take the matter to the Lord Chancellor?"

Sir Dudley's blue eyes widen at this suggestion. "To Lord Eldon? No, I do not think it is necessary to involve him at this juncture. I will bring it to the Vice Chancellor, who will confer with the appropriate ministers to decide the best course of action. I hope you can trust me to see it through," he says, presenting me with the strident ridge of his brow as he tilts his head down, as if he expects me to refuse.

Why does he expect it?

Because I have not been very clever at hiding my disappointment. The tools I have been given to deal with objectionable statements—fluttering my eyelashes coyly, giggling sweetly—are inadequate to the situation and I do not bother to employ them.

My expression reveals my thoughts.

Embarrassed by my churlishness, I assure him without hesitation that I trust him implicitly.

And I do because Holcroft trusts him and he has shown himself to be intelligent, honorable and steadfast.

Would I have trusted Kesgrave more?

Well, yes, of course.

He is a *duke*.

Nevertheless, the problem is uniquely specific to the Chancery Court itself and the seemingly endless ways it allows corrupt activities to seep into its structure. In that sense, it does seem more logical to allow a man who is part of the system to *fix* the system.

"And what is to be done with Brooke?" I ask. "He is not a clerk to be fired and fined, and as the architect of the scheme, he deserves a harsher punishment than the loss of reputation and money."

Sir Dudley agrees wholeheartedly with my assessment and promises Brooke will be made to stand trial for his crimes. "The Crown takes bribery and fraud very seriously. As we do not yet have evidence of murder, I cannot speak to that outcome. But I do urge you to keep in mind that taking up residence in Newgate is a distinctly unpleasant experience regardless of the cause, and if he is truly responsible for the death of one man or even many, I think rotting away in prison is a more egregious punishment than hanging. The latter is painful but brief."

His observation is entirely reasonable, and, yes, yes, I agree that enduring year after year of privation and confinement is a horrible way to live out the rest of one's life. And yet it reminds me again of the unsatisfying conclusion to which my murder investigation has been brought.

Bea got to sweep across a terrace with a torch at the ready to subdue a killer who had tried to hurl her body over the top of the balustrade. Her dress was scorched in the process and her hair was remarkably disheveled and somehow she still managed to end the evening as the future Duchess of Kesgrave.

She captured a murderer and the most eligible parti in the whole of Britain *in one night*.

It simply does not seem fair.

She is a plain woman of six and twenty years of age.

By rights, she should not even have been on the terrace to confront Lord Taunton. No, she should have been sitting quietly in a corner somewhere with the other companions and spinsters.

I am the one who should be in the center of the room, and yet I am being shunted to the side.

And it is not as though I begrudge Bea *one iota* of her happiness. The feats she has managed to accomplish at her advanced age are astonishing and that she has done so while hobbled by her vast limitations makes her a true original.

It's just that I thought I could have a little of that originality for myself.

No, please, do not say it.

I know I am absurd.

Men have lost their lives, and I am brooding because I did not get to wield a torch.

I am every silly name Papa has ever called me.

Sensing my frustration, Sir Dudley says with rousing determination that I have still done a very good thing. "There might not be any compensation for Brooke's past victims, but thanks to you, Miss Hyde-Clare, he will have no future ones. I hope you can be satisfied with that."

Since he seems vaguely troubled by the prospect of my disappointment, I smile brightly and assure him I am quite pleased.

Content with my response, he nods firmly and requests specific information on how to locate the secret compartment so that he may direct his people to find the additional evidence. Holcroft explains that the Roentgen lock mechanism is released by lifting the gargoyle statue on the shelf.

That is all he says: gargoyle statue.

He does not mention its gruesome bat wings.

He does not describe its terrible porcine grin.

Sir Dudley makes note of it on a slip of paper to ensure he does not forget any of the details. When he looks up from the sheet, he notices the clerk is still hovering near the entranceway and calls to him. I think he is going to reprimand him for daring to eavesdrop, but instead he chastises him for being coy.

"Good God, Harkness, you dunderhead," he says peevishly. "If you wish to remind me that I owe you a letter for Mr. Martin, it would be far easier if you came out and said it, rather than loitering like that at my door."

Harkness ardently denies that this is what he is doing as Holcroft announces our departure. "We have already taken up too much of your time. You clearly have much work to do and we are in your way."

"Yes, yes," the Master of the Rolls agrees, but he refuses to allow the demands of his position to deprive him of a proper visit. "You have yet to tell me of your mother's health, and I have not heard a word about your father's cabbage crop. You know I am fascinated by his farming experiments. You will remain, and Harkness will go as soon as I write this letter."

The clerk turns a bright shade of pink and insists it was not his intention to interrupt.

"No matter, no matter," Sir Dudley says dismissively. "We all do what we must. Come in here, Harkness, and wait while I dash off this note. It won't take above five minutes. But I am not inviting you to tea, do you understand? You may pour yourself a cup if you desire, but this is not a social occasion. I do not want to hear about your mama's health, although I do worry about her catarrh."

Harkness cannot accept his offer, however, because there are only three cups, and realizing this, Sir Dudley calls for Chivers to supply not only another cup but also a fresh pot of tea. Then he sits down at his desk to write the letter. His clerk hovers awkwardly by the table, darting us embarrassed glances.

Sir Dudley is just finishing up the letter when Chivers returns. He slides the note into an envelope and hands it to the clerk, who scurries quickly away. Then he sits down with a heavy sigh and apologizes again for the interruption. "I wish I did not have to write that letter, but business is business."

"Of course," Holcroft murmurs. "We understand and should really allow you to get back to it."

I am no more inclined to linger than Holcroft. The hour grows increasingly late, and there's no telling when Mama will overcome her aversion to the sickroom long enough to peer through a crack in the doorway.

But Sir Dudley won't hear of it.

No, he has discharged his duty faithfully and now wants the pleasure of a proper visit.

"Tell me how Mr. Caruthers fares. I hear that you visit him regularly and refuse to allow him to wallow in self-pity."

Holcroft's expression darkens at the mention of his disgraced cousin, and he says with a tinge of bitterness, "Yes, I have shirked none of my responsibility there."

The resentment of his tone disconcerts me because in all of our conversations about Mr. Caruthers, he has displayed only patience and concern.

Sir Dudley's heavy brows descend even further as he regards his oldest friend's son with concern and says he would expect nothing less from him. "Of course you have held steady in your support. I am sure your family will come around. Your father, for example, has always been the most reasonable of men."

Holcroft allows this to be so but observes that his cousin and his wife are less generous in their understanding.

"Alas, yes, I know," Sir Dudley says, "for your father has frequently complained of them. Your mother's relatives, I believe. And how is Chester?"

"He is excellent, sir," Holcroft says, explaining that his youngest brother is now attending Balliol at Oxford.

"Charming," Sir Dudley says with a brisk nod before asking about other members of the Holcroft family.

And there are *so many* members of the Holcroft family.

I pour myself a fresh cup of tea as Holcroft reports on the health of his mother, another brother, a parcel of sisters, three grandparents, two uncles, one slightly dotty great-aunt and a beloved stallion called Lucifer, who almost ran down Sir Dudley in a field behind the Holcroft ancestral home.

True to his word, he actually wants to know the details of the senior Holcroft's farming experiments, and there is a lengthy question-and-answer session on the moisture levels of soil.

Finally, I am unable to withstand the anxiety of worrying about my mother and rise to my feet. "I am sorry, Sir Dudley, but my conscience cannot allow me to distract you from your work any longer. We must leave you to it."

Sir Dudley glances at the clock and, noting the hour, apologizes. "Oh, dear, I seem to have let time run away from me. My only excuse is that it has been far too long since I visited with your father. I hope I will have an opportunity to see him soon."

"I know that would delight him to no end," Holcroft says as he stands.

"Perhaps I will write him a letter this very eve," Sir Dudley says, escorting us to the entrance of his office. "As soon as I have information about this business, I will send you a note, Sebastian. In the meantime, if you have any other concerns, I hope you will not hesitate to contact me."

"We will, thank you," I say, "and thank you again for your help."

He demurs graciously, and one of his associates, the clerk seated nearest to the door, scowls with impatience. He is ready for us to be gone, as is his colleague at the neighboring desk.

I am sure our presence was not *that* disruptive.

Sir Dudley yelled only the one time.

Amused by the clerks' irritability, I step into the hallway just as Harkness returns from delivering his note to Mr. Martin. He dips his head in acknowledgment, and matching the gesture, I discover my mood is curiously light. The heaviness I brought into the cluttered office is gone, and I realize it is relief at having placed the burden of Brooke on more capable shoulders.

It does not seem fair that relief can come so easily. It is

not that way for everyone. Mr. Chambers, for example, who has to live with the ravages of Brooke's venality. Or Mr. Gorman, who does not get to live at all.

Eagerly, I propelled myself into the mystery of Mr. Davies's death, scarcely grasping what that meant. I thought it was a lark. Justice is an adventure!

Now a second man is dead, and I still get to walk away.

That is neither justice nor a lark.

It is the sad reality of life, and yet my relief remains pervasive. The story may not have followed the narrative arc I had imagined in my head, but the plot advanced.

I like to think I advanced as well.

Chapter Thirteen

Make no mistake: I am flirting with Holcroft.

How did it happen?

Honestly, I am not entirely sure.

When we boarded the carriage, we were silent. It was not a sullen silence, I don't think. We were not specifically *not* talking. Rather, we were both consumed by our private thoughts.

What was he thinking about?

It is impossible to speculate. Perhaps he was trying to understand how he had become so deeply engrossed in such an unpleasant business that had nothing to do with him. Maybe he was considering which waistcoat to wear to his club that evening.

I was struggling to comprehend the complexity of my own emotions—how I could feel at once relief and shame for feeling relief.

The carriage jerked and began to roll down Chancery Lane. I grasped the leather strap to steady myself, and Holcroft, as courteous as ever, held out a hand to offer his support.

It was just a passing gesture, his hand fluttering in midair for only a second before returning smoothly to his side. But it struck me then how resolutely he had been there, near, his hand always ready to dart out, during the whole of this absurd enterprise, with its shoehorn compartments and hideous gargoyles and indolent valets who hide bottles of port behind heavy velvet drapery.

Suddenly, all at once, he seemed to glow with a sparkling goodness that glimmered from somewhere deep inside him, giving him a vaguely angelic appearance despite his dark good looks. And those eyes, those verdant and fascinating emerald green eyes, gleamed so brightly I almost had to look away.

It was just a trick of the light.

Truly.

The carriage had driven past a gap between two buildings, and for a moment the sun spilled brilliantly into the conveyance.

A mundane occurrence, to be sure, and yet utterly transforming.

No, not transforming.

Revealing, because all it did was make plain what I already knew.

Feeling only relief, I let go of the strap, leaned forward in my seat and asked about the design of his curricle.

He responded with technical details, expounding on the various mechanisms that make it a particularly well-sprung vehicle.

My fault, I thought, because I was not clear about what I meant.

But when I explained that I was asking about the curiously dashing colors, his face lit with sly humor and he said, "I am building up to the colors. You do not describe the perfection of the rose by starting with its petals."

Well, actually, you do, don't you?

You describe the color first, then the silkiness of the texture. You absolutely do not enthuse about the majestic straightness of the stem.

I did not quibble, however, and he continued to describe the marvels of his curricle. I fluttered my lashes as if transfixed by the information, which I was not but neither was I bored.

And now I am flirting.

Mr. Holcroft knows it and is flirting in return.

It is a little disconcerting because I assumed flirting is either beneath his dignity or beyond his ability. Why else mar the delightful perfection of the waltz with conversation about the weather?

But to my delight neither is true, and I feel a warmth suffuse my face as he asks me if I enjoy visiting the park during the Fashionable Hour.

And we are not passing through a patch of sunlight.

Indeed, we have just turned onto a particularly dark, narrow lane.

"I very much enjoy a drive through Hyde Park," I say, tilting my eyes away from the window to look at something far more interesting than the slender shops lining the street. "Alas, I never get enough opportunities."

I am angling for an invitation, and there is nothing subtle about it.

Holcroft does not mind at all, for his grin widens as he laments the misfortune of my circumstance. "If only there was some way I could help rectify that."

I respond with a giggle, which is remarkable.

Not the giggle itself because I giggle all the time.

But the sincerity of the action. I actually *feel* gigglish.

Mama would be mortified.

"I am happy to assist you in coming up with ideas," I

reply. "I am sure this problem is not beyond both our faculties."

"Your generosity, Miss Hyde-Clare, is humbling to—"

The carriage halts suddenly, jarring us both, and Mr. Holcroft breaks off in surprise as my head slams against the back of the seat. He lurches to my bench with a confused expression as he reaches out a hand to make sure I am all right while his eyes take in our surroundings. As if perceiving something I cannot see, he stiffens abruptly just as the carriage door swings open and the sandy-haired clerk from Brooke's office looks in.

"Everyone all right?" he asks.

His tone is genial, convivial, as if he is genuinely concerned for our welfare.

I open my mouth to say I am fine, although I can feel a bump forming on the back of my head, but before I can speak Holcroft snarls.

Calmly, the clerk tsk-tsks at the angry sound and says, "You should watch yourself, Holcroft, or someone might get hurt."

He says *someone* as if it could indeed be anyone, but then he rotates his body toward me and I see the gun he had trained on Holcroft. Now it is aimed in my direction, and I know who he means.

Me.

I might get hurt.

In the pit of my stomach an oily wave rises and crashes fiercely as if on a craggy shore, then it rises again and crashes again, more ferociously.

I am going to be ill.

God, yes, violently and viciously ill.

Any second now.

I can't. I can't.

One sudden movement and Altick shoots.

It is almost impossible to breathe deeply with the rock lodged in my chest, so I settle for shallow breaths.

Does it work?

No, not at all.

The queasiness just intensifies.

While I struggle to hold on to two wafers and a biscuit, Mr. Holcroft nods and raises his hands in front of him to show he has nothing to hide.

"My driver?" he asks evenly.

"Unconscious but alive," Altick says. "If you follow my instructions, he will stay that way. I bear him no grudge."

Oh, but the way he says it, with the emphasis on the word *him,* making it terrifyingly clear against whom he *does* bear a grudge.

My stomach roils again.

The frequency of my shallow gasps increases.

Am I going to faint?

Is that really the sort of female I am?

Swooning at the first hint of danger?

It's just a gun, I tell myself. It's just a gun.

But I don't know how that is supposed to make me feel better.

It's *just* a gun?

As opposed to what—a cannon?

"Good," Holcroft says. "That is good. Stanley has nothing to do with this. Neither does Miss Hyde-Clare. Please let them both stay here while I come with you."

Altick scoffs at the assertion. "Oh, I think Miss Hyde-Clare has plenty to do with it. The missing Mr. Davies, after all, is *her* friend."

The chill that runs up my spine at these words is remarkable.

Why is that?

Why do I feel a fresh wave of fear at his words? Nothing

he has said is new information to me. I already know that all roads lead back to Bea's beloved clerk. Two moments, present and past, linked by death.

Holcroft smiles wryly and regards Altick with condescension.

A gun mere inches from his heart and still he manages to project disdain.

"Miss Hyde-Clare is a fool who has no idea what is going on," he says coolly, "and you are a fool if you believe otherwise."

In fact, Miss Hyde-Clare knows *exactly* what is going on, and she twists her face into a look of utter terror before saying the silliest thing she can think of. "What is happening, Mr. Holcroft? Why is Mr. Brooke's clerk aiming a gun at us in such a menacing fashion? Did you do something horrible to him?"

Fluttering my lashes as if profoundly confused, I switch my gaze to Altick, keeping my eyes away from the gun. I cannot think if I look at the gun. "Is this about money? Is Mr. Holcroft deeply in debt to you? Did he lose a great sum to you at vingt-un? I told the wretch to stop gambling. He is terrible at cards and completely hopeless at mathematics. Do tell me the amount and I will make sure it is delivered to your home as soon as possible. I have access to unlimited funds, you see. You may not know this, but I am related to the Duke of Kesgrave. He is quite besotted with my cousin and will do anything she asks."

My breathless chatter accomplishes nothing.

As soon as I finish speaking, he says with contempt. "Nice performance, Miss Hyde-Clare, but you were in the meeting with Grimston. Both of you were."

The meeting with Grimston.

Shocked that he could know anything about a meeting

that ended only ten minutes before, I look at Mr. Holcroft and ask, "What is happening?"

Before he can reply, however, Altick says with a delight that bears a distressingly close resemblance to glee, "He is discovering that his father's school chum is not quite the reliable friend he thought him. Old Grimy isn't exactly the ethical proponent of justice you supposed him to be. He is just as greedy and self-interested as the rest of us. More so, in fact, because he has no qualms about having people killed to protect his interests. Which is not to say that he doesn't feel badly about the whole thing. I am sure in some sliver of his heart he is cut up about it. The note he addressed to me, however, concerned only the business aspect of the act. Now come," he says, gesturing with the gun. "We have lingered here long enough."

Neither one of us responds.

Why does Holcroft stay rooted to his spot?

I have no idea.

Perhaps he is too shocked by the revelation of Sir Dudley's villainy to move.

Maybe he is too busy replaying our recent visit in his head to hear him.

I am incapable of movement.

The moment he declares his intention to kill us, every muscle in my body leaves me. Suddenly, my bones are like jelly.

I am a plate of blancmange.

There was only a hairbreadth between knowing his intentions and hearing them, and yet my heart tumbled as if falling into a yawning chasm.

It lies on the bottom now motionless.

Altick, his eyes focused on Holcroft, leans deeper in the carriage and presses the gun against my side. "I said come."

Holcroft's nod is almost languid. "A splendid idea. This

conveyance grows confining, and I would appreciate the fresh air," he says, offering his arm as if to escort me to dinner.

Not a hint of trepidation crosses his face as he looks at Altick.

Not even the tiniest trace in the flicker of his lashes.

How is he doing that?

Does he feel no fear or is he simply that skilled in hiding his emotions?

I cannot mimic his affect.

The terror is plainly written on my face.

"No, no," our captor says, declining Holcroft's offer on my behalf. "You will exit one at a time. The girl first."

It is all very well for Altick to decide I should climb out of the carriage, but there remains the troubling matter of my inertia. I feel fixed to the seat, as if someone has applied a strong adhesive to my bottom.

"Miss Hyde-Clare?" Holcroft says with gentle concern.

Gentle concern for me.

When moments ago he discovered that his father's oldest friend has arranged for his death as callously as tossing away a cravat that has one too many stains to be redeemed.

No matter, no matter. We all do what we must.

That is what the blackguard said, wasn't it, as he sat down to write his monstrous note.

It turns out Harkness's protestations were sincere after all. He had not intended to interrupt our meeting. Sir Dudley merely seized on his proximity as a convenient pretext to compose the letter ordering our execution.

My heart hammering—yes, yes, my *heart* has no trouble moving and so painfully as well—I stare helplessly at Holcroft.

He stares back, his green gaze serene.

Serene.

Not panicked.

The nausea does not subside, but my muscles tighten. I slide forward in the seat and slip past Altick as I disembark. He grabs my arm to keep me close as Holcroft climbs down.

"Now, that wasn't so hard, was it?" Altick says mockingly. "Into that building there, number twenty."

Dirt from the road kicks up as wind gusts through the alley, causing the sign on the haberdashery across the way to knock loudly against its pole. The narrow lane is oddly more confining than the carriage itself, with its rundown buildings seeming to hold each other up, like a line of exhausted dancers after a vigorous set.

Although the alley itself is not entirely bereft of people, it is devoid of concern. The man working the till in the clothing shop darts his eyes toward the window, then resolutely looks down. Even if he cannot perceive the small gun trained on me, he can see Holcroft's driver lying unconscious on the bench, his wrists and ankles tightly bound with rope and a cloth stuffed in his mouth.

Holcroft takes a step toward his driver to confirm he is all right, and Altick orders him to move away. "I told you he was fine and will remain fine. But I guess you're just going to have to trust me on that," he says, chuckling at his own sally.

I begin walking toward the decrepit structure, looking over my shoulder with regret at the driver.

If he wakes up...

If it's in time...

The hope is forlorn, and even as I see—or think I see—his eyes flutter lightly, I know it makes no difference to our survival. He is bound and gagged, and the haberdasher wants nothing to do with us.

"If I had known you were having us over for tea, I would have brought a tin of biscuits," Holcroft says as we approach the building.

"This decrepit structure isn't my home. I would not be

caught dead here. You, on the other hand..." Altick trails off meaningfully as he unlocks the door. "*You* like to bring your lightskirts here to satisfy your prurient tastes, as more than a dozen doxies will be willing to attest after your body is found. You always knew it was a little dangerous to come here with your gold pocket watch and fat purse, but that was part of the appeal. Oh, yes, the threat of a hedge-bird making a run at you really got your juices flowing. As I said, your tastes are prurient. Poor Miss Hyde-Clare. If only she understood the danger she courted by associating with you. And everyone thought you were such an honorable gentleman. At least now they will know the truth."

A sour smell assaults me as Altick closes the door and grows worse the deeper we step into the house. A particularly acrid stench hits me as we walk past a room to the left. My belly roils again, and I pause to grip my stomach. Altick makes a disapproving sound and orders me to keep moving.

"Upstairs," he says, "where the bedroom is. It has been prepared for you. Holcroft is considerate in that way."

Resisting the provocation, Holcroft marvels over the clerk's ability to pull his scheme together so quickly. "Sir Dudley sent you a note...what...only a half hour ago?"

The first step creaks as I begin to climb the stairs. The farther we get from the door to the left, the less awful the house smells, and I cannot help but wonder what dead thing is inside the room. It has to be a rat or a small bird. Maybe a stray dog that wandered in and got trapped.

It cannot be a person!

No, not a human being beginning to rot.

"You are correct," Altick says. "I received the note from Grimy about forty-five minutes ago, which left me enough time to arrive at his building just as you were climbing into your carriage. I followed on foot for a few blocks and then overpowered your driver when he stopped to allow a fruit seller to pass with his cart. Knowing you were involved, Grimy assumed a permanent solution to your meddling would be needed and instructed me to prepare. I knew what you were up to the moment you introduced yourself and began asking about Davies with his absurd scar."

He shakes his head as if unable to conceive how anyone could fail to recall a law clerk with such a significant deformity.

"And then I saw Gorman slip you that note and I knew for certain you were investigating Brooke," he explains. "Ah, but that was a shock to me. Up until that moment, I never had any reason to suspect Gorman. He seemed so earnest and determined to impress Brooke. I just thought he wanted my job, the sycophant. Now I realize he was cozying up to the boss to gain his trust. The fool probably gave it to him. I still do not know what Gorman managed to discover. He would not say a word to me."

I gasp. "You killed him!"

"Yes, but only because he left me no choice," Altick says as we reach the landing of the first floor. "I tried to discover what he knew without hurting him, but once it became clear that he had arranged a secret assignation to tell you everything, I had to act quickly. What if he knew about Brooke's arrangement with my employer?"

"Your employer?" I repeat, mystified. "But you *work* for Brooke."

"No," Holcroft says, "he works for Grimston. Did he secure the position for you?"

"I worked for years for Brooke before Grimy came along," Altick says. "Paid me a pittance too, which is why I was more than happy to protect Grimy's interests for a fee. He approached me a year ago when he brokered his deal with Brooke. He did not trust him not to undermine him, so he recruited me to keep tabs on him."

The information is so astonishing, I halt in the middle of the corridor and stare at him in the dim light from the room up ahead. His sandy hair is disheveled, giving him a benign younger brother appeal. I can scarcely grasp the fact that he is the assassin who jabbed Mr. Gorman with such precision and assurance.

"You work for the Master of the Rolls," I say, "who pays you to make sure Brooke does not betray their corrupt agreement?"

"You know exactly what is going on, Miss Hyde-Clare," he says with a hint of admiration. "You're not a fool at all."

Beside me, Mr. Holcroft groans quietly, as if I have thoughtlessly unraveled the complex scheme he was painstakingly constructing. I appreciate his optimism, but in this case it is sorely misplaced. Altick is not persuadable. He will not suddenly decide to let me go because I am a pretty ninnyhammer.

No, the only way Holcroft and I will leave this dilapidated building alive is if we prevail physically over Altick.

That is it.

Our only option.

Nothing else is viable.

I cannot say why knowing that helps me to think better, but it does. It calms me down. It allows me to see all the individual threads of the plot and weave them into a single strand.

Will comprehending the full story help me to live?

No, not at all.

But words are life.

Every syllable he utters is another breath of air I get to draw.

"Thank you, Mr. Altick, for the compliment," I say in my best ballroom drawl. "But I must confess I am quite baffled by the arrangement between Sir Dudley and Brooke. Their jobs seem at odds, and I cannot comprehend how working together can be mutually beneficial."

There is nothing subtle about the tactic, and I am not surprised when Altick chuckles at my attempt to delay the inevitable. He nudges me forward, pressing the gun against my side as he directs me to turn right into the bedchamber.

"Your final resting place," he says with snide pleasure, "so I hope you like it."

There is nothing to like. The ceiling is low and stained with curly patches of mold that look like the beginning of a design. Rosettes, perhaps, for the trim of a ballgown. The walls are pink, faded almost to white, and pocked with holes where the plaster has peeled. The floor is also crumbling with boards so rotted you can see through them in places, and the windows are bare except for a few wispy strands of fabric that hang from forlorn curtain rods.

In the center of the room is a mattress with a yellowed sheet, its edges frayed and torn.

My final resting place.

A wave of nausea overtakes me, so intense I almost double over.

The only thing that keeps me upright is the thought of Altick's smirk.

My effort is useless, however, because Altick chuckles anyway, and Holcroft steps forward, alarmed, I can only assume, by the sudden pallor of my face.

It is not possible to feel this swoony and not be entirely white.

"Buh-buh," Altick says, raising the gun so that it is now aimed at my forehead. "I've already warned you about this, Holcroft. Stay back."

The gun seems larger now that is directly in my line of sight, more lethal now that I can see the decorative pattern on the silver handle.

I cannot fathom the ornamentation.

Why make an instrument of death pretty?

Unable to bear the lovely delicacy of the design, I close my eyes and grasp the doorframe for support.

Delighted by this display of weakness, Altick decides to indulge my curiosity as he shoves me farther into the room.

Why?

Perhaps because extending the prelude heightens my suffering and therefore his enjoyment. Delay is an exquisite form of torture.

Regardless of his motive, he launches into a detailed explanation of the scheme. "As Master of the Rolls, old Grimy hears cases and renders judgment. But he is only a subordinate judge and his rulings are dependent on their being accepted by the party involved. If a litigant chooses to pursue the matter, he can bring it to the Lord Chancellor on appeal. And it is on that opportunity that Brooke's entire plan hinges, for it's a very costly process to appeal. Generously hearted Brooke hates to see a client throw away his money but of course will press the suit if he thinks the case is likely to prevail. I trust it goes without saying that he always thinks it is likely to prevail?" he asks with a taunting grin.

The smile might be disingenuous, but his pleasure is real, and I cannot tell if it is our impending deaths that delight him or the ingenuity of Brooke's scheme.

With a tilt of his head, Altick waves the gun and gestures for me to enter the bedchamber. Reluctantly, I release my grip on the doorjamb and take one hesitant step inside. The floor is unsteady, with loose planks that wobble and shake. A beam is so unmoored from its surroundings I imagine jumping on one end and sending Altick soaring into the air like a child on a seesaw.

Slowly, Holcroft and I draw closer to the hideous desecration in the middle of the room.

"To ensure an appeal is necessary," Altick continues, "he pays Grimy to rule against him. It is an arrangement he has also set up for a small cadre of solicitors whom he trusts. Grimy draws a tidy profit from the practice while Brooke lines his coffers, so he is understandably keen to protect it. As you are the only two who know about Brooke's secret compartment, I'm sure you comprehend why your continued existence is so untenable to him. After I take care of our business here, I am to go to Brooke's and retrieve the rest of his evidence, which will further solidify Grimy's position. In one stroke he will be able to protect himself and keep the clerks in line."

The bed is worse up close. Many of the yellow stains are speckled with brown spots, and a small battalion of ants march across the far-right corner. I cannot imagine how anything can become so filthy. Is it the product of years of disregard or did terrible things happen in this room?

"He cannot have the pair of you running around producing evidence of Brooke's corruption," Altick says, shoving me slightly as I pause about a foot from the bed. "I imagine Grimy is quite cut up about the ugly turn this venture has taken. From what he has said, I do believe his affection for your father is genuine, and he is probably sorry for the grief his dear friend is about to experience. Losing one's heir is terrible enough but to discover at the same time that his seemingly honorable son was actually a defiler and a scoundrel..."

Altick clucks in disapproval, and while he is basking in the depravity of his plan, I dart a glance at Holcroft. It is an awful thing to imagine how your death will be received by the people who love you.

My own parents will promptly fall in line with Altick's version. Gulled into believing Bea's mother and father died in the most sordid way possible, they have already shown themselves to be susceptible to salacious explanations.

But Bea won't be fooled.

No, she will see through the film of filth Altick has laid over this scene in an instant.

Holcroft meets my gaze with steady eyes—the same steady eyes with which he examined Mr. Gorman's corpse, the same steady eyes with which he tucked me behind the curtain in Brooke's study.

Always, always, those steady green eyes contemplating the world serenely.

And somehow even now, despite the desperateness of the situation.

Is it an inability to perceive the whole truth or a determination to thwart it?

Almost imperceptibly, he nods.

I don't know what that means.

How could I possibly know what some vague gesture in the middle of a death struggle signifies?

Churlishly, I am annoyed that he expects me to understand the implication. We are not army generals who have strategized offenses together for years. I can only assume it's a sign that he is going to try to save us.

Be ready, he is saying.

I am ready, yes.

If Altick is going to kill me here, in this wretched little room, with its stained walls and rotted floorboards, then I might as well make it as difficult as possible for him. Perhaps the bullet will lodge in a place that does not align easily with the story he intends to tell. Maybe I can do something that will help Bea figure out the truth.

Good God, *help* Bea solve my own murder!

Inconceivably, I want to laugh.

And not just laugh, *laugh riotously* like a patient in an asylum staring up at the moon.

But I hold it in, pressing a hand against my belly, and blink several times to let Holcroft know I am prepared.

Whatever happens, I will be ready.

Altick, oblivious to the moment of communication that passes between us, continues to lament the tragedy that is about to befall the Holcroft family. "Will your father go so far as to remove your name from the family Bible? Probably not. But forbidding mentions of your name? I would think yes." He cackles, delighted by the prospect as he pushes me even closer to the bed. My legs are now pressed against the mattress, and I wonder how the events will play out. Will he shoot me where I stand and let me fall back onto the bed? Or will he arrange me on the sheet and then pull the trigger?

Do my thoughts seem dispassionate?

Yes, I think they are oddly dispassionate.

Possibly, this is how my brain has decided to deal with my imminent death, by pretending it is a curiosity to be examined or an equation to be solved.

It is so different from the moment at the Western Exchange, when time itself seemed to stand still.

What a wondrous mechanism fear is, the way it distorts and deforms reality.

Altick rattles on, but it is hard for me to pay attention because of the distance my brain has created. I see his lips moving, the grim smile, but his words are vague.

Something about giants.

Something else about great falls.

And then suddenly it all snaps into focus as Altick says: "Holcroft the Holy, who turned in his own cousin for double dealing."

Stunned, I turn to Mr. Holcroft and say, "*You* turned in Mr. Caruthers?"

It is only a trice, a mere fraction of a second, but briefly and assuredly it is as if we are in the drawing room of a fashionable London hostess, discussing the latest *on-dit,* and Altick has suddenly realized that the ineffable joy of sharing news of the scandal belongs to him. His guard drops as a look of anticipatory delight sweeps across his face.

An instant, yes, but it is all Mr. Holcroft needs and his fist flies out of seemingly nowhere to strike Altick on the jaw. The assassin's head whips back as he lurches to the left, and the gun discharges like a crack of thunder.

I feel the shot in my bones.

It is a brick wall that slams into my body.

Everything hurts.

Altick snarls with anger, his face turning a furious red, as he swings his torso around and bashes Holcroft with the pistol. Blood trickles down Holcroft's face from the gash above his left brow.

"*Run!*" Holcroft roars at the top of his lungs.

It's a baffling order.

Clear, yes, of course it is clear because a murderer is bent on ending us both and he does not know how long he will be able to stave him off.

Run to safety.

That was the message that was in his eyes.

I understand *that.*

But save myself when I am already lost?

When even now I am weakened from a bullet hole in my...in my...

Where exactly is my wound?

I have no idea because *everything* hurts.

Altick grunts as Holcroft lands a blow on his cheek, blood begins to seep out of his nose, and I realize I have not been hit.

The bullet missed me.

Run!

Run at once out of this room and down the stairs and through the hallway and into the bright glare of daylight.

Run to the haberdashery and scream your head off until the indifferent man at the till looks up.

But my legs don't move.

They don't budge at all.

And it is not terror that keeps me rooted to the spot.

It is shame.

Running away while Holcroft literally fights for his life!

I would not be able to live with myself.

His nose bleeding heavily now, Altick throws himself at Mr. Holcroft, pitching his entire weight forward and propelling them both to the ground. Again, he thwacks Holcroft with the gun.

Another gash.

More blood.

Dazed, perhaps, Holcroft heaves himself up with a fierce swing of his legs, dislodging his assailant. Altick lands on his back and throws the pistol, which hits Holcroft in the eye, dulling his vision. Then the clerk grins as if he knows something nobody else does and digs a hand into his pocket. Mr. Holcroft, recovering his sense, wipes the blood from his sight and leaps on top of him.

He punches him square in the face, but it isn't enough.

It will never be enough because Altick has a second weapon: another gun, a knife, something. He came here to kill two of us.

Frenziedly, my gaze sweeps the room—stupid, empty room, with its grotesque bed in the center—and lands with frantic hope on the curtains.

I dash across the room to attack the drapery with some half-formed thought of using the curtain rod like a lance or spear, of running Altick through like a knight at a joust.

No, no, that won't work. The top of the window is too high, and the scraps of fabric are too flimsy to tug. It *might* succeed if the plastic is so rotted it crumbles like sand.

Rotted!

Pivoting desperately on my heels, I turn around and run back to the entrance to find the loose board, the one so unmoored from its bearings that I imagined jumping on one end of the plank and hurling Altick into the air.

I feel it before I see it, the wood beam rattling beneath my feet the moment I step on it.

Yes, yes, it is loose.

Perfectly loose because it yields at once to my pull.

Clutching the board in both hands, I spin around. Holcroft and Altick are on the floor by the window, grappling for control of a knife that is perched a mere inch from the former's neck. The clerk is grinning. It is a vicious grin, angry and determined and confident that triumph is at hand.

If he could just...shove...the...blade...into...the...jugular.

Holcroft's own lips are pulled tight in a grimace, and his face is bright red from exertion. The effort of holding off Altick makes the veins in his neck pop out, as if presenting his enemy with a clearer target.

Frustrated, Altick shrieks furiously, incensed that Holcroft is making it so difficult. Why can't he be a good little victim and just let him plunge in his knife!

I'll show you difficult, I think, striding across the floor with the plank held high and whacking him over the head with it. The knife clatters to the floor at the same time Altick drops back, his eyes shut.

Scarcely comprehending, Holcroft glares up at me pugnaciously, as if expecting an attack from another front. His green eyes are wild now, hostile and turbulent, and although I want to stand there as long as necessary to provide him with the same serenity he gave me, movement in the doorway claims my attention.

Tightening my grasp on the beam, I turn to confront the new enemy, my face no doubt the picture of pugnacity as well.

But it is Bea.

Bea and the duke.

It makes no sense—their being here in this hovel in...in... God knows what part of town.

And yet it makes perfect sense because this is exactly what Bea does: follows clues, deciphers mysteries. I knew she would find my murderer; I just did not realize she would do it before he had completed the job.

Calmly, then, because it all somehow seems preordained, I point to Altick, who lies unconscious on the floor, and say, "There. There is the man who killed Theodore Davies."

Bea is stunned.

Yes, stunned beyond anything I have ever seen on a person's face before. Her face turns completely white and her brown eyes appear to pop out of their sockets as though dislodged from a gun. "Theodore Davies does not exist. I made him up."

Chapter Fourteen

✦

I argue.
I argue. I argue. I argue.
Mr. Davies not exist!

What a staggeringly outrageous thing to say!

Am I an *utter* nodcock?

Am I a *complete* goosecap?

Is this her true estimation of me—that I would be swayed by the most facile Banbury tale anyone has ever told?

My heart is pounding, my hands are beset with splinters from the rough plank I am holding, and Holcroft is bleeding from several wounds on his head because *Altick just tried to kill us*.

Why?

Because we asked him about Mr. Davies.

All of this was set in motion by our inquiries into the dead clerk.

Obviously, she is denying the truth out of a misguided sense of responsibility.

Bea is still trying to protect me.

Of all the absurd things in the world!

Can she not see that there is nothing left to risk?

All the danger has been exposed. All the mysteries uncovered. All the punches thrown.

The murderer is *literally* lying at my feet on the floor.

But old habits die hard.

The longer Bea speaks, the more elaborate her story grows. Somehow Miss Otley from the Lake District is pressed into service as the reason she made up the lie in the first place. "I was trying to elicit her confidence."

Each new detail is a study in implausibility.

The notice in the *London Morning Gazette* announcing Theodore Davies's death?

"I visited the newspaper office myself and placed the item," she insists. "I was desperate for your parents to stop looking for him because I knew eventually they would find out the truth."

"That he doesn't exist?" I ask cynically.

"Yes!" she says fervently.

Although I am disheartened to discover her true opinion of my intelligence, my tone is gentle as I say. "You are a lovely cousin to worry about me so, but I don't think you understand how far out to sea the ship has sailed. This man *has confessed* to killing Mr. Davies."

Bea, her manner agitated in a way I have never seen before, says, "That is impossible. He could not have killed a figment of my imagination."

Holcroft stares agog as we quarrel, blood dripping off his face as he tries to make sense of the argument. "Mr. Davies is not missing? You are not trying to find the man for whom you nurture a passion?"

My patience already strained by Bea's denials, I glance at Holcroft peevishly because I had forgotten that he had jumped to that absurd conclusion. What had I ever done that would allow anyone to believe I could *nurture a passion* for a law clerk? Every action I have taken since the day I entered society has been in pursuit of the opposite. I have tried repeatedly with little success to nurture a passion for a titled man of great wealth.

Irritably, I say, "Mr. Davies is my cousin's former beau, not mine. I've never met the man."

"Because he does not exist," Bea says sharply.

Altick groans.

"Here, I will show you," I say, walking over to the assassin and tapping him several times on the cheek to return him to his senses.

After a moment, his eyes flutter open and he regards me with confusion. He is awake but insensible.

Kneeling fully on the floor, I grab him by the upper arms and tug him into a seated position. His head bobbles to the side, threatening to topple him, so I push him against the mattress for support.

Then I lean back to consider him.

He seems steady enough.

Matter-of-factly, I say, "Are you with me, Altick?"

His awkward nod is unsteady but confirms his coherence.

"Very good," I say. "Now please tell my cousin how and why you killed Theodore Davies."

His head lolls to the side and he stares at me blankly through one swollen eye. "Who?"

Clearly, the blow to his head disoriented him. "Theodore Davies. The clerk who worked in Brooke's office with you."

Altick shakes his head. "I know of no one by that name."

Is he toying with me?

Oh, yes, he is toying with me.

He must have heard enough of my conversation with Bea to know this is the best way to provoke me.

Resisting the urge to scream, I remain calm and remind him that he has already admitted that my investigation into

Mr. Davies is what alerted him to the true reason for my visit. "You said you knew everything the moment I asked about him."

Altick manages a half-hearted sneer. "No, *you*, you daft woman. I did not think twice about you. It was Holcroft."

Holcroft?

What was Holcroft?

No, no, that is only a distraction.

He is still taunting me.

"You do know him," I say heatedly. "Just minutes ago you called his scar absurd."

Altick's eyes blink shut as a thick smile flits across his face and he mutters, "Absurd detail. Only a silly, romantical girl would think that was convincing."

His head flops to the side again.

He is only pretending to sleep to deny me satisfaction.

Roughly, I grip his shoulders and begin to shake him. "Altick," I say angrily. "Altick!"

Beside me, Bea drops to her knees and lays her hands on top of my own to still them. "I am sorry, Flora," she says softly as I continue to tug at the unconscious man. "I am so very sorry. I never meant for this to happen."

It is the way she says *this,* with so much heartfelt regret, that finally penetrates my brain.

Slowly, I loosen my grip on Altick's shoulders and stare at her in bewilderment. The color has returned to her face so forcefully she is now bright red.

Bright red, I realize, with embarrassment.

But for herself, not me.

Oh, but if she is mortified by *telling* the lie, what does that say about me for *believing* it?

Murmuring soothingly, Bea turns me away from Altick and pulls me into her arms. I am taut, resisting, unsure. But she persists, running her hand gently down my back.

It is, I realize, the first time she has ever reached out to me with affection. Our relationship has always been so distant, and that is my fault.

That is partially why we are here.

Why did I really want to figure out who killed the former love of her life?

To make amends.

To say, I know I was a terrible sister for so many years but I am going to do better now and to prove it, here is my first act of atonement: Mr. Davies's killer.

Mr. Davies, who never existed.

The tears come slowly, like intermittent raindrops, and I am not sure if they are caused by grief or humiliation. I feel both emotions in equal measure.

Bea tightens her grip on my shoulders for a moment, then loosens it slightly and says, "I believe this is the first time in my life I have been called a silly, romantical girl. As a spinster of six and twenty years, I believe I am deeply offended."

A giggle escapes me because it is true. Nobody in our family had ever described her as such, even when she *was* a girl.

The knot in my belly begins to unravel, and I lean back on my heels to remind her she is a duchess. A look of genuine surprise crosses her face, as if this detail actually had slipped her mind, and I realize none of us are exactly who we think we are.

I am not a heroine who embarked on a daring adventure to solve an impossible riddle.

I am a fool who propagated a farce.

Altick moans as his eyelids flicker, and it strikes me that I am not quite that either. No true farce ends with a murder attempt.

I might have stumbled into the hornets' nest backward, but that does not make the swarm any less real.

The whimpering increases as Altick struggles to open his eyes. I wait while he blinks furiously in the light that streams through the window.

When his gaze is focused and still, I ask him what he meant when he said it was Holcroft.

His expression turns surly, and I can almost picture him sticking his tongue out like a small child. Why should *he* help *me* understand the situation when I am trying to lead him to the gallows?

The silence stretches, and I repeat the question.

No response.

Bea, her tone almost bored, calls to her husband and asks him to please induce Altick to reply so that she does not have to make the effort herself. "I am comforting my cousin and you appear to be in need of a task."

Although it is not clear whether Altick realizes it is the august Duke of Kesgrave who has been summoned to persuade him to comply, he withers beneath my imposing cousin-in-law's severe gaze.

Sulkily, Altick says, "Everyone knows Holcroft the Holy for the sanctimonious crusader he is. So opposed to corruption he will report even his own cousin. As soon as he introduced himself, I knew he had got wind of Brooke's various arrangements and was determined to bring him to justice. Grimy's participation would be revealed. I could not allow that."

It is shocking.

Yes, yes, Mr. Davies is a figment and my queries were useless, but it is still utterly astonishing to realize it had been Holcroft the entire time.

Holcroft.

Every step of the way.

He could have told me the truth about Mr. Caruthers.

At any moment he could have said, "By the by, Miss

Hyde-Clare, I did my dear cousin a wretched turn as required by my rigid code of honor, so if something seems inexplicable or vaguely wrong about our investigation, it could be that I am infamous for my integrity."

But that is not fair.

Nothing in our investigation seemed inexplicable or vaguely wrong.

Unaware of my interest, Holcroft the Holy wipes away blood that is dropping into his eyes, then holds his hand awkwardly in the air, uncertain what to do next.

Wipe the blood on his other hand?

Smear it on his coat?

It is the first time I have seen him at a loss.

Kesgrave, noting his confusion as well, hands him a hand-kerchief.

Holcroft accepts it gratefully and looks up to discover he is the center of everyone's interest. Although he appears to have been too distracted to have paid proper attention, he says, "Gorman thought it too."

"Gorman?" Bea asks.

"An investigator hired by the son of one of Brooke's clients to prove the solicitor had cheated him out of thousands of pounds," Holcroft explains. "He drew the same conclusion as Altick and assumed I was there to find proof of Brooke's corruption. That is why he passed me the note. He wanted to exchange information, not just give it."

"This was yesterday," Bea says, "at the Western Exchange? Was that where you were supposed to meet him?"

Am I surprised she knows?

No, not at all.

Having charged into the room at the very moment I felled my enemy, she has already proved herself thoroughly conversant in the details of my adventure.

Nevertheless, one does want to know *how* she is so knowledgeable.

"Nuneaton sent around a note this morning asking if you were all right after the excitement at the emporium yesterday," she says. "He thought it was quite odd that you were in the company of Mr. Holcroft, as he did not realize you were acquainted. I thought it was curious as well so I invited you and my aunt for tea this afternoon. To her regret, she was compelled to decline because you were bedridden with oyster poisoning, from which you had been suffering for fully a week because I had not the courtesy to delay my wedding until you were well enough to attend safely. As your oyster poisoning had been a ruse from the start, I knew that you could not be suffering horribly in your bedchamber like Aunt Vera believed. I asked Kesgrave to locate Holcroft, which he did by sending out footmen to scour London for his carriage."

"Eggs," I say as a ghost of a smile forms on my lips.

"Excuse me?" Bea says.

"I am suffering from food poisoning caused by a plate of rotten *eggs*," I explain. "Although I am not as skilled in subterfuge as you, my dear cousin, I do know enough to vary the source of my illnesses. Last week's ailment was caused by oysters. *This* week's illness was caused by eggs. But you know Mama. It is so difficult to get her to listen."

As Bea does in fact know this, she merely nods and says, "So Gorman, believing Holcroft was engaged in the same pursuit, arranged to meet you at the Western Exchange. He was murdered before that meeting could happen, presumably by Altick here?"

"We missed him by only moments," I say, shivering slightly at the grisly memory of his freshly killed corpse. "He was in too much of a rush, I think, to search Mr. Gorman's pockets because we found a slip of paper with an address on it, which I believe he planned to give us. The address was for his client, a Mr. Chambers, who hired him to prove that Brooke cheated his family. From him we learned of Mr. Gorman's direction. We searched his rooms and found all the information he had compiled on Brooke, which was considerable. He even recorded in minute detail how he was going to break into Brooke's residence and locate the evidence. From there, it was an easy thing to follow the instructions and locate his secret compartment."

"Easy!" Holcroft says with an admonishing shake of his head. "It was only easy because your cousin has a remarkable ability for locating secret compartments. She did it twice today."

I blush.

How can I not?

He had owned himself impressed by my skill earlier, but that was before he learned the horrifying truth about Mr. Davies. That he is able to retain even a modicum of respect for me after everything he has heard is bewildering.

Too embarrassed to make eye contact with Holcroft, I glance down at my hand, which is still clutched in my cousin's grasp, and say that it was merely luck.

Holcroft is doubtful. "Both times?"

Before I can respond, Altick cackles harshly and says, "You lot must take me for a real rum corker if you think I'll believe for a second that *none of it was intentional*."

Fully sympathetic to his exasperation, I rush to assure him that *some* of it was intentional. "The investigation itself began with the faulty premise that Theodore Davies was an actual person, but once Mr. Holcroft and I set foot in Brooke's office, the die was cast. *Iacta alea est,* as Julius Caesar said," I add specifically for Bea's benefit. It is always a delight to watch the surprise dart across her face at my unexpected displays of erudition.

Slowly, I feel my mortification fading.

LYNN MESSINA

There is nothing outrageous or foolish in my subscribing wholly to the existence of Mr. Davies. What possible reason would I have to doubt the veracity of Bea's story? She had so many details at her command and appeared genuinely distressed by the topic, as if unable to discuss the man she had loved and lost. She knew everything about him, even down to the color of his darling children's hair (light brown with touches of blond).

And her inserting a death notice in a newspaper just to stop my parents from looking for him?

That is beyond imagining.

Nobody would doubt something they read in the *London Morning Gazette*.

(Except perhaps a gossip item by Mr. Twaddle-Thum. A headless chef, for goodness' sake! Surely, *that* detail is an exaggeration.)

Even if believing in Mr. Davies *was* appallingly gullible, it led to a greater truth, one that has still yet to be properly dealt with.

To that end, I turn to Kesgrave and inform him that I have made a good start but there is still much work for him to do.

He receives this news calmly. "Is there?"

"Chancery Court is a den of corruption and thievery," I explain, rising to my feet and offering a hand to my cousin, who, I notice, is looking exceptionally well now that the unbecoming blush has left her cheeks. Her dull brown hair is unusually vibrant in shiny curls that fall softly around her face. And her dress is an exquisite ivory silk gauze decorated with a pattern of embroidered green leaves that grow dense on the flounce and neckline.

To be sure, marriage agrees with her.

But so do the designs of Madame Bélanger.

Although there is never an inappropriate time to admire a

well-constructed walking gown, I return my attention to Kesgrave. "We will take care of Grimy...Sir Dudley Grimston, who is Master of the Rolls. He is rotten to the core and instructed Altick to assassinate us. Holcroft and I will testify to that, but I am sure Grimy will issue vehement denials. There is no cause to worry. Additional evidence of his crimes is forthcoming."

Kesgrave is amused by the confidence in my tone. "Is it?"

"Yes, Holcroft and I will retrieve it as soon as he is feeling well enough to travel back to Calvert Street," I reply. "There is a secret compartment in Brooke's study behind his shelf. You open it by releasing the Roentgen lock, which is hidden in a hideous gargoyle."

Dabbing the wound on his forehead, Holcroft says he is ready now.

Oh, but the gash in his forehead looks deep and I wonder if he should visit a physician first.

He dismisses my concern with a brisk wave of the hand. "I am as eager as you to see this matter through, Miss Hyde-Clare. Sir Dudley is a lifelong friend of my father's and I cannot rest until I have delivered proof of his treachery into the hands of the Lord Chancellor himself."

"Let us go," I say.

But Bea objects to the plan on the grounds that it is too dangerous. "What if Sir Dudley sent another henchman to retrieve the evidence against him?"

I thank my cousin for her concern but assure her it is not necessary. "Altick was going there next. After killing us, he was charged with fetching the documents. And Brooke will not pose a problem either, for he has a meeting at five-thirty with a man named Stanton."

Bea accepts this argument with a nod and then raises another concern. "It is five o'clock now. If my aunt has not discovered your absence yet, it is only a matter of minutes until she does. You must return home before she summons the authorities."

It is true, of course. Mama is a dear, but she is inclined to panic.

Abruptly, I turn to the duke. "Kesgrave, can you be a darling and send a note to Portman Square?"

It is not the question he is expecting. "A note?"

Yes, I nod firmly, a note. "Something brief that says I am visiting with you and the duchess for the afternoon."

Bea rolls her eyes impatiently and insists a missive would never work.

Taking offense at this excessively pessimistic response, I remind her that I have supported her in all her exploits regardless of how fruitless they appeared. "Your courtship of the duke, for example. That seemed utterly hopeless."

Now Kesgrave laughs and thanks me for persisting in the face of futility.

I assure him it was the only thing I could do. "The poor dear was so smitten, it would have been cruel to dash her hopes."

Bea glares at both of us, then reminds me that a note will not prevail because Mama had already refused her invitation to tea, citing my illness. "I cannot tell her you are at Kesgrave House after she has told me you are confined to your bed."

"Use your duchess seal," I say with another exasperated look at Kesgrave.

After all, his wife is supposed to be the clever one in our family.

"Excuse me?" she says.

"To fasten the missive," I explain. "Use your Duchess of Kesgrave seal. It will look marvelously official, and Mama will be cowed into believing whatever you tell her. You know how easy she is to intimidate."

Bea looks like she's prepared to argue, but instead she

presses her lips together as if smothering a laugh. And I see it in her eyes, the thing that has always been there, her irrepressible humor, although I had not known her well enough to recognize it for what it was.

She has been laughing at us for decades, which is only fair because we—all of us (but especially Russell)—are ridiculous.

"Is the matter settled now or do you have another objection?" I ask impatiently.

"No more objections," Bea says, her tone begrudging. "You may proceed with your evidence gathering. I am trusting you, Holcroft, to see to her safety."

"I will see to my own," I say reassuringly.

Bea sighs, "I know. That is precisely why I am worried."

"You're going to have to stop doing that," I say as I rise to my feet.

"Doing what?" she asks.

"Treating me like your younger cousin," I explain. "I have solved my own mystery now. Wrested from your very grasp."

Although she seems prepared to argue, she merely shakes her head and instructs me to visit Kesgrave House after we have retrieved the evidence. "I would like to hear more about your investigation into Mr. Davies's death. Mr. Holcroft, you are invited as well. I am still not clear how you became involved in this matter and would appreciate a better understanding."

Holcroft accepts the invitation as he slides the bloody handkerchief into his pocket. "I would appreciate a better understanding as well, your grace. Until a few minutes ago, I was under the impression that Mr. Davies was missing. The news of his death is a great shock to me," he says, then turns to Kesgrave and apologizes for leaving him Altick to deal with. "It seems indecorous to incapacitate an assailant and then rush off before the authorities arrive."

Altick takes issue with the description of his state as

weakened and mutters mostly incoherent threats that he intends to follow through on as soon as Grimston arranges his release, a comment that leads me to think he does not actually know who Kesgrave is.

"The Runners are on their way," Kesgrave says. "I sent my driver to fetch them. And your driver is all right. He was hit hard on the head and will most likely have a terrible headache, but he was awake when we arrived and able to give us your direction. Once the Runners are here, I will leave them with my groom and fetch the magistrate myself. He will apprehend Grimston at my bidding regardless of the evidence you produce. On that you may rest assured."

Holcroft nods firmly and thanks the duke for taking control of what is surely a very bizarre situation.

Although I admire Holcroft's desire to be gracious, I assure him it is not necessary in this particular instance. "Kesgrave and Bea do this all the time. I do not think a week has gone by since they met when the duke did not have to summon a Runner."

Bea smiles and admits my observation is not wildly off the mark. "It is not once a week but far more frequently than is decent."

Holcroft laughs and bows over Bea's hand. "It was a pleasure meeting you, your grace, and I congratulate your husband on making an excellent match."

If Holcroft were trying to earn my goodwill, he could not come up with a better way than complimenting Kesgrave on the wisdom of his choice.

As we are leaving the room, Altick scrambles to his knees and then tries with little success to rise to his feet. Bea, sighing wearily, asks him to please share the details of his escape plan so that she may explain its futility point by point and spare them both unnecessary effort.

Resenting her condescension, he growls in response.

Although Holcroft seems amused by the exchange, his expression turns dark as soon as we turn into the hallway. "I told you to run."

"You did, yes," I say, ignoring his anger as we approach the staircase.

"He intended to kill you," Holcroft says furiously. "As soon as he finished with me, he was going to run you through with the same knife. And yet you stood there *gawking* like an idiot."

Obviously, I understand why he is angry. Holcroft the Holy with his rigid code of honor wants to save everyone from themselves. And comprehending a little of the way he thinks now, I am almost certain he blames himself for the entire debacle. Not only was it his presence that sparked Mr. Gorman's murder but it was his trust in Sir Dudley that almost got us killed.

But it is not his fault—it is Altick's, it is Sir Dudley's—and I will not allow him to claim responsibility for their villainy.

I cannot.

Because if it is his fault, then it is mine.

I am the one who was standing in front of Lyon's Inn for ten minutes trying to work up the nerve to identify the man who killed a phantom.

A figment of Bea's imagination.

My mortification is fading, yes, but it will be a long time before I shed it entirely.

It will also be quite a while before I stop reexamining the events of the past two days through the strange, unsettling prism of truth and marveling at how different everything looks in hindsight.

Disquieted by the sensation, I say with deliberate frivolity, "Not like an idiot. Like an ingenious young woman with a unique ability for finding secret compartments."

Holcroft's expression remains stark and he refuses to

respond to my teasing, saying with fervent disapproval that my talent for moving gargoyles had no purpose in that awful room. "Unless you were able to will one into existence so you could bash him over the head with it, but that is arguably a different talent."

His mockery is so aligned with my thought, I smile and say, "But that is what I did."

He is still not in the mood for levity. "What?" he asks irritably.

"The plank from the floorboard," I say. "I bashed him over the head with it."

On the last step of the staircase, he halts suddenly and stares at me.

Oh, no.

His face is serious again.

Quickly, I try to come up with another absurdity.

It should not be difficult.

According to Papa, my head is *filled* with them.

But my mind is drawing a blank.

"You will allow me to apologize for putting your life at risk," he says sternly.

I nod because the look on his face is too intense for argument.

But I also say, "Only if *you* allow *me* to apologize for putting *your* life at risk. As I was the one who arrived at Lyon's Inn first, my guilt is older than yours and must take precedent. Only a cad would try to usurp my claim."

He smiles faintly at this assertion and considers me silently in the dim light of the wretched hallway. His green eyes are as verdant as always but now they spark—oh, yes, they do—with something I cannot name.

Curiosity, perhaps.

Hope, possibly.

Affection, almost certainly.

An odd sort of butterfly sensation flutters in my stomach.

"What if I am a cad?" he asks softly.

Now *there's* an absurdity.

As if Holcroft the Holy could be anything but good.

"Then I will reform you," I say lightheartedly. "I believe the secret to a successful rehabilitation is to visit once a week without prior warning."

"If that is the remedy, then I must assert in full caddish fashion that while your claim might be older, mine is more severe," he says.

His tone is teasing, but his gaze remains somber. His eyes darken, deepen, and my heart trips as I realize he is going to kiss me.

Here.

In the hallway of the dilapidated house where we both almost died.

Suddenly, the stench from the corridor wafts toward my nose, that odor of a dead...bird...mouse...something, and I take a step back.

No.

This is not happening.

My first kiss will not take place in the shadow of that horrid room.

Oh, but it *will* take place soon.

The thought makes me giddy and I smile brilliantly at Holcroft despite the noxious fumes emanating from the room down the hall.

He feels it too, the happiness of anticipation, and takes my arm as we resume our march to the door.

"But first we must discuss your diet," I say.

Ah, now *there* is an absurdity.

Papa would be proud.

"I beg your pardon!" he exclaims in surprise.

And it is delightful, his confusion, his inability to understand fully what is happening.

"Yes, and rightly so," I say. "Now tell me, this kipper habit of yours—is it daily or weekly?"

He objects to the question on the grounds that it is nonsensical.

"You cannot make that determination if you do not know the topic of conversation," I point out reasonably.

"Very well, what is the topic of conversation?" he asks.

"Your fondness for fish," I reply.

He shakes his head and asserts that my comment is even less logical.

"Tell me, Mr. Holcroft, will you always be like this?" I ask.

"Like what?" he asks, riled by confusion.

"Unwilling to acknowledge your love for kippers," I reply.

"I do *not* love kippers," he insists.

"Truly?" I ask suspiciously. "Or are you just telling me what I long to hear."

"Miss Hyde-Clare," he says on a heavy sigh as we step out of the house, "I cannot imagine why in the world that would be something you long to hear."

And he glares at me with exasperation.

But not just exasperation.

Fierce exasperation.

Feral exasperation.

In my stomach, the butterflies take flight at the wild green of his eyes.

The alleyway is also grim. The ramshackle structures block out all the sunshine except for one narrow shaft that is sparkling down on us.

On Holcroft.

Creating a halo.

Unable to resist, I lean forward and kiss him.

His lips are soft and yielding. I feel the tautness of his

surprise, then the sweetness of his surrender. When I begin to pull back, he tugs me closer.

It is, I think as the heat from the sun beats down, the only way to end a story.

***

IT'S THE END, YES, BUT IT'S NEVER *REALLY* THE END. Bea and her duke return for an eighth adventure in spring 2021.

About the Author

Lynn Messina is the author of more than a dozen novels, including the Beatrice Hyde-Clare mysteries, a series of cozies set in Regency-era England. Her first novel, *Fashionistas,* has been translated into sixteen languages and was briefly slated to be a movie starring Lindsay Lohan. Her essays have appeared in *Self, American Baby* and *the New York Times* Modern Love column, and she's a regular contributor to the *Times* parenting blog. She lives in New York City with her sons.

More Mystery!

Some Romance!

Anything can happen in Regency London, as five headstrong and passionate women defy propriety and find love with powerful lords as determined as they are.

***

Love Takes Root series

Made in the USA
Monee, IL
03 June 2022